I Loved a German

by Anton H. Tammsaare

translated by Christopher Moseley

Vagabond Voices
Glasgow

The original Estonian edition was published in 1935 as *Ma armastasin sakslast*, and this edition was translated from the edition published by Eesti Riiklik Kirjastus, Tallinn 1964.

Translation copyright © Vagabond Voices 2018

This translation first published in July 2018 by

Vagabond Voices Publishing Ltd.,
Glasgow,
Scotland.

ISBN 978-1-908251-83-1

Printed and bound in Poland

Cover design by Mark Mechan

Typeset by Park Productions

The publisher acknowledges subsidy towards the translation from the Estonian Cultural Endowment

EESTI KULTUURKAPITAL

The publisher acknowledges subsidy towards this publication from Creative Scotland

ALBA | CHRUTHACHAIL

For further information on Vagabond Voices, see the website, www.vagabondvoices.co.uk

Introduction

A.H. Tammsaare was born in 1878 into a poor farming family, the fourth of twelve siblings. Serfdom had been abolished in 1861, and his father Peeter was able to buy a farm, though the land was either stony or marshy. If we take as our indicator *Vargamäe*, the first volume of his monumental pentalogy in which Indrik can be identified with the author, peasant life was slowly improving in that part of the Tsarist Empire. Tammsaare was born Anton Hansen, and added the name of his family's farm to his own. His father was hardworking, built farm buildings on his land and made furniture and household utensils. He could also read and write, and newspapers were delivered by bicycle during the summer months.

When he wasn't working, the young Tammsaare would spend his time getting muddy, observing insects and watching birds. This dreaminess was accompanied by an aptitude for study, and the family decided a little late in his teenage years to fund his education and he went to secondary education in Tartu from 1898 to 1903. And from 1903 to 1905, he worked as an editor at the Tallinn newspaper, *Teataja*. In Tallinn he was able to witness the Russian Revolution of 1905. While many Estonian writers supported it in part as a means for their own emancipation from the empire and German landowners, Tammsaare took a more cautious approach, supporting some of the aims but rejecting violence.

In 1907 he enrolled as a law student at Tartu University, but in 1911 he was unable to sit his finals, as he became very ill with tuberculosis. He was moved to Sochi on the Black

Sea and then to the nearby Caucasus Mountains, where his condition improved. On his return to Estonia, he lived for six years on his brother's farm where he encountered another life-threatening illness and underwent surgery for an intestinal ulcer. Unable to work, he threw himself into his studies and mastered foreign languages: English, French, Finnish, and Swedish.

He might have remained in the country writing articles and translating books, had he not met Käthe Veltman during a trip to Tallinn. They shared interests but when she turned up at his brother's house with a newspaper containing the announcement of their marriage, which she'd placed herself, he was not amused and it was nearly a year before their marriage became a reality and he moved to Tallinn, where he would continue to live until his death in 1940. This move and the responsibilities of a family increased his literary output dramatically and he would be a prolific writer to the end.

I Loved a German was published in 1935, and superficially it concerns the "ethnic" (by which we mean linguistic) divisions in Estonian society since it had been annexed by Russia during the Great Northern War (1700-21). Like the Swedes before them, the Russians left intact the social structures under the German hegemony established in the Middle Ages. Hence German remained the language of culture and trade, the aristocracy was principally German, and the government and bureaucracy was Russian. The majority Estonian-speaking population was excluded from power and until 1861 effectively excluded from the cities and educational establishments. Analogous situations also existed in the Anciens Régimes of eighteenth-century Europe, though the French Revolution had removed a few of them and unsettled a great many more. Tammsaare's life coincided with continuous change in these complex relationships, but in the Baltic States the final stage was sudden and complete, because both the Germans and the Russians were weakened after 1918. But was it so complete? Formally it was, but the human mind takes time to adapt to sudden change, and in part that is what this novel is about. Erika, the Baltic German granddaughter of a now dispossessed German landowner, and Oskar, the Estonian son of a hardworking peasant, have difficulty in navigating their courtship through the often unconscious prejudices and assumptions that govern their behaviour and expectations.

The novel is not of course incomprehensible to readers unfamiliar with such situations, particularly those unused to polyglot societies, as problems of fast-moving social change are still with us. *I Loved a German* could be interpreted as a nationalist novel: Estonians have to become masters in their own land, and grow out of their residual subservience. It's true that Tammsaare, a convinced pacifist, made an exception for the Estonian War of Independence. History had provided a unique opportunity, and Estonians had to take it. Equally you could argue that it is an anti-nationalist novel. The Estonian nationalist who appears towards the end of the first volume of his pentalogy, *Truth and Justice*, is not a positive figure. The author appears to be distrustful of his conviction and simplification of complex issues, and perhaps the latent bigotry. The personal level of our relationships remains the starting point for much of Tammsaare's thinking, and there's no doubt that the two young lovers are genuine in their sentiments, however innocent and self-analytical they undoubtedly are, as their anguish over lies and half-truths demonstrates. The primary obstacle to their love is national prejudice. This is already present in their early encounters, walks in the park under the moonlight not for romantic reasons but because Erika is ashamed of her worn gloves and other signs of financial constraints. Their different social backgrounds are often referred to: he apparently upwardly mobile and she downwardly mobile, but his finances are still in the worst state. Both are keen not to reveal their true situation, but when she starts to talk, she does confide in him.

The real turning-point in the novel is Oskar's decision to ask her grandfather for permission to marry her. He is convinced that man-to-man he will be able to persuade the dispossessed German nobleman (who presumably was compensated for his loss). The meeting turns out to be a complete disaster. Much of the conversation between Oskar and Erika or between Oskar and her grandfather revolves around the fact he has become a *Korporant*, a member of a *Korporation*, which is a social organisation for university students and a sign of social status, expressed through the right to wear a particular kind of coloured cap. This would have been the almost exclusive domain of young German men and now it had been opened up to Estonians. We're talking here about privilege more than national identity, though in pre-independence Estonia they were clearly interlinked. The arguments can occasionally appear arcane, but isn't this true of all social prejudice? The grandfather is clearly incapable of assessing the new reality and to some extent he admits to this. Tammsaare is too good a writer to make him a caricature, and this condescending and occasionally obtuse man is capable of expressing some interesting ideas and is motivated by genuine love and concern for his granddaughter.

Following this encounter and an argument with Erika, Oskar starts to question his own love and asks himself whether he was more interested in the upper-class connections than in Erika herself, though this appears not to be the case after the final twist in the story. Oskar, the narrator of his own account he occasionally calls a "novel", writes, "What was so terribly provocative was our long-humiliated and mutilated sense of ourselves as slaves when we tried, even outwardly, to be the masters of slaves, which we hid within ourselves [p. 30]," and perhaps even more revealingly, "My love must surely smell of coarse bread and a dusty granary, and that's why it's so precious to me. My reason tells me to defend the break-up of the manorial lands, but my emotions tell me to cling compulsively to them, as do all my contempraries [p. 30]."

I Loved a German is not so much a nationalist or anti-nationalist novel as a novel about nationalism and our socially ingrained prejudices which are so difficult to shake off even when the world around us has changed dramatically. I would hazard a guess based on my reading of the novel that Tammsaare was an exponent of civic nationalism *avant la lettre*. His concern was to salvage Estonian culture from the ravages of history and not to defend some mythical "ethnicity". What is certainly the case is that this is a complex novel that imparts a number of paradoxes concerning both nationalism and more generally the human condition.

Finally a few words about the novel's structure and style are in order. It is occasionally a discursive novel, though not on a grand scale. There is, for example, an amusing digression into the difference between writing in the evening and writing in the morning. The manuscript story is that Oskar started to write this autobiographical account after nearly all the events had occurred (i.e. before we or he know what happens to Erika after the split, which is revealed in her letter that ends the book). This manuscript is found after he too has disappeared, and it is handed over to Tammsaare who decides to publish it under his own name and writes an introduction, which of course is actually part of the novel. For some this may appear overly elaborate, but this and Oskar's habit of calling it a novel undermine the text and that must have been intentional. There is something theatrical about the novel, and the conversations with the landlady and with the grandfather, which form the backbone of the novel, could easily be transferred to the stage. The encounters between the lovers are more typical of a realist novel, with detailed descriptions of the weather, the time of day and their walks. The landlady, who the lovers detest because she embarrasses them unrelentingly, is Estonian and proud of it. Tammsaare clearly finds her ridiculous, but she too is not a caricature. There is some humanity underneath her bluster and bullying. The Estonian maid, on the other hand, is a subdued character and treated with contempt by everyone, including Oskar, but it is revealed in the fictional introduction that she is the one person who had the greatest understanding of people and events. This does not become clear to readers until the end when they have the knowledge to make the judgement. Another reason why this is one of those novels that deserve to be read more than once.

Allan Cameron, Glasgow, June 2018

I Loved a German

To The Reader

Some time ago a certain young man vanished – it isn't known exactly when, why, where or how. He must have been of a fairly ordinary stamp, for otherwise his disappearance would not have gone unnoticed. At least with death, an individual appears more extraordinary when at the funeral mourners remind each other of what a great person he was, even though he was born small and weak, and lived mostly like an insect under the tree-bark. But with a missing man – this missing man, I mean – there wasn't a single clue as to where to search for him. The people with whom he lived in town supposed that he had temporarily moved to his father's farm, but there they were convinced that he was still living in town. And when it finally transpired that he was neither in the countryside nor in the town, it was too late to start a search. The police were informed, but they said that it is difficult to search for and find a person if there are no indications of a crime related to his disappearance. In order to assist the investigation, the lady with whom the young man had lodged brought the police a manuscript he'd left behind. But on closer inspection of the manuscript it emerged that it too lacked indications of criminal activity. For even if it were assumed – which is not very likely – that the young man had put an end to his own life or that that the actions or words of a young lady had incited him to do so, that would not have been of the least significance, for that young lady is dead, and the police do not pursue crimes committed by the dead. Moreover, the civilised world has not regarded suicide as a crime for a very long time, but rather as a certain act of personal freedom and independence, and therefore anyone who encourages suicide cannot be prosecuted in law, especially not when the encouragement is an element of a love affair.

To sum up – the manuscript did indicate a particular psychology, but not criminal one such as the police deal with, and therefore it was returned to the landlady. After she'd talked to the man's relatives, the landlady turned to me because she had heard that I have a keen interest in every kind of psychology, whether criminal or not. As I read the manuscript, I became gripped by various aspects, not least the question of how much the events described correspond to reality. As I continued, this question came into ever sharper focus, especially because in places I found remarks in the margins of the pages, added in pencil and badly erased, such as "a lie", "not right", "fantasy", "exaggeration", "quite the opposite" and so on. Likewise the margins of the manuscript were abundantly decorated with question and exclamation marks. Discussing it with the landlady who brought it, I found out that most of the markings were hers, but some were by her assistant. The two of them had read the manuscript several times, both alone and together, and tried to correct it where there was an outright mistake or a misunderstanding. Generally, though, she said, the story corresponded to the truth, and in that sense the present book has a striking authenticity: it could almost be life itself; in other words, it was born to be a story.

As time allowed, I tried for my part to help adjust the manuscript in accordance with the guidance from the landlady and her assistant so that no one should have anything to say against its authenticity. Adjusting it turned out to be very easy, for mostly there was so much contradiction between the landlady's and her servant's opinions that finding a golden mean was a mere trifle. If, for example, I asked the landlady, "Was there anything special about Miss Erika the young man seemed to see in her?", she would reply, "That's made up! Erika was a perfectly ordinary German girl, a bit naive, a bit wooden and stiff, but of course she wasn't without a certain attraction as young girls generally have." The servant answered the same question: "The young miss was much, much nicer than she's portrayed in this book; the writer couldn't have had any gift for poetry. I came to love her, and I cried my eyes out when I read here that she had died." I went on to ask, "Does the letter at the end of the book appear to be genuine?" and the landlady gave this reply: "The letter must be a forgery from beginning to end, or altered in translation, apart from the handbag, because she really did have that with her once" – whereas the servant replied, "The young lady might actually have written a letter like that, only I don't know anything about the bag and the things that must have been in it." Finally I was interested to know what they thought of his coloured student's cap and some other aspects of his life, and I got this answer from the landlady: "I don't have any opinion on that, because those are mostly my and my husband's opinions, which the man vanished wrote down." The servant said, "Well, no, what is there to think! When it came to the colours of his cap – well, he was in a better class and position, wasn't he? Like some Russian or even a German." Nearly every question produced the same result. But as to the young lady having pimples on her face and her blonde hair really being a little curly, both were of the same opinion.

You might ask, Why is the book appearing under my name? Before we try to explain that, I have a duty to assure you: everything possible has been done to bring the actual author's name to light as soon as a suitable moment arises. Initially his identity has to remain unknown, because it's obvious that, if the people and events described here are at all true, the use of the author's actual name could be detrimental to him and the other protagonists, all of whom are still alive with one exception. The death of the young man himself has not been established, although it is possible. Yet if some pseudonym had been considered, that would surely have been the first time that a dead person or a suspected dead person, hid behind a false name. Up to now there have indeed been false deaths, but no false names of the dead.

Use of my name as the author of the book was prompted on the one hand by economic considerations and on the other by literary and artistic ones. The former were emphasised understandably by those who were hoping for an income from the book, the latter by me personally. You see, I thought that if the book appeared under the young man's real or assumed name, the protagonists' origins would be uncovered, and other things would inevitably come to light. Thus a great deal would be added to literary science drawing attention to the writing but lessening interest in the book itself. It is strange that people are more interested in the location of Carrara marble or some kind of clay than in the images shaped from such marble or clay. People are forever being seduced by the logic that a work of art is explained and appreciated if it is known what it is made of and where its material came from. So it is quite understandable that we had a writer living among us who thought that no great works could be created, if there weren't any factories manufacturing fountain pens used by people like us.

Since the book is now appearing as a work of my own, scarcely anyone will believe that there is anything true about it. They would rather think that it is all made up, purely fiction and imagination – that never in the world did there live such a student and *korporant*, such a landlady, such a servant, such a "German girl" or her grandfather. However mistaken that opinion, the reader will equivocate: firstly they have a chance to evade the literary-artistic science which examines, instead of a created image, holes in the clay, shards of marble or fountain pens, and secondly

6

they will get a taste for the real life you get in fiction. This last point is especially important because the history of the young generation, and even more so the historical novel and cinema, take immense care to ensure that fiction is accepted as reality.

By using my name we were also attempting With my name we were also considering achieving certain results in literary policy. If the book had appeared under some stylish new and unfamiliar name, critics would certainly have expected something new or unfamiliar in it. And if they didn't find it, they would have said, "What's the point of this stylish new book and name, if everything else is old?" It is quite certain that they would not have found it, for finding something new in a book, if its author is not your friend, is just as difficult as seeing a thing you've stumbled into – only philosophers can manage that. But would any philosopher in Estonia behave like a critic? It would have been even worse if the newness of the name had been matched by the same kind of content, because neither a reader nor a critic like new things: for the former it spoils the entertainment expected of reading; for the latter it makes it more difficult to write reviews priced by the line. Therefore the critic, whether old or young, functions by force of nature like a guardian. Whether a biped human, a quadruped dog or a feathered bird in an Indian village, he makes a loud shrill noise when he smells, hears or sees anything unknown and strange. By putting my name on the book, we hoped the book would have a relatively ordinary reception: the old guardians would growl appreciatively on getting acquainted, looking downwards so to speak, because the maker always stands on a lower level than the consumer or critic of the object; the younger ones, who don't know me, raise angrier voices, smelling something foreign which does not need to be appreciated, merely disdained.

Finally the landlady was able to convince me that the appearance of the book under my name would be useful not only to the book, the reader and the publisher, but to me as well: to the book for its literary credentials, to the reader for being more to their taste, to the publisher for business reasons, but to me for moral ones. She said I had always written about love without encouraging moral improvement, as if this were some sort of unnatural phenomenon. This book could be read as a story of how a love can remain within moral bounds if it is the right one. If the book bears my name, there will of course be gullible people who think, however wrongly, that it was written by me, and thus they could quite easily conclude that I too subscribe to a moral basis for love. That would be useful to me too, she argued. And the benefit to me would be even greater, and my rehabilitation on the basis of love would be more complete, so for that reason she wanted me to make certain adjustments to the text. For a start I should erase the scene where the young man seizes the helpless girl by the waist in the park, although he himself has fallen to his knees. Secondly, instead of a "German girl" I should put in a "fine Estonian lass", because there are still some among them who have natural curls in their blond hair, thus protecting the fictional value of the book. Thirdly, instead of the German grandfather there should be a stout old Estonian gentleman. Fourthly, the entire letter should be removed, or at least only those parts that speak of the child and the spirit should be left in, because, she said, real love was only concerned with those two matters. When I objected that this would distort the truth, because this book is a factual account, the lady replied, "That's of no importance. It may be a factual account, but such things should be left to the holy book and the newspapers; a book that appears under someone's name should be moral." I went to great lengths to ensure this book was published as the young man had written it. If it really does bring me misfortune, as the landlady predicted, there is nothing I can do about it; I have acted according to my conscience.

In short, the names are the only pure fiction in this book, both those of the author and those of the protagonists; all the rest are things that happened here in Estonia. Where a name is missing, it is at the wish of the relevant person. For example, the landlady did not want a pseudonym for herself, and remains without any name at all. Her husband followed the same practice. Their will be done. The servant's name is what she chose for herself, with her mistress's approval of course. The inventor of the young man's name is his sister. I deleted the grandfather's name on my own initiative. I hope this hasn't detracted from the book's value too much.

As editor of this book, I have nothing more to say; the rest will become clear in the reading, and anyone who doesn't read this book will require an explanation. May God have mercy on them.

I give the floor to the young man who vanished.

A.H.T.

"Every educated person can write at least one novel – a novel about himself." I've read those words somewhere, I remember it clearly. But I've forgotten where.

It's very probable that I've read those words several times, because I've noticed that words are like announcements: they have to be repeated, otherwise they don't catch your eye or stay in your mind.

There's a reason why things happen like that: some thoughtful words appear first somewhere in a book, then in a magazine and finally in a newspaper. But the order of appearance might be the opposite: first in a paper, then in a journal and finally in a book – as a serious scientific study or a respected novel which schoolchildren have to read.

For as education grows from year to year, people are writing clever things all over the place, so that you hardly know any more what you should take up to read. So for an educated person the only intellectual relaxation and treasure house is the cinema, which doesn't make you yawn or put you to sleep.

And yet the written word must have some importance in the future, there's no denying it, or at least for now, and until educational institutions have been completely reformed. Since ancient times they've seen it as their duty to get young people used to reading boring books – only boring ones of course, on the correct assumption that the interesting ones will be read anyway, like it or not.

Apart from that, strangely enough, there are still people in the world who like to read books and other writings only when they're bored. Even their tastes have to be satisfied.

And my last point: the written word is important for recording those things that don't stick in your mind: such as the first sentence of these lines, so that everyone can look back at will and see who used it the first, second, third time and so on. Such a record could accommodate the names of all the films in the world, so that an educated person won't have to go and see the same film again for the tenth time.

I wrote the above lines yesterday. I spent nearly half a day composing them. Actually I wanted to write something else, but that's what came out. I realised once again that writing is a complex activity: I'm doing the writing, but someone else is doing the guiding.

Moreover, the lines I wrote don't deal with the matter at all, but they might as well be left in. They could be left out too, it's a matter of indifference – except to me, for whom those lines would be lost.

If I leave them in, my excuse may be the fact that the novel is a realm where one talks about what doesn't concern the principal themes of the book. This is especially true of psychological novels.

Every novel has its own story, plot and psychology. The story is what is told, but might also be left untold, as has often happened recently. The plot is what is considered or meant by the story, or what is said intentionally or unintentionally. The psychology, though, can include everything that comes to mind in the telling.

So my lines from yesterday are part of the psychology, because they came to mind – except that they came to mind even before I started to tell my story.

But the reader shouldn't infer that I definitely want to write a novel – let alone a psychological one. I am of the opinion that if novels in general were to die out tomorrow, only the authors would feel the loss, including their royalties and sometimes a few prizes that some people might count as royalties.

As for my intention to compose some sort of novel with its own story, its own plot and its own psychology, there are special reasons for that, which I will set about explaining shortly, in an attempt to be as precise and factual as my inexperience allows.

I am at present twenty-five years old, of average height and with blue eyes which are not large or expressive. There is no beard or moustache to speak of, since I either get shaved or do it myself when forced to, although I don't like doing it myself, as shaving can be painful.

My hair is black, but with a sort of indefinite tinge that makes it different. I won't speak of my eyebrows, because I'm not sure of them these days. One might also say the same about my hair. Generally speaking of colours it would be most correct only to specify whether they are natural or artificial.

The general shape of my skull is oval, but with a certain inclination or pressure toward the back of the neck, which is said to be the seat of reason – something that so far I haven't made much use of. The jaws have a musculature as if fate had marked me to be a biter, though I don't actually have an urge to sink my teeth into anything. Today, for instance, it's now past twelve o'clock, but I haven't eaten yet and I don't know when or where I'll get anything. It might seem strange to some people, even incredible, but nevertheless this is the case: I have jaws and teeth, I have a stomach and an appetite, which would like to put food in the stomach, but there is no food. At the same time the market is piled high with foodstuffs; I went there yesterday to take a look, because I had a cent or two in my pocket. I walked through row after row of stalls selling berries to admire their abundance and freshness, and sniff their almost entrancing smell. In some places I even asked the price, where the garden strawberries were especially fresh and plump. When an old woman wanted to measure some out for me, I said I'd have to take a further look at the market and the prices, because I needed to buy a large amount. I chose the plumpest and most appetising strawberries, and I asked the old lady what they cost because I wanted a taster, so I would know later where to buy them from. She couldn't sell berries for less than a cent, she said. I gave her two and moved on. The woman shouldn't have been thinking about the money; no, it was only a question of knowing what the berries tasted like. That's what it should be. But a beautiful berry eaten on an empty stomach just seemed sickly-sweet and plain watery. I felt very sorry to have wasted my two cents.

When I had suitably distanced myself from the rows of berries, I went to where they sell bread – black, brown and white – from tables behind which stood large carts or vans piled with supplies. In my pocket I counted out a handful of money to work out what to buy and how much. In the end, however, I didn't buy anything here either, because it occurred to me there would be no point in carrying all that bread home, when right by the courtyard at home there is a shop where you can buy the same thing just as cheaply.

Generally it isn't appropriate or polite for an educated young man in the street to carry a little packet whose shape reveals to everyone that it contains a piece of bread. It's a different matter if your packet contains sweet buns, cakes or a tart – quite a different matter, because that implies certain relationships, acquaintances, adventures, delicacy and love. A piece of bread only speaks of hunger, which everyone considers to be a vulgar and crude thing demeaning to everyone who encounters it.

So I headed home and bought from the shop – not the one by the courtyard, because I have very old bills there, but another one, a bit further away, around the corner – four hundred grams of dark bread and a herring, which I took between two fingers and held like a carcass away from myself, so as not to soil my clothes. Then I hurried half-running up to my room, locked the door behind me, sat down on a chair and munched on both the bread and the herring. True, there was a mouthful of bread left over – that I devoured dry in the middle of the night, when I was already lying down.

In winter, when my landlord's family are at home and live on the first floor below me, it's possible for me at least to get boiled water from their kitchen, but now when everyone is on their summer holiday apart from my landlord, whom I rarely see, I have to be content with cold tap water. Even in winter, getting the boiling water wasn't just a matter of going and asking, or taking, for I had to enter into a friendly relationship with the maid which sometimes required more obligations than I was willing to take on. Never mind, one way or another I was able to arrange it and quite often she came up from the kitchen with the water and something hot or cold to eat, food that she found off-putting. I objected with all my heart to these additional things – I say really with all my heart, because it was humiliating and repulsive to me – I was angry with the girl, I cursed her, but it didn't help. In the end I had to give in and swallow the pill.

On the first occasion I couldn't object, so great was my hunger was so great, but I couldn't bear to look at her tearful eyes. And if she'd been a little older or prettier, I wouldn't have accepted a pork chop with fried potatoes either on that first occasion or later – and having to eat them like a thief. But the girl was youthful, about seventeen or eighteen, quite childish in her appearance, shabbily dressed, almost filthy, the slippers on her feet always full of holes and almost without soles, her face oblong, her nose longish, her mouth too big, her front teeth sparse and stumpy, her gums too prominent when she laughed, her eyes small under black brows.

In truth, her brows were the only part of her whole being that nature had not given her niggardly – her brows and maybe her hair, because it was black, a quite beautiful black and naturally a little curly. But otherwise it was quite pitiful to look at this poor creature either walking or standing: her neck was short and thick, her shoulders broad as if they belonged to a man, her waist too low, her legs too short, her whole body below the average height. So when she stood in her mundane shabbiness or wretchedness by the door, supporting one shoulder against the doorframe with her darned stockings in her torn slippers, holding a plate with another upturned one on top of it, wearing a soiled apron and her hair clustered on her head and with tears in her eyes, looking away as though she and not I should be ashamed, I felt such a deep pity for her that I might have accepted a dead frog or a rat from her and bolted it down, simply because she was what she was. For no other reason than the manner in which she stood at the door. Because if she had said a little earlier those words that she only said when I had started eating the chop and the potatoes, I would certainly not have accepted her gift. But no, she was silent until I'd half finished the plate and said, "The landlady has nothing to do with this; it's my portion, which she gave to me."

"But didn't you have anything to eat," I cried pushing the plate away.

"Young sir, I can't eat pork chops anyway," she replied. "I always give them away to someone else – to the cat or the dog."

The morsel congealed in my mouth and my tongue reached for my palate. For this wretched girl I was replacing a cat or a neighbourhood dog! I didn't know where to look. But when I did finally turn to her, I realised that everything she had said was a lie. The only true part was that she had brought me her tastiest morsels, and in their place she was gnawing on a bit of dry bread and sucking on a herring's tail.

"Why are you lying to me like this?" I asked.

"No, sir, I'm not lying. I can't eat such greasy stuff; I'm used to the lean," she explained.

If that was true, then I was still playing the part of the cat or neighbourhood dog who gets what isn't good enough for humans. But nothing could be done about it; half of the chop and half of the potatoes had gone now, and the rest was going to follow them.

Later with a full stomach as I laid myself out comfortably on the divan, my thoughts turned again to the girl, as she had leaned at first against the doorpost, a plate under her apron. And now she seemed to me, if not as some sort of beauty, at least no longer as ugly – pleasant, at least. And I tried to understand what is beautiful and what is ugly, what is pleasant and what is unpleasant. Of course I didn't come to any conclusion. It only occurred to me that the landlady had engaged the girl mainly because of her ugliness and wretchedness, because she didn't consider pretty maids to be suitable objects to have about the house, and above all she was wary of the neat manner of their dress. "These days nobody wants to work once they've got themselves some glad rags," she would assert, and that conviction of hers must have been the reason she only let in ragamuffin girls like that one. I was amazed that even an experienced landlady like her could be so wrong about people, about men and women. Even though it made no difference that Loona might have been, like everyone else, made to be pitied, laughed at, joked about or found fault with, she could still stand by the door like that and see that she could please any man, even be beautiful in his eyes?

For the past couple of days I haven't been able to write a line – I wasn't at home. Three evenings ago, I went out following the incident I've just related to satisfy my hunger one way or another, and had rotten luck in the literal sense of the word. I only got back at about three or four o'clock this morning, and although the clock will soon strike three again, my head still hurts and I feel giddy. I was supposed to go out again, but for some reason I started rereading what I had written.

In my present state of mind, I'm struck by only one thing: I should have been clearer about my purpose of my writing, for why else would I have deviated so badly from my original intention? I started by describing my own appearance, but as soon as I got to the jaws and teeth, everything was suddenly forgotten, and there followed pages and pages only about food and about who brings me food one way or another.

One thing I haven't mentioned is that Loona's explanation for bringing me food was of course all a lie and a deception, but not in the way I thought – quite a different one. Nor did the landlady make a mistake in choosing Loona as her servant, and I was wrong about her knowledge of people. But there's a time and a place for all that.

Now I'll return to my own appearance, and tell you: perhaps I was right to break off my description last time, which due my hunger. I very much doubt that a person's outward appearance can be linked with their inner self. If I, for example, have a flat nose, who can definitely conclude from that that I can't have the same natural qualities that some hook-nosed people have? You can't. So why should I emphasise my flat nose so much?

It's a different thing when it's a question of women and love – quite a different thing. Women think that only straight-nosed and hook-nosed men are noble, so to speak, and that their love is to nobility as a bee is to honey. Simply ridiculous! As if nobility couldn't be found behind an African wide nose. Several researchers testify that it's to be found there in much greater numbers than amongst hook-nosed Europeans. And when my acquaintances assure me that I have a real Finnish nose, what I want to know is whether there's any nobility such a nose? And does that nobility have anything to do with love? But then I ask, what is nobility anyway, and what does it mean to be in love?

So much for flat and hook noses, and therefore I won't say any more on the subject, except that my broadish nose constitutes, along with my jaws and my shoulders, and especially my feet, a certain artistic whole: they all correspond to each other and are in balance. My gait, in particular, is of that kind: a little broad and longish, a little clumsy and angular. It is for wise heads to decide what to make of this, because they love to make mistakes, so that even wiser ones will have something to rectify. I do have three teeth – two lower molars and one front tooth at the upper right, just next to a canine, that have been filled, but I don't think that affects my nobility or my knowledge; it only affects love, especially if the filling doesn't fit, is made of bad material or has fallen out. Anyone who doesn't know that knows nothing of love, just like those who think it doesn't matter what shoes you wear.

A shoe is more important in love than a nose or personality, and the shape of the tip decides a person's fate in temporal and eternal life much more than the flatness or curvature of a person's nose. I have noticed this. Someone else will notice something else, and that is for them to write about. So I have the perfect right to say that I wear size 43 and 44 shoes alternately, whereas the only right size would be 43 ½, but those, the half-sizes, are not to be found anywhere. That's why many older people pine for the old Russian times, because they were widely available then. The most suitable are the shoes with a wide toe, as can be inferred from my previous arguments, but I also wear those that are sharp as arrows, if fashion dictates it. So I'm not going to create a principle for myself about the toe of a shoe, just as I have no firm principles about human relationships, but I do think that if shoe toes keep changing their shape more and more often, then people should also change their principles more and more often, or even cast them aside and only follow fashion, which is perhaps the most modern principle and world view. The cobbler and the tailor have to calculate the direction of culture and the level of education.

My education is such that it can be called secondary or higher, as you wish. In my own opinion I have a higher education, because I have spent two and a half years at university and sat the Latin examination there, and I have documentary proof of this, if needed. I took off the fox fur and I was awarded the colours, so I am a full member of the graduate community. I left the university at my own wish, because I could no longer find any friends who wanted, were able or dared to lend me any more money.

But through friends I became an intern at a bank for a few months, and afterwards obtained a permanent position at a ministry, which I lost because there were men and women, older and younger than me, who could prove that they had a greater right to my position or that they were better suited to it. So here I sit in my attic room for the umpteenth month, waiting for better times. Thank God the owner of this old two-storey wooden house believes in better times; otherwise he would have had to throw me out long ago and taken on a new lodger, someone enjoying slightly better times than I am right now. I pay ten crowns a month for the room, but I haven't paid it for three months. The owner evidently believes that I will pay my debt one day. May God keep his faith firm and perform a miracle, so he won't have to be disappointed in me or in other people.

So it'll take a miracle for the landlord to get his rent from me soon, but I may get out of my present situation by more worldly assistance: I could go home to the farm. But that's not what I want, for a hundred reasons, and those reasons don't only concern me, but also my father and mother, my sister and brothers, in fact all my family, friends, acquaintances and associates. Despite all that, returning home to my parents' embrace would require a degree of heroism or desperation from which there would be no escape. Thus I've decided to find a way out by writing the only novel that every educated person has to hand – for am I not an educated person? – that is a novel about myself. For God's sake, let no one think that I believe I have a special talent or power, that I'm hoping for the arrival of some holy spirit in whose light everything will be done almost painlessly, as if by itself. No, I believe first of all in work, especially as I've read that one particular genius believes his works are ninety-nine per cent perspiration and one per cent inspiration. Now if geniuses bring about their works almost purely through labours, why can't I? And anyway where is the man who can say where the work ends and the talent begins in the case of modern novels? That is only for coming generations to decide, or not even for them. Nowadays the proof of a talent is the work done, which is like a talent. That's why no first prize is ever given for even the most divine poetry, but it's given for a great novel, however mediocre it may be. Talent is a gift from God and it would be immoral to reward anyone for what God has given them.

If I had some special gift which is called a divine spark, would I be troubling my head or heart about such worldly things as privation and hunger? Wouldn't I warble like a skylark so that everyone would envy my great *joie de vivre*? Out of my tears and great sadness that sometimes snare my heart, I would make something that creates the illusion of an earthly paradise everyone would yearn for. Now, when I lack that divine spark, I think for the umpteenth time as I write these lines about how at six o'clock the doors of the grocers' shops will close and I haven't yet put anything between my teeth today, and I don't have a crumb in the house to put there. For ages I've been fretting about going to the shop, but I'm still writing, although I know that in the end I'll have to go anyway. And today I can go – not to the shop directly outside the courtyard, because I don't have enough money to pay my old debts, but I'll go to the one around the corner with my head held high.

Does anyone know why some people grow the nails of their index or little fingers long? I grew the index fingernail long on my right hand, although I didn't know why I was doing it. But today my eyes were opened while I was eating: the long nail on the index finger is a great help in skinning smoked Baltic herring. It can be wonderfully adept at removing skin, even from a half-dried herring. Having arrived at this conviction, I couldn't resist wondering how every senseless thing in this world has its own little purpose. The same should apply to hunger and privation. Where in

21

the world could you put old crusts of bread, dried sprats, rancid herrings and stale hunks of rye bread if there weren't people going hungry and living in privation? No, there would be nowhere to put them, and no one to sell them to, and they would go to waste, which would do great harm to the economy. But now, thank God, everything moves on, everything bears fruit, whether it be half-rotten apples or mouldy strawberries, worn clothes or galoshes with holes, scrap iron or dog-chewed bones.

As I ate, marvelling at divine order and dispensation, it appeared to me suddenly that throughout my whole life I have seen nothing but privation and hunger, and that it alone rules the world. My common sense tried to reject this, but I still felt this was right. Since childhood I have heard of nothing but privation and hunger. When my mother went to give straw or hay to the animals, my father always said that whether a lot or a little, she would have to give something, because a long winter lay ahead. Even in the spring he insisted that you had to be careful, because no one could be sure that the animals would find something in the forest. Even with the greatest care, there was always privation and hunger in the spring, and no one knew where to get fodder for the animals. The heifers had sometimes to be driven into the swamp, where they would gulp great mouthfuls of dry grass from the tussocks, and scattered clumps of reeds which stuck out here and there.

It was the same with people's food: there was always talk of rationing, always calculation of how long this or that would last. And it didn't last: very often the shortages would come. Of course there were times when they feasted, eating and drinking several times and beyond reason, but now it seems to me that that happened because tomorrow, and the day after, there would be so much to give up, and so they caroused today, just to get their fill of food and drink for once. Maybe everyone who eats and drinks too much in the world does it because of fear of the morrow, which may bring, if not hunger, then at least privation. There is still something today, there is still enough for today, so let's eat and drink and be merry, because no one knows what the future may bring.

But I didn't fight, did I? And my companions didn't fight, at least I didn't notice anything and nothing like that affected me. We had never seen our own mother's and father's heifers and piglets, and words about a struggle for a better future went in one ear and out the other, without affecting us in the least. And how were we supposed to fight from a school bench? By great learning? But we noticed too early that this better future that our fathers and mothers thought about at home would not fall into our laps because we'd got an education, quite the contrary: the better future would be tasted by those who haven't learnt a thing, or who have, while learning, seen fashions, amusing pastimes, polite social activity. Those who acquire things are acquisitive but proper learning lessens acquisitiveness. This was the unavoidable conclusion we had to draw from our experience. Real learning trains the conscience, but we were growing up at a time when everyone was behaving as though such concepts were a logical error in need of urgent correction. Learning was supposed to awaken our mind and spirit, but everyone was living as if the mind was a silly fairy tale for children, and the spirit was only awakened by alcohol. Some teachers said that we had to learn so as to gain a sense of responsibility for our families, our relatives, our acquaintances, the whole Estonian nation and the homeland, because our whole future depended on responsibility, but we didn't understand, or we forgot it when we saw that it was the irresponsible ones who were harvesting the fruit we'd been sent to school to obtain. Why worry our heads about it? So we could go bankrupt, like everyone else who had studied before us? Did our fathers and mothers study along with their piglets out in some remote forest, by a bog or on a hillock, so that we could learn to go bankrupt? Were they interested in science or art? Are they interested in it even now? Is that what they saw in our better future, and why they fought for it?

No, no! Not even my sister and brother are interested in such things. Even today they see nothing more in my studying than the investment of retained capital, which should bear as high an interest as possible. Father and mother, sister and brother, relatives and friends, acquaintances and strangers, they all have one notion: school is a place where a person is prepared for usury. No one knows really where or from whom the profit should be taken or can be taken, but everyone thinks they know that you go to school only so that one day you will earn as much as possible for as little effort as possible. Moreover, everyone has a strange presentiment – originating from who knows where or when, you could even say from a strange dream – not only that people who've been to school earn a lot of money for easy work, but that their school attendance affects the welfare, prosperity and abundance of their fathers and mothers, sisters, brothers, relatives, friends, and even their steers, heifers, piglets and chickens. They too all want to earn more for less effort, they too can start to eat and drink better, so that none of them will ever even dream of hunger and privation again.

The ancient story of the bizarre tragedy of the world was repeated. People spoke of education as some sort of Redeemer or Messiah, leading us to some higher and more ideal kingdom, but everyone was expecting an earthly Canaan, running with milk and honey. The world has surely always been that way, talking of one thing and thinking of another. And that is surely because nobody is content with what they have, they always want more, as if eternally gnawed by hunger or feeling anguish from privation. Somewhere far in the south there live tiny little white ants which wander indiscriminately from place to place, destroying everything organic in their path. They chomp up hundred-year-old furniture into pulp, and one fine day a person finds they are not sitting on a chair or sofa but a pile of dust. That's what white ants are like, but do they differ that much from humans? Haven't they also wandered for centuries from country to country and from continent to continent, and haven't their pathways been littered with destruction? The ant is driven by hunger, but the human? The human driving force is hunger, which it has endured from the lands where its history is known. Even today, people confront people and nations confront nations, beating their breasts and trying to scream to outdo each other with proof that they are hungrier than others, and thus they have a greater right to wander around like the tiny white ants, seeking food and turning to ash and dust everything that happens to be in their path.

And so the idea settled down in me as I smeared butter as thinly as possible on a piece of bread, as I'd decided that a hundred grams should suffice for at least four meals. Evidently the natural tendency to save and stretch things out, inherited from my parents, was unconsciously at work in me, because I knew, as they did with their piglets, that a long and slighter hunger is better than a brief and horrible one. But until today I had never thought about it. None of us who went to school thought about it. At least we never talked about it among ourselves. Somehow we did our schoolwork, mostly making a face that said that we were doing it for someone else, not ourselves. We needed to play, have fun, go somewhere, look at or listen to something or simply wander around town, especially at forbidden times. We were all of the opinion that what was expected of us was pointlessness or senselessness invented by our parents, and pursuit of the forbidden was the only right and proper task in life. For if this wasn't the case, why did those who no longer went to school go to those places we were forbidden to enter? Places frequented even by those who were supposed to monitor our walks, amusements, activities and acquaintances.

You could almost say that we were forced into something that we didn't want or need and which everyone was trying to dodge, and they tried to take away from us everything that pleased us, tempted us and attracted everyone who wasn't under the supervision we were. Even the cinemas couldn't advertise themselves, they had to always stress that they were forbidden for young people. So why couldn't we change our caps or simply hide them away so that our monitors couldn't identify us as schoolchildren? Why couldn't we change into apprentice tinsmiths, painters or joiners, so that we could get to see what was forbidden?

Those forbidden things could be necessary, that I don't dispute, because I still don't have a certain yardstick to measure when this or that food or drink, play or film, game or amusement is harmful to a person, when it is useful, when it is indispensable. But one thing I do know for certain: we didn't believe a word of what we were told about the harm or benefits of things, substances and amusements. We didn't believe it because those who taught us mostly didn't live according to their teaching. And those few who acted according to their teaching mostly became targets of other people's; they were quite simply ridiculous.

The same thing happened to our classmates when they tried so hard to bear in mind all sorts of prohibitions and restrictions: they were sissies, mother's boys. More than that, they were suspected by the teachers of cringing, of telling tales, of all sorts of meanness. Nobody believed that any of us would be unaffected by such circumstances and things which day by day increased our passion – our peculiar hunger. Over the years we came to the conclusion that what they were doing was nothing less than irritating and enticing us with something sweet and tasty, but instead of giving it to us just saying, "You'll have to wait." But the others didn't wait.

If anyone had asked us directly what was driving our hunger, we would have been at a loss for an answer, or at best would have answered: everything. And by "everything" we would have meant the glittering entrance of some cinema, or the door of a theatre with people pouring in, some rude novel, some ambiguous or obscene ditty somewhere in a poetry collection, an advertisement for a pub in a newspaper, a string of pearls glittering under furs around the neck of a fine lady, lips painted bright red, the laughing mouth of a woman approaching on the street, jazz music and dancing and some kind of nightclub, known by whispers to only two or three people. These were what surrounded us and what assailed our eyes and ears with every step, even though they were banned. This gnawed away at us day after day. This was what nurtured our hunger for something almost nameless, and yet we longed for a time when we could start to slake our hunger. We were waiting for that time in the same way perhaps that our fathers' and mothers' steers and heifers did, when in spring they bellowed in front of a half-empty fodder rack and they itched to get to a pasture and fill their mouths with as much of the last tussocks as would fit in their stomachs.

Our forgotten pastures should have been a university – or rather, not a university as such, but what's associated with it, what's around it: independence, freedom, doing one's own thing, and just idling and loafing. Some had relatives, some had friends, some had acquaintances who had already been at university for quite a while and yet still hadn't passed any examination or had passed pitifully few. What is more, we knew that in going to university you could get through an examination even without opening a textbook, just by cribbing study notes. To talk and think about all this felt just like manna from heaven compared to the eternal cramming and tests at school. So we went to university safe in the knowledge that now the holiday would begin, now it would be relaxation, entertainment and pleasure, and now we would have everything that had allured us and yet been kept away from us. Our cup had been filled to the brim, and there was nothing left to do but lift it to our lips and drink as deeply as possible.

Many, very many feelings we had like that. So what is there to wonder at, if we pushed our way into the *Korporationen* when we entered university? They were said to be, since ancient times, a nest of youthful carefree fun of every kind. Why otherwise would all the sons of our Vons, our barons and counts have gone there? They were supposed to know the meaning of pleasure, which means a carefree, joyfully dissipated life. Relatives and friends had been telling us this since we were born. God, they thought, had piled all the troubles and pains onto His parishioners, while at the manor the endless feasting just had to go on. The parishioners lived in constant privation, even hunger, while at the manor there was endless abundance, wealth and style. But now there were no more manors, there were just the parishes and the parish householders. What happened to the pleasures and joys of the manors, theirs style and wealth, their dissipated life? It couldn't just vanish from the world, as it had been admired and envied too long for that, and it was too tempting and alluring. Our fathers would talk with pride about the time they sold a steer to the manor stables to be fattened – and why wouldn't it tickle them, when their sons and daughters were wearing the same sorts of coloured student caps, having now become the objects of special pride and the emblems of the anticipated life of revelry as it was once lived in the manors.

We had taken over the manors, and now we were hurrying to take over their way of life too, not only among the young students, but in the towns, villages and farmhouses. We wanted to feel like real landowners, lords of our demesne, and we didn't know how to express that desire any better or clearer than by trying it ourselves and being pleased that our progeny were also trying to live like their former masters and their progeny. We did what we could to carry on the manorial traditions, manners, ways of life, outlook, the whole ethical and aesthetic attitude.

Most of our manors were burdened with debts, and we took this as a model too. Most of the young people from our manors left university without completing any courses, being satisfied with merely studying; but we couldn't do anything else if we wanted to be the proper heirs to the manors' heritage. The young manor folk lived only for wine, women and song – well, our generation also wanted to kick up their heels. And the wealthier the country pile, the richer the manor, the more they felt obliged or called upon to follow the customs of the inherited manor in every respect.

And when the hard times came – as come they must, living like that – and the bankruptcies started, the young people were blamed, and that's where we are now. I've had first hand experience of all this. Once the spiritual baggage of the manorial class was being taken over, was there anyone anywhere among the younger or older ones who sounded a note of alarm or stood in their way? Even today a girl's eyes light up when young men put on their coloured caps. Fathers, mothers, sisters and brothers still feel a little ashamed or humiliated when a son, daughter, sister or brother turns up at home without that coloured cap. Not a single living person has ever asked me what I was studying or whether I had studied at all, but everyone wants to know which *Korporation* I was in and what we got up to. The main thing is this: do we live as the landed gentry did? Do we have the same customs, the same songs? Nobody wants to know if I speak German, but everyone wants to know if we sing in German. Do we drink in German?

There's another thing that I've never been asked: have I been in love in German? I'm quite amazed I haven't been asked this. But perhaps that's a good thing. I wouldn't have answered anyway, or I would have answered with silence. For this is the subject I've been meaning to write about from the beginning, and am finally getting round to, while up till now I've been talking about vacuous psychology. Has it somehow plumbed so deep into my soul that no force on earth can make me talk about it? Even if I should one day marry out of a great love, which I don't believe I will, I wouldn't feel obliged to confess it, because actually nothing has happened or come of it, and the great majority of girls, especially if they have worn the cap for a few years, would regard me as a bit stupid if I wanted to confess it to them before marrying in my own so-called novel. "Oskar, you really are a little ridiculous," my bride-to-be would say, "what's the point in telling me such things as if I were some uneducated village girl. We don't even pay much attention to such things these days, because we're becoming cultured, even without university and a *Korporation* cap."

Of course this is the case, I don't deny it. But the real heart of the matter doesn't lie there, but somewhere else, perhaps in the first pages I wrote. That essentially my novel took shape and came about for precisely the same reason that I and so many others rushed to join a *Korporation*: we were under the spell of the past. What was so terribly provocative was our long-humiliated and mutilated sense of ourselves as slaves when we tried, even outwardly, to be the masters of slaves, which we hid within ourselves. If the slave within us over the centuries had not continually pushed himself upwards, we would not have been able to put our masters' caps on, when the chance came. What would have been the point? What kind of satisfaction would we have had, if we'd felt like real masters? But we were the sons and daughters of our own folk, their flesh and blood. The smattering of education we had acquired had only slightly affected our brains; our emotional life was completely untouched by it. Our ideal was inherited from the past, and included coarse bread and communal granaries.

My love must surely smell of coarse bread and a dusty granary, and that's why it's so precious to me. My reason tells me to defend the break-up of the manorial lands, but my emotions tell me to cling compulsively to them, as do all my contemporaries. It is hard to break with the past so suddenly. In our hearts we circle around the empty dwelling places of our former masters, as if our consciences are troubling us. It's like murderers feeling sorry for their victims. But I don't feel any pity when I think of my love.

I wrote that last sentence at one o'clock at night. It's now six in the morning. For some reason sleep deserted me early today and I was up and dressed before I realised why I was doing it so abruptly. But reading the last sentence from yesterday, I feel that it simply isn't true. When I think of my love, I do feel sorry for something, though I don't know what. Why then did I write the opposite last night? Did I want to mislead, reassure or console someone? And if so, whom?

Perhaps I should never read in the morning what I wrote in the middle of the night; the morning and the night do not understand each other, or rather they misunderstand each other. But this morning I didn't read only the last page from yesterday' I read everything else I've written. There isn't much content there, but it's about myself and that's the subject, since I wanted to write a novel about myself.

As for the cult of the coloured cap, here I would like to defend myself and my fellows much more passionately this morning than I did last night. In my opinion there's no objection to be raised against me or the others. We haven't done anything that wouldn't have pleased ourselves, others or indeed the whole country; we have represented the country and people as they were. We didn't have any support from rich farmers in their grey baronial pomp: that came from every starveling cottager, peasant and tenant, every tailor, cobbler and saddler, every shopkeeper, businessman and industrialist, and every prophet of truth, palm reader and card sharper; if you want, every lawyer, doctor and pastor, every engineer, factory owner and banker, and every man of the people, public figure and politician. They all felt lifted up by the ears when their daughters and sons, relatives and acquaintances, or even they themselves pushed that coloured cap on to their heads. So why do people try to sling rocks at us for helping to pull the whole country up by the ears? If anything, they should have accused us of not doing it energetically enough.

And I wanted to do it and be personally responsible. I would have set all the wheels in motion so that the old German *Korporation* would finally abandon its lofty isolation or be forced into liquidation. I would have made it clear that it was wrong to see us as belonging to an Estonian *Korporation*, which would have been change in name only. In spirit we were the same *Korporation* as before. We were dreaming of the same superior position as our predecessors. All of us, like every person of sense, wanted privileges and favours, we didn't pay particular attention to the sciences and the arts, but we perceive them as having a practical purpose or being an amusing recreation. We didn't want to feel responsible to the country or the people, as we were mainly thinking of ourselves. And if these words didn't influence people, I would have said, What? Don't you trust us? Are you demanding real evidence? All right, gentlemen, what are your demands? Will you be satisfied if, one fine day, we announce that everyone is a traitor to his country who doesn't defend the corporations and their principles? Or do you want something more? That's what I would have asked them if I had had the opportunity.

And yet I probably wouldn't have asked such questions at the time I was only a student – I'm only asking them now. In those days I didn't have this novel to write and – who knows – maybe it's this novel that's provoked the foregoing questions and ideas in me. Maybe! I say this because we've always had love, and it's even more fickle of us to abandon our own fatherland, mother tongue, nation and mentality. So it's downright odd to hear that some people are trying to prove that we've become sober-minded, businesslike and practical – even in matters of love. Is it really sobriety, adherence to the facts and practicality when, even today, people abandon their fatherland, mother tongue and nation for love? Quite the contrary: it's romanticism, it's self-denial and it's heroism.

And we're the only ones who can sort things out in our homeland, and not a single German or Russian. Is there anywhere in all the Baltic lands a single German or Russian who would have betrayed his fatherland, his mother tongue or nation for love? No, no, my dear ones, only we, the original inhabitants of the Baltic lands, are capable of that. Nobody has loved us in our homeland for a long time, we have only been subject to pushing and pulling, and so we have come to learn, in our own skin, how much a human being needs love. That's why we've begun to love foreigners in a self-denying way. Such a love is characteristic of the slave; the landowner loves selfishly. Evidently we still feel like slaves in our own country. The great doctrine of love was once passed down through women and slaves; both our men and our women have loved like slaves. Great love creates in our homeland a countless number of fortresses belonging to foreign nations, which cannot be destroyed by cannon fire from the fatherland, because love can only be overcome by death or even greater love.

But I don't think even death would be worthy of my love. At any rate, her second love, whose consequence was marriage, did not do anything to my love. I often have the feeling that the marriage would have been no hindrance to Erika's return, and that her return could happen in the near future: why, how or when? I can't answer that. Even this morning, when I came back from the shop with half a litre of milk, a rye bun and a hundred grams of ham, I sat down at the table, started eating and was about to put a sliver of ham on my bun with my finger, when I suddenly felt that Erika was sitting there with me, watching me eat, and I asked myself if I really should take the piece of ham from its wrapping where she could see me, and I decided that on no account could I do that. And I got up from the table, took the little plate, knife and fork, and tried to eat my wretched breakfast as if I were sitting with my beloved at a banquet table.

As I ate, my eyes fell on the coloured cap hanging on a little peg on the wall, and the question sprang to my lips: how could I not be ashamed, as I ate like some rubbish collector or ditch digger, picking at a herring or skinning a sprat with the nail of my index finger, and how my habits have changed at the mere thought of the woman who thought it better to leave me here? Why am I actually fighting for this cap and its traditions, if it doesn't make me a whit better, neither when it's on my head nor when it hangs on a peg in front of me? And why didn't I put up a fight for the woman who makes me a new man at the very thought of her? Perhaps it was because winning over a woman involves "culture", which I didn't have, whereas winning a cap required nothing more than borrowed money and empty vanity? Or maybe winning a woman also means money and vanity, but in much larger amounts than I had at my disposal, or could hope for in the future? But love? My love and hers? Or was she not in love? Was I the only one? No, she was also in love; I felt it then and still feel it now, but with the difference that for me that love was the whole world, and for her it was merely a part of it. For my love I was prepared to forget everything else, but she would only love if everything else was left to her as well. That's how it was with her, as if it were an empty and peripheral thing in our lives.

It began one and a half years ago. I was living in this same room, but not as I do now – rather a little more comfortably. My income was small, but it was assured and at least enabled me to lead quite a decent life, in that those with an assured income have no hindrance to getting a loan and paying it back. I would eat lunch with the family, and that bill was paid in full. When I lost my job, I was forced to give up those lunches too. This didn't affect my love, because it had developed to the point where it could continue even without polite lunches.

My landlady was one of those rare women who still love children. For this reason she was regarded as slightly ridiculous or "funny", as someone called her. Her love for children went so far that she tried to treat everyone like children. First of all, her husband, the children's father, had to put up with this. Even I could not escape such treatment when I wanted to eat lunch here. Equally Miss Erika had to submit to it, but she was treated as a slightly older child who taught German and the piano to the younger ones. The landlady didn't love adults because they weren't obedient enough, especially in these times. So she wanted to ensure that her little family always came to her, like obedient little creatures scampering around her. If her husband pulled a face, she would explain: "What's it to you? You don't bring them into the world or raise them. You have to be brought up yourself, and kept in check. And as for hardship, don't say a word about it! You've no problem in getting fed. Our little shack and the farm can raise more children than I can manage to bring into the world. It would be different if we had twins or triplets as some people do. But there are none in our family, and I don't think you've any either, do you?"

"None in our whole clan that I've heard of, thank God," replied the landlord.

"Thank God indeed!" agreed the landlady, and went on to explain, turning across the table to me, as if I required some of her practical wisdom: "Because it would do no good if several came at once; they would all grow big at the same time. So it's better if they come one at a time, so that the line doesn't run out. I'm planning to live to at least seventy, and only rest for the last five years – until then I'll have to have someone to push and pull around, so they know how much I love them."

"That's a nice love to have!" sniggered the landlord.

"So what's your way? If you love someone, then keep away," she replied.

"That's more like it, yes," he said. "Leave people in peace if you love them – why keep pushing and shoving?"

"Young man, is that your understanding of love too?" she asked me, and since a large mouthful prevented me from answering immediately, she continued, "You're still young and inexperienced in life, so listen to what I've got to tell you: from my experience of men, all of them understand love incorrectly. They all say roughly the same as my husband does: if you love someone, leave them in peace. Young lady, do your men say that too?"

"Oh madam, I don't have a single man!" replied the young lady, blushing all over and casting a glance at me, as a sign of thanks for my just having offered her a pickled cucumber.

"I don't mean your man personally – I mean men in general in your society," she explained.

"I'm very rarely in contact with society, or not at all," she said evasively.

"You mean that men are the same everywhere," the landlady concluded from this, "you're only embarrassed to say it, young lady. They neglect their women."

"But what if they don't like women?" the young lady now ventured, and my gaze passed involuntarily over her shoulders, waist, arms and hips, as much of her as could be seen sitting at the table. She noticed my appreciative gaze and blushed again.

"Heavy-boned, like me," I said to myself, feeling something passing through my heart – a little jerk or shudder, a tiny warm flash. As I realised later, this was the start of everything that followed.

"What! Don't like them!" cried the landlady in reply. "But how can they like them when the woman doesn't wait and doesn't hang around? No miss, that is not how it works. You're young and you don't know men. Believe me and learn this lesson: if the man doesn't show interest, then we have to do something. We have to make it clear to the man that he loves us – then he'll start to behave as he should."

"What are you talking about! The girl is only young!" the landlord chided his wife.

"You're saying that I was old when I got involved with you?" she asked her husband. "No, my dear old man, I too was only young then, but without me we would never have become a couple, because you were so in awe of my parents' house that you would never have dared take the first step, although you'd been in love with me for ages. It's true – that's how it was. And I was only twenty-six then…"

"The young lady isn't twenty-six yet," said the landlord as a counterargument.

"How old are you really, young lady?" the landlady now asked, and when she noticed her embarrassment and blushes, she went on, "What is there to be ashamed of – we're a family! Society is another thing. Take no notice of the young man, he won't be the one courting you, or even if he did want to woo you, you won't be going to him. So tell me, boldly, how old are you?"

"I'll soon be twenty-three," she now replied.

"Already!" I thought, as I looked into her face.

"Well, you hear, old man, the young lady is already twenty-three and I was twenty-six; a couple of years make no difference. So young lady, bear in mind what I tell you: you've got to take the initiative yourself – men are so strange and funny these days. Men used to buy themselves wives, but now they're dead against it if they have to pay for anything."

"Women used to be different," her husband chimed in.

"Men must have been different then too, that's the main thing," parried the lady.

"Women used to be harder-working and more obedient, then…"

"So you mean I'm not hard-working?" she asked her husband.

"Well, but are you obedient?" he countered.

"Who do you think I should be obeying?" she challenged her spouse.

"A woman should obey her husband if she wants the man so much to marry her," he explained, slightly evading the question.

"If a man buys a wife, I suppose she obeys him," opined the landlady.

"Nowadays she doesn't anyway," said the landlord.

"Oh, she'll be obedient then," maintained the landlady. "But if I have my own home, why should I obey my husband?"

"Can't you do it out of great love?" I interjected in the family banter.

"Yes, you can obey your husband out of love," the young lady added.

"But if the husband wants to put you on to a mortgage, could that be done out of love?" asked the landlady.

"Maybe you could do even that out of love," I replied.

"Well, young man, you don't know what love is," said the landlady with conviction. "It's out of love that a wife has to keep a watch on her husband and guide him, so that he won't fall into other women's snares, because that would make the him unhappy, as well as his wife and children too. And you know, men are like that – any slag of a woman can twist them round her little finger, no trouble at all. That's how it is with love in this world, take note of that, young people!"

Nobody argued with her any longer and so the meal continued in silence. For some reason we were a little embarrassed. The young lady was bent over her plate, and seemed to be hurrying to finish the food her landlady had offered her. She declined to take any more, although the host was pressing her to do so. I also declined, as if I were following the young lady's example.

"Go on and have some food!" the landlady told me, "then the young lady will dare to take some more."

"Maybe I could, for the young lady's sake," I half agreed, and started to hand over my plate.

"No, no, not for my sake, I can't eat any more, I really can't," she rushed to assure me, and motioned as if to leave the table.

"Then I won't eat alone," I said and resolutely withdrew my plate.

"These young people today are certainly stubborn," said the landlady almost angrily.

"You're a funny person," said the landlord, trying to turn everything into a joke, "you talk about love all the time, and then you want the young people to eat."

Days passed without any sign that anything romantic was burgeoning between me and Miss Erika. Various illnesses occurred in the family that kept a couple of the children for a few days in bed, and so the young lady didn't eat with us at the table, but in the bedroom where she tended to the sick children. The landlady insisted on her eating at the table first and taking meals to the children afterwards or, better still, giving them to the children first and then coming to the table. But she definitely wanted to eat with the children, as if to keep away from the table and our company. This was very keenly felt because nursing and feeding the children were not really her duties, but she did it on her own initiative and she took on the responsibility. The landlady also felt that the girl was deliberately keeping away, and this offended her a little, because she went to great lengths to make sure no one insulted her, her family or her household.

"The old haughtiness is still there," remarked the landlady with a glance of mild reproof, when she thought that the eight-year-old boy and six-year-old girl didn't realise what the fuss was about.

"Listen, what's it got to do with haughtiness when she's sitting with your sick child?" remarked her husband.

"I can decide in my own house when and how my sick child is sat with," she retorted.

That is where the conversation ended. But the landlady had evidently not forgotten it, and some sort of secret worm was eating at her heart. And when the children's illness passed, so that the whole household could sit at the table again, she kept on offering me and more especially the young lady, more and more food to eat, and when finally the latter jokingly tried to claim that she must keep her waistline, because slimness was now the fashion, our landlady retorted, also jokingly, "Why are you so worried about your waistline? You're better off eating your fill; then you'll feel much more confident. We might not have a manor, or a castle, or a country mansion here, but thank God, we do have food – no shortage of that! And I like it when people are pleased with the food I make."

The landlady added this last sentence only after a little pause, having taken note of the effect of her previous words. For me they were like a whiplash in the face, to say nothing of the young lady, who seemed to turn red to the very lights of her eyes, so that even the children noticed the sudden change in her face, and the six-year-old daughter cried out in amazement: "Mamma, mamma, look how red miss's face has gone!"

"I've had a headache since this morning and now I'm suddenly hot and flustered," said the young lady, trying to excuse her blush.

"The children have been sick – now it's your turn," said the landlady.

"Oh no, my lady, I'm not getting sick from them, it will be over soon," she explained.

"But remember, young lady, that if anything more serious happens, you won't come in, you'll infect the children, God forbid!" intoned the landlady.

"Don't worry about that, my lady," the girl assured her. "I'll keep my promise – if I really get sick, then…"

"Very good, very good," the landlady interrupted her.

"But now we can get up from the table, everyone's eaten and the children can start working."

So we got up, and the young lady disappeared into another room with the children. Now the landlord said, turning to his wife, "Why do you treat her like that? She's very nice."

"How do you mean 'like that'?" she asked, as if she didn't understand.

"Well, all that about food, manors and country houses," he explained.

"I can talk about what I like in my own house," she said.

"But when it hurts others... You could see how the girl blushed, even the children did..."

"The children might be the only point you're right about," she opined, "but anyway – why should I be so delicate about it? Let them think a little about what service means."

"Have no fear about that, my dear woman, they think about that right enough."

"Well, I want to think that they think a great deal about it too," she now explained and, turning to me, she asked, "Mr *Korporant*, do you also think that I shouldn't have said it?"

"My lady," I replied, repeating the term used by the young lady, "I don't know whether you should have said it or not, but I wouldn't have said it myself."

"Well, thank God, at least you're fair!" cried the landlady triumphantly. "Of course you wouldn't have said it, and if I had been you, I wouldn't have said it either. You're right there. You're a man, and you're young as well, and a member of a Corporation to boot. If I were in your place, I might even get to love the young lady; at least I would try and see if she would start to love me."

"Yes, yes," grinned the landlord, "you go on about love, and then you talk to her like that!"

"Leave love out of it – you don't know anything about it!" she told her husband.

41

"Of course I don't," he agreed, "but you do. You think that the girl can be loved for her fair hair and blue eyes, and you can't forgive her for that."

"You think I'm jealous of the girl, do you?" she asked.

"Jealous of her pure heart," the landlord laughed, but you couldn't tell if he was joking or serious.

"What use are blond locks and blue eyes when your face is full of pimples like the young lady's?" said the landlady with mock pity, and this touched a raw nerve with me, because I too had felt some pity for the young lady when I first saw her pimply, flushed face.

"Love comes, pimples go, love goes, pimples come," said the landlord, half-joking, half-serious as before.

"What are you so pleased about today?" the landlady asked her husband, but he didn't answer immediately. First he gave a hearty chuckle and only then did he explain: "It's not that I'm pleased, but the way you get so worked up about that girl is something I find ridiculous. Shouldn't we be recommending some face cream for those pimples of hers? Mr Corporation Member, you might take on that job!"

"This is becoming a criminal case, I'd better go!" I joked, and I left the householders there and went up to my room. I couldn't rid myself of the feeling that it really had become a criminal case. I kept on thinking that I had once compared the young lady's bone structure to my own and then felt a little tug at my heart. I kept seeing her blond head, which really did have some natural curls, and her blue eyes and pimply face. I couldn't help it and could get no peace at all. Finally I went out and mooched around the town for hours, hither and yon, as I used to do as a student, when I didn't want to be at home and had had enough of sitting in cafés. Whether I did it consciously or not I still can't say, but I came back at just the moment when the young lady was supposed to leave the household. We came across each other on the stairs, I doffed my cap, she wished me

42

good evening, but we both – at once – stopped on the same step, as if we had something to say to each other, yet we remained silent and the next moment continued on our ways, I upward, she downward. But after a couple of steps I stopped again and called out quietly, as if in secret, "Miss!"

"Yes," she replied, turning around, looking up at me readily, as if she had expected my call.

"Could I come and keep you company?" I asked.

She started to laugh in a strange way, lowered her eyes and spoke hesitantly, as if doubting something: "I don't know…"

But I was already coming down the stairs, saying, "Let me come, miss, I so much want to. Of course, if you have special reasons why I shouldn't come, then…"

"No, why should I?" she cried, as if embarrassed. "No, no, please, if you…"

She didn't finish – we both stepped on to the street.

"I wanted to beg your pardon for something, ma'am," I said, although why I called her "ma'am" I don't know. Her eyes turned to me with a shocked expression, as if she were seeking a sign of mockery or a grin on my face.

"Beg my pardon?" she wondered. "I don't recall you doing…"

"Not me, but the landlady today at the lunch table," I interjected.

She blushed on hearing those words in the same way as she had before, and it was embarrassing for me to recall this to her mind at all, the more so as it didn't concern me in the least. I don't know what devil it was that drove me to say something like that. But there was nothing to do about it now, I had to continue, and so I explained: "I just wanted to tell you that I don't condone such treatment, I condemn it, and as a gentleman I should have stepped in to defend you at the table, but I couldn't, I didn't know how to."

"It was nothing," she said.

"But miss, why try to make it into something other than it

really was!" I cried, with a certain with a certain impatience and reproach. "The landlord started talking about it as soon as you'd left."

"Oh really?" she asked in surprise, though I don't think she was surprised at all, but only suspicious of everything I said. Although I didn't understand why I chose to use those particular words, I openly declared my position: "Forgive me, miss, but I feel that I've been a bit of a fool. You don't believe a single word I'm saying, and you don't believe me because the one who treated you so unfairly is Estonian, and I, who am trying to ease this injustice somehow and put it right, am also Estonian, while you are a German. Isn't that so, miss? If there had been some young German man at the lunch table today in my place, listening to what I heard, and if he had gone out walking and talking with you, you would have reacted quite differently."

"You're the first Estonian who's talked to me like this," she said.

"Don't you want to talk to me like this, as you've never done with an Estonian before?" I asked.

She didn't reply, and we continued walking side by side in silence. After a while, I sought her eyes and found her dejected face; she swallowed spasmodically and I realised that she had tears in her throat. She was doing everything in her power not to let them into her eyes.

"I apologise with all my heart for daring to upset you," I said when I saw this, "but I suppose it's best if I go."

"Please stay," she replied, adding after a little pause, "I'll be all right in a moment."

So we carried on side by side in silence, keeping in step, which was easier because she was wearing low-heeled shoes and so her pace was just as fast as mine.

"Why do you take it so much to heart?" I said at length, to comfort her in a comradely way, as if walking side by side at an even pace had given me courage.

"I don't," she replied. "I've got used to it already."

"So this happens often?" I asked.

"I don't know about often, but it does happen," she explained.

"You don't get used to a thing like that," I countered.

"I do, believe me, really," she assured me. "But when you started talking to me like this, it was unexpected, and I didn't know what to do. And if I don't know what to do or say, I tend to start crying."

"Life's difficult, isn't it?" I asked in an off-the-cuff way, but she replied quite seriously: "No! Why should it be? Grandfather is always asking me whether it's hard for me, and he doesn't believe me when I say that it isn't. Grandfather decides by his own experience. But I don't know about what used to be, hardly anything at all, and even what I do know I increasingly forget with each passing year. A couple of years ago we visited the estate we once owned in the country, and there we were shown around it. The changes were pointed out to us, but what really stuck in my mind was the orchard – yes, I remember that and it was big and beautiful. But otherwise – new settlers everywhere, and most of the park had been broken up, grandfather explained. For him of course it was a different matter, as he lives only for what used to be."

"How simply you put it," I said for something to say.

"So what's to be done?" she asked. "Parents – it's much harder for them of course. My brother, for example, he can't help it, he has to go several times a year to his old home in the country, summer and winter too, and every time he comes back, he says how beautiful it was. Thank God I'm younger, it's much easier for me."

Suddenly she seemed to wake from a dream, looked at her watch and said, "But now I really must run home, grandfather has been waiting for ages!"

"Can't I come any further with you?" I asked.

"No, please, no further, I'll go alone now. Thanks for coming."

"But might I come tomorrow or the day after?" I had to ask.

"Will you want to?" she asked back.

"Only if you let me."

"Me and my kind – nobody wants to be with us. My cousin explained to me once that we are too bony and wooden; Estonian girls are much more interesting."

"Is that possible?" I started laughing.

"Yes, my cousin said so," she affirmed gravely.

We shook hands and parted.

From that first walk I brought back with me a sort of disappointment. I couldn't explain the cause of it. Perhaps it was the directness and openness with which she responded to my openness? Or was it those final words about her own and others' "woodenness"? Perhaps the final effect on me was when we shook hands, and I felt as I left how strong and rough her hands were. They were a worker's hands, but with longer fingers than I have usually noticed.

The consequence of all this was that as I came home I almost regretted that I had asked permission to accompany her on the next evening as well. But I consoled myself with the fact that asking permission like that did not oblige me to do anything; it was a matter of simple courtesy.

The next day at the lunch table I tried with varying degrees of conviction to appear as if nothing special had happened between me and the young lady. I observed that she was doing the same. But our efforts were evidently overstrained, and the landlady seemed to notice something unnatural in our exchanges. Finally she couldn't restrain herself and expressed her suspicions to me: "Mr Studious, please be more attentive and polite to the young lady; her bread ran out long ago, but you don't seem to see or hear anything."

"Sorry," I replied, "but miss doesn't love to eat dark bread at lunchtime."

"You still have to offer it," explained the landlady. "And since when were you so well acquainted with what the young lady does or doesn't love?"

"Are you going on about love again?" interjected the landlord. "Yesterday you made us all lose our appetites – today you're doing the same thing."

"I didn't start on about love today – it was Mr Studious," she retorted to her husband. "And don't you interrupt other people's conversation – I'm asking since when has the young gentleman known what the young lady does or doesn't love. Let him answer me. What did they teach you in the *Korporation*, if you haven't learnt to answer?"

The young lady cast a furtive glance at me which I took to mean that she was awaiting my answer with a certain tension.

"That the young lady does not love bread with her lunch," I finally responded, stressing the word *not*, "I know because she has never accepted the bread I've offered her; what the young lady *does* love I haven't the faintest idea."

"Oh yes you have," said the landlady mischievously. "You must know that if you offered her chocolate, she wouldn't refuse you. All young girls love chocolate."

Again everyone became uneasy and silence followed. In that general silence I decided to myself that I wouldn't accompany her today. But when she rose from the table to leave, and cast a glance at me in which I read the question "Are you coming today?" I strove to reply with my own look without further ado: "Of course I'll come." That is what happened later, except that we didn't meet on the stairs as before, but on the street, several scores of paces away from the house.

"Why does the landlady always try to steer the conversation around to love?" she asked me straight away. This was unexpected and took me aback. But I quickly pulled myself together and replied frankly, giving a joking nuance to my tone: "Apparently she wants to tease us."

"Does she know something already?"

"No, she doesn't, but she guesses."

"So quickly!" she cried in amazement, adding, "I behaved at lunch as if everything was as before."

"You were very sweet," I replied.

"Was I sweet, really?" she asked, and I felt this came from her heart. To make her happy I assured her: "Very!"

"It's terribly nice to hear something like that about myself; I'm always hearing it about other people," she laughed, but I felt she meant it seriously.

"That can't be so," I contested.

"But it is, of course," she assured me. "I don't even have time to be sweet. At home I have all my indoor work and then I give lessons as well, because the family doesn't give me enough of them. And the kitchen makes my hands ugly and breaks the skin on my face – who can be sweet like that? We have a charwoman who comes twice a week for a couple of hours. In the evenings I'm tired, so that if I have to read something aloud to grandfather or play chess with him, I sometimes fall asleep. But our boys don't like tired girls, they want to be able to carry on, have fun and laugh. There are enough like that among the Estonians, so that's where they look for them. And I don't have any pretty clothes either, they barely cover my body. You can't be sweet if you're bumbling around the rooms with an apron on. I'm changing, and I'll be pretty indifferent to my looks if I live the way I'm having to. Even grandfather notices it. He's said to me a few times that a young girl mustn't be so careless about her looks, because then others won't care about her either. Everyone's becoming careless, the men are too. But it isn't good when even the men are indifferent to a young girl."

"Does your grandfather really tell you that?" I asked.

"Several times he's said it," she assured me, looking me in the face. But she must have surmised suspicion in my eyes, because she rushed to reassure me. "He really has said it.

But you'd have to know my grandfather, then you'd believe me. He is, you know, of an age a bit like – you understand? But that's what I like most about him. I like him more than anyone else in the world. He's the only person I can really talk to. My old aunt, who also lives with us, and all the other people are so cunning and worldly-wise that I can't get on with them. Are your people so terribly clever too?"

"How should I take that?" I wondered.

"Your girls for example, who go to university and wear the coloured cap; I've seen them on the street – are they terribly clever? Do Estonian boys like clever girls, the kind that know how to smoke and drink? Do you like them?"

There were so many questions at once that I didn't know which to answer. And as I thought about where to start, she said, "Of course you don't want to answer, you're afraid of hurting me. You like clever girls too, but you don't want to tell me that, because I'm not clever at all. Well, and then…"

"No, miss, it's not like that," I contested. "For a start, I don't understand why you think you're not clever at all."

"Well, listen, what cleverness can there be about a girl like me, working at home with an apron on, and then teaching little kids the piano or their ABC book?"

"The fact that you can ask me that only goes to show that you aren't so very…" I didn't dare to finish the sentence, so she continued, with a laugh that came from the heart: "… that I'm not so very silly. Thanks for being frank! Now at least I know that you think the same of me as so many others do: I am silly, but not so very much. The only person who thinks differently is grandfather. He never calls me silly, only 'immature'. He always says, 'Dear child, whatever will become of you and how will you end your own days, when my eyes have been closed? You, poor creature, won't get anywhere, you won't see or hear anything, you'll be knocking around at home or fussing over those lessons. But that's not how a young person matures.' So that's why I want so much to know what those mature people actually do and see. I once asked my brother, when he finally came home, but he replied it wouldn't be decent for a young girl of my age to hear or talk about it. That was about two years ago, and when you started talking like that to me yesterday and I started crying, my only fear was that you'd leave me there and go away. Because I thought straight away, as soon as I heard your words: thank God, now I've finally met the right person! If he can tell me things like that to my face, then he'll definitely tell me other things; I only have to dare to ask. So everything had to depend on me – on my courage. But it was a pity that..." She stopped.

"What was, if I may ask?" I interjected, because I wanted so much to know what the pity was.

"I don't think I should tell you that."

"Tell me, please," I begged.

"It's about you – I'm afraid of offending you."

"I forgive you everything in advance – just tell me."

"It was a pity for me that you are a Corporation member," she said then.

A hot wave surged through my whole body as I heard these words, as for the first time I understood very clearly that I had begun to love this girl, and her words generated a fear in me that I might lose her for no other reason than that simple reason: a coloured cap hung on a peg at my place. It was downright ridiculous how it affected me, that she suspected me because of those colours. My love for her must have already been very deeply rooted. This love might perhaps have been already within me before I felt it at all. It might have been latently coursing through the blood of my ancestors for centuries, unconsciously of course, a burning hatred, a worshipful adoration and a flaming love, centuries old. Now it welled forth into consciousness, saw the light of day in me. And not because she was walking and talking with me, but simply because she was who she was. At once I felt that I was in love with her bones and limbs, her gait, her eyes, into which I didn't dare to look, fearing all the time to reveal my inmost self.

"Now you see, I shouldn't have said it," she concluded, when I didn't know how to react to her in words.

"Quite the opposite!" I cried then, "it's very good that you said it. But won't you explain to me why you feel sorry for me as a Corporation member? And are you still sorry?"

"I still am," she replied as if delaying, thinking over whether she should have said it or not.

"But why?" I asked insistently.

"Aren't the Estonian corporation members about the same as the German ones?" she asked in reply, and when I tried to deny it, but couldn't find quite the appropriate words and proofs, she asked again: "But why would you be in corporations if you didn't want to be? Don't you have *Weib, Wein und Gesang?*"

"We do, but ...," I wanted to explain, but she interjected impatiently, "Better not to say anything, because you'll say it like a *Korporant*. I've talked to the ones I know, I know very well. You can't know anything anyway. You simply evade the issue, because you're a *Korporant*. You'd say that a corporation member can't talk to ladies about everything. A *Korporant* can't talk to ladies about men's things, you all say that. But tell me – can other students talk to ladies about everything? You do have other students too – you're not all in the *Korporation*? Or, you arrange everything, as we do, so that no student may really talk to ladies about anything, because you have to be polite, you have to be gentlemen. So maybe you understand why I was sorry that you are a corporation member. Or rather, I wasn't sorry for you, but for myself, that's how lost for words I am. At first I was so glad that I was getting to know an Estonian student..."

"I'm no longer a student now," I interrupted.

"Have you already graduated?" she asked.

"No, but..."

"You mean you left because you lacked money, I know

that. But surely you'll get some money again and then you'll carry on studying. Anyway it doesn't matter whether you're going to university or not, you're still a *Korporant* and that's what's important to me. For I would be so very pleased if I'd got to know someone else who wasn't one; we do have people like that ourselves."

"So why is it so important to you that there is someone else who isn't in a *Korporation?*" I asked.

"I told you," she replied. "It's not worth talking to a *Korporant*, because he's a gentleman, but if I want to become more mature, how do I talk to a gentleman?"

"So what would you like to talk about?" I enquired.

"I don't actually know what about," she replied. "Whatever would develop me so that I wouldn't be so silly any more, as everyone else thinks, even you."

"I don't think that," I tried to contend.

"I'm sorry," she said convincingly, "but you're only saying that because you're a *Korporant*, though actually you think something quite different. When our boys say, for example, that Estonian girls are more interesting than ours, because they're supposed to be more mature, then I have asked several times – what should we talk about then, to be interesting, and to prove that we're mature? What do you actually talk about to Estonian girls? But they reply, 'About everything.' Well, so talk to me about everything, I say. 'I can't, with you, because you're not mature and it's not interesting with you.' So we debate, like squirrels on a treadmill. And that is why I thought that if I got to know an Estonian boy, I would start chatting with him so that I would soon become a more mature person. I thought I'd take the bull by the horns and say to the Estonian boy, Talk to me now so that I'll become a bit more mature. In the end, let him treat me like … let him swear, as you did to begin with…"

"I beg your pardon – I didn't swear!" I said.

"You said you were playing the fool," she explained. "But

how can you be a *Korporant* and a fool at the same time? Isn't that swearing?"

"I was talking about myself."

"Doesn't matter, swearing is still swearing, even though you explained that you were doing it for me. I was terribly afraid that you would soon call me a fool, and I decided beforehand that no matter what you call me, I will bear it sweetly; perhaps it will make me a little more mature, as grandfather wishes. But you wanted to leave. Then it occurred to me that you're a *Korporant*, and I felt terribly sorry for you."

"Now I'm starting to understand you a little," I said. "You have some sort of peculiar conception of Estonians and Estonian students. You think there's something bold, crude and robust about them, but at the same time cunning, smart and cynical."

"I really don't know whether it's like that," she said. "But don't your women members of the *Korporation* seem very bold, as they sometimes walk down the street, their caps over their eyes or tilted on their heads, and their hair hanging loose. The other students are perhaps even wilder, but I don't recognise them without their caps on. And yet you shouldn't think that I mean it badly – not at all. A mature person, a woman too, I suppose, must…"

"… be bold and sturdy," I interjected, but with a certain hint of irony.

"Exactly," she affirmed, "bold and sturdy."

"And isn't what you say a demonstration that you too can talk about interesting things?" I added.

"You're wrong," she replied with conviction. "I say what I think. Of course, my opinion might be silly, as it usually is, I don't deny it, but it is my opinion. A month or so ago I had a chat with one of our *Korporanten* about much the same thing. He too called some women bold and sturdy. But when I wanted to know who these women were, he wouldn't answer. Yet I, as is my wont, stupidly asked him what kind of women the *Korporanten* liked to sing along with, when drinking their wine. Of course, I asked that because I wanted to be more mature. But he started explaining things in such lofty and idealistic terms that I didn't feel any more mature; I'd heard it all before and read it in books as well. So I said to him, Why don't you take me or someone like me along to your drinking sessions, if wine and women are such ideal things? Take me, for goodness' sake, if you're a gentleman, take me along with other women and gentlemen, so that I can learn about maturity among the gentlefolk."

"Did he take you?" I asked with a smile.

"No," she replied simply.

"So why not?"

"It wasn't for ladies, he explained to me. But I answered straight away: am I a lady, if I scrub away all day in my apron and teach the ABC to kids? Do ladies ever do such things? Or if they do, are they ladies for long? A lady is always a lady, he replied. And a lady must always remain silly and immature, I concluded. At that point he left me there, because he said I had a wicked tongue. He was no great loss to me, because I hadn't matured one little bit with that kind of talk. Always the same thing: I'm a lady and therefore nothing is good for me, and since nothing is good for me, I won't mature, and because I'm immature, I'm not interesting, and if a girl isn't interesting, she can only hang around with her grandfather and aunt; no boy will find her attractive. You could stay like until you're a grey-haired old maid and start to shrivel."

"But I'm starting to love you, I do love you already, I've loved you from the start," I said quietly, almost indifferently, as if I were merely pointing out a fact. I don't even know why I said it, because I might just as well have said it the next day or the day after. But I must have felt that I had to say those words anyway, and therefore I was saying them then, so that they would no longer trouble my heart or scorch my soul. Of course it was downright stupidity to declare one's love for anyone, let alone when you're a *Korporant*, as she kept emphasising, and when you love someone so madly and rashly as I loved her.

Even today, when I try to understand or explain my declaration of love, I can find no reason other than what must have been the uniqueness of my love at the time. I had previously declared love half a dozen times, but I had always thought of it as a customary or polite gesture, and I had had enough patience to wait for a suitable place and moment. Today it happened on the street in the midst of passing and approaching people, who might even have overheard my declaration. I had taken nothing into account.

Another factor that determined my declaration may have been that she was at such pains to stress her regret that I was a *Korporant*. Evidently I wanted to prove to her that it didn't matter that I was in a *Korporation*, I could still behave in an extraordinary manner even in an exceptional situation. In other words, I was trying to rehabilitate myself and win the young lady's trust, respect and interest, even if she regretted the excessive sociability of a *Korporant*. She suspected something of the kind in my actions, because, while at first she couldn't believe her ears, looking at me inquisitively as if I were mad, her face then turned bright red, so that even her ears glowed; she soon collected herself and said, trying to smile, as if it were all a huge joke, "Does every Estonian *Korporant* declare his love on the street, or are you the only one?"

"I don't know about others, but this is the first time I've done it," I replied.

"You mean you've declared your love in other places before now?" she asked with a little sting in her tone and a slight tremble in her voice.

"Always other places before now," I assured her seriously.

"Why do I have the honour of getting it on the street?" she asked. "Is it perhaps because I'm a German? Or am I not enough of a lady, after what I've said to you?"

"Please have mercy, miss, and leave off that tone and those words, if you have even a speck of what I see and believe in you. Or do you think it would have been better coming at the lunch table?"

I saw actual terror in her eyes, but the freezing of her lips and the movement of her nostrils cannot have come from that. Instead of blushing, a pallor spread over her whole face. She kept her eyes lowered, twitching her eyebrows, as if trying the brush aside tears. Thus we continued our walk silently for a while. I only noticed that she mechanically changed her pace, to keep in step with me as her companion. After a while she asked, as if in curiosity and fear, "Is that how it comes out then?"

"Not before now, only today," I replied.

"But that's terrible. Just think what would have happened if you'd said the same thing to me at the lunch table. It would have been really horrible."

"Love is sometimes horrible."

"Love should be beautiful," she affirmed.

"It is beautiful, it's so beautiful that it gets horrible."

"So beautiful that it gets horrible," she repeated to herself slowly, as if pondering whether these words hid some idea, or whether they were just like so many other words.

"Love is beautiful and it makes you happy," I said. "Walking beside you and talking like this, I'm happier than ever before, I'm the happiest person in the world."

"Do you really believe what you're saying?" she asked, with a sort of happy sigh.

"My words are only a little drop, a tiny speck, of what I feel for you, for the fact that you exist at all, that the two of us are together. I don't have words to say what's inside me. If I were a poet, a singer, composer or anyone, and I could express it in any way at all, what I feel and how, then I would be world-famous overnight, we'd both be carried aloft, we'd be drowned in gold."

"Do Estonian girls talk about love like that too?" she

asked, as if she wanted to draw me down from the heaven of emotions into the earthly everyday.

"I don't know," I replied, "I only know I said those words for the first time."

"But you said at first that you've loved before, declared your love before."

"Please don't ever remind me of that," I said. "There is only one real love in anyone's life, and nothing else counts."

"There is only one real love in anyone's life," she repeated like a distant echo, and I felt her drinking in and tasting every word, every syllable, every letter, every sound. After that she asked me in quite a different tone, "But what did they reply to you, the ones you declared your love to?"

"I've never declared my love in quite that way before," I replied.

"You must have said something!"

"Please – I can't answer that today, maybe some other time. I can't even think about that today."

"Now you're becoming a *Korporant*, a gentleman again," she said, "now, just when things are getting so interesting. I'm so sorry about that. But what's even worse is that grandfather is waiting at home, I have to go."

"Right now?" I asked, and my voice and actions must have betrayed alarm, because she started to laugh and said, "Now, now, it's only till tomorrow, tomorrow at the lunch table we'll see each other. But it's terrible – what faces we'll have tomorrow! The landlady is bound to read everything in them."

She reached out her hand to me, I took it in my own two, and pressed it to my lips with such force as if I were about to leave her forever there. Her long fingers crunched a little, and were shot through with a pulsation, from pain or some other cause, I do not know to this day.

"You shouldn't kiss my hands," she said, making a slight attempt to draw it back, but she let it rest on my lips, "they're what I use to scrub the floor with."

"I'm ready to kiss those floors that this hand has scrubbed," I replied in a kind of drunken stupefaction, when she finally released her hand from mine.

She turned and left. I stood as if dumbfounded, staring after her. After a few steps, though, she looked back, and seeing me still there, she stopped, as if uncomprehending. I don't know what I concluded from that, but the very next moment I leapt towards her.

"Tomorrow I'll try to tell some lie to grandfather," she said with a shameful smile, "and then we'll have a little more time – shall I?"

"Erika, you're an angel!" I cried, calling her by her name for the first time.

"Good heavens, not so loud, other people will hear!" she implored. "And don't hope for too much; grandfather won't let me be alone for very long."

"I could climb to the top of Oleviste spire and shout to the whole town that you promised to lie to your grandfather for my sake!" I declared, without curbing my enthusiasm.

"You're frightening me!" she said, starting to laugh, and ran off. I stared after her until she vanished behind the next street corner.

Yesterday Erika had expressed the fear about how our faces would look when we appeared at the lunch table, and all evening and half of today I had assured myself that I wouldn't come to lunch at all, because I might not have the right amount of control over myself, but when lunchtime arrived, my feet led me unthinkingly into the dining room. Yet it all went more easily and smoothly than either of us had dared to suppose. Today the landlady paid no attention to us, because she was preoccupied with cooking and food preparation.

"Well, my dear masters and porkers," she began, full of good cheer, "today I've made you a joint of roast veal, so hold on to your tongues – otherwise they'll go into your stomachs when you start eating. Each of you can toss on your oat gruel as much salt and butter as your heart desires, I did it myself just for the children; otherwise the boys will empty the box before the older folks even get a look at it."

And there was nothing to be done; even if the boys wanted to put their own butter on it, promising to do it very sparingly, they had to be content with what their mother gave them.

When the roast appeared on the table, the landlady turned to Erika and said, "Miss, let your plate be the first one today."

"My lady, what about the children? I can wait," replied Erika.

"No, no, young miss," said the landlady, "today you're the first, because it's for your sake I've been slaving over the roast. On other days the children can get served first, and then the grown-ups."

Erika's face coloured as she handed her plate to the landlady, no doubt fearing who knows what bomb exploding with the woman's next words. But nothing came that was worth worrying about. Today the landlady was extremely delicate and polite.

"You're not interested, young lady, in why I've taken so much trouble and devotion just for you over the roast today?" she asked, adding, "Carrot and turnip as well? White beans? Today I've put a double portion of brown butter on them."

"No, my lady, I'm interested in why today I have the honour of…"

"Not honour, but gratitude," interjected the landlady. "And not only to you, but gratitude to all German ladies."

"But I'm not a lady at all yet," laughed Erika, breaking into the landlady's words.

"If you aren't one already, you will become one, because a nice young miss like you will never be an old maid; men simply won't leave you alone, you'll see. And once you're a lady, then remember today's roast, the cabbage and carrots, the beans and everything else that's still to come. They've been made from your recipe. Not yours personally, of course, but German ones in general, I mean, from German ladies in the good old days. From when my mother sent me into service with them, more or less like you now, with us. Not that we were in desperate need of it, because we had our own nice little home then, but my mother said to me, Off you go, you'll get to know things that'll make you smarter, and you'll learn about what you need in life. And I've never regretted that I went into service. Whatever was bad about it I've forgotten, because that's how I was – not used to carrying bad thoughts in my head – and what was good I've held on to. So if today's meal, miss, is at all tasty for you..."

"Everything is marvellous, my lady," interjected Erika.

"Well, so it should be, because it all comes from German ladies and the good old days. And finally..."

"And here comes the moral part of the story," declared the landlord.

"Finally the moral part always comes if you're a housewife and a mother, and if you are no longer a housewife or mother, there is no need for it any more," said the landlady with conviction. "And really it was..."

"... the Lenten sermon about fasting that I wanted to give," chuckled the landlord, again intervening in his wife's flow, while trying to trickle some brown butter from the bean bowl on to his plate, as a result of which the beans poured on to the plate, the table, his knees and the floor.

"Listen, stop chiming in to what I'm saying," said the landlady, turning to her husband, and seeing his treatment of the beans, added, "You are a pig, not a bit cleverer than your boys, always leaving leftovers under your feet."

"Nah! If you haven't served in a noble house, food is one of things that..." the landlord was about to make a silly joke, but the landlady stepped in: "Then listen to your wife's Lenten sermon about food, about preparing and eating it. That's the whole moral story here – today's roast, along with the potatoes, fresh cabbage, beans and turnips and carrots."

"Pickled and fresh cucumbers, cauliflower, pasta and tomatoes are missing," noted the landlord in a matter-of-fact manner.

Now they all burst out laughing, so heartily that even the landlady had to join in, like it or not. Only a while later did she manage to say, "Now try and talk seriously at the dinner table! They're all laughing and joking. And yet there's nothing to laugh at here. Would you laugh if you didn't like your meal? No, you'd all have glum faces. But haven't you ever been interested in how tasty food is prepared?"

"I've never been," replied the landlord, lifting fresh cabbage to his mouth, "I'm happy to leave those matters to the servants."

"But if there were no more servants?" asked the landlady.

"Some will be found," replied the landlord.

"But there aren't any who know how to or want to."

"Well, if there aren't any servants, then the women and ladies themselves do it," said the landlord.

"No, my dear man, there's a shortage of servants because there are no longer any proper ladies of the house, no housewives – that's the whole issue. You think just like other men, that you open some new soup kitchen and in come the serving people. But they don't. A servant only comes from a house, remember that. When there are no ladies treating housekeeping as important any more, how can there be servants who know their skills? Now ladies regard it as a personal insult if someone dares to think that they're interested in housekeeping, but at the same time everyone complains and expresses amazement if a complete stranger isn't enthusiastic about the mess they've been paid to clear up. What a terrible injustice! You pay the poor creature fifteen or twenty crowns a month, and she doesn't into raptures about your duster or the sooty bottom to your pot."

"They're very right not to, because a machine can clean up dust, and you can cook with gas or electricity with no soot," remarked the landlord.

"Why then do people go to London to learn cleaning?" asked the landlady.

"They go to London for the English language," he explained. "Don't you want to send your daughter there when she grows up?"

"I do, but on one condition: before going, she should learn to clean the bottom of my little pot at home, and then let her go to London to clean grime, or she'll come back as soon as she can! Straight back even wilder than when she left, and then there'll be nothing gained from the English language. No, my little piglet…"

"Now listen…" her husband tried to interject.

"Shut your mouth for once," shouted the landlady, "because the dinner table is the only place where you're dining with us all, otherwise you'd run off straight away, as soon as I start to say something. And I'm happy to call you a porker, because you run like the piglets to the trough, without knowing where the food comes from or how."

"But chickens don't know that either," cried one of the children.

"Chickens do know," contested the other. "Haven't you seen how they lift their heads up and watch if something's going on?"

"Quiet, children!" cried the landlady. "Don't interrupt when mummy's talking. When I was small, I wasn't allowed to open my mouth when grown-ups were speaking."

"That's why you're trying to keep them quiet now," remarked the landlord.

"You're not a bit smarter than your children," said the landlady to her husband, almost angrily. "Let me tell the young lady what I have to say; it will interest her, won't it, miss?"

"My lady, it'll interest me very much," Erika confirmed.

"I think it will interest you to know what an Estonian lady thinks of you and how she appreciates you. And I appreciate you very highly. The German lady I worked for was perfect and a proper lady of the house. She kept and cherished her kitchen and her home."

"So, now we've come to the matter of love, and now you can't be sure any more what will come or how it will end," I said to myself, and threw a glance at Erika, but she didn't notice it, because her eyes were fixed, whether out of interest or a sense of duty, on the landlady's lips, and the word "cherished" seemed to leave her quite indifferent.

"And since the lady of the house loved her home and kitchen, she learnt to love her maid too. The German lady had respect for the titles of lady and housekeeper, and therefore the position of her assistant, her maid, was worthy of respect as a decent calling in life. Not like nowadays. A housewife is now a lowly creature among women, and her assistant is regarded as lower than some night-soil man."

"Mummy, what's a night-soil man?" interrupted her little daughter.

"You are silly!" cried her younger brother. "That's the one who cleans up after others."

"But then Loona is a night-soil man, she cleans up mine and..." The daughter wanted to explain in her bright voice, but her older brother put his hand over her mouth and they were suddenly quiet. The children burst out laughing, even the little daughter laughing along with the others, as her mother carried on talking: "You see, from a very young age! Where do they get it from? You silly child, if you talk like that about Loona, then I'm also your night-soil woman, a cleaner for all of you."

"A proper lunch table conversation with white beans and fresh cabbage," noted the landlord mockingly, while I said to myself, "Doesn't matter about the night soil, as long as it's not about love."

"Dear man," said the landlady, now turning to her

husband, "if I have to pay your charwoman day after day, then I may dare to talk about it, even at the dinner table. And I demand respect for my work, like any other person. You think of course that paper smeared with printer's ink is grander than a pan smeared with grease."

"It's not just me, the others think the same," declared the man, who was very proud of his position at the office.

"But why do you complain that there are no other housewives apart from one or two and that no one wants to go into service any more?" asked the landlady. "Why do you cry that there are no children any longer, when you all prefer smeared paper to the smeared pan? Paper won't feed your children. If I weren't so superstitious, I would say, Thank God, my children have so far escaped serious illnesses and all sorts of complications only because I have kept a hold of the pan and pot handles when I was cooking and boiling food for them. You, my husband, are healthy only because I have fed you myself, otherwise you would be stooped there in the office suffering for ages, or you might even have kicked the bucket. But of course I don't say that, because I'm afraid that as soon as I say it, everything will fall on me and my children that I had just been thanking God for avoiding. God doesn't want to be thanked for the things we can worry about. Illnesses and diseases are in the soup pot, not in God's hands."

"Then a new faith ought to be created, the religion of the soup pot," said the landlord.

"Well, it would be more useful to believe in a soup pot or a greased pan than in smeared paper or any sort of tubs and vessels where you keep women's paints and colours that men admire," the landlady lashed out now like a whip at her husband's stare. "A German woman, since I am talking about her, was the mainstay and the keeper of her home and hearth; now everybody is enthusiastic about those women who are masters at breaking up homes and hearths. And I tell you, my dear young lady, that if the German men had been as virtuous as the German women, you would not be sitting at our table now. Because…"

"For God's sake, please, no politics!" said the landlord, as if outraged.

"What about politics?" replied the landlady, who had evidently got into her stride, "I'm only saying what I personally think."

"Nobody believes that you're alone in thinking this; everybody is convinced of this general opinion. It's what Estonians think," explained the landlord.

"No, my dear man, listen to me first. Then you'll see that ideas like this can only be held by a few Estonian women familiar with the steam of the soup pot. You see, I think that if German men had been as clever and virtuous about their affairs as German women have been, they would have all gone with our men over beyond Narva and near Pskov, but not down to Võnnu. No one would have gone there if they'd been equal to their women. And if they had all been beyond Narva and near Pskov, our history would certainly not have taken such a sudden turn. Or what do you think, Mr Studious?" she turned to me while I was staring wide-eyed at her, "might our history have been different, if all the *Korporanten*, even the German ones, had gone beyond Narva together and over near Pskov?"

"I don't know," I fumbled for an answer, "but it seems to me that the whole supposition…"

"… rose from the steam of the soup pot, eh?" interjected the landlady. "All right! So why are you a *Korporant*, Mr Studious?"

"Leave those questions alone!" the embarrassed landlord reprimanded his wife.

"Let me ask now," replied the landlady, "I do want to hear how Mr Studious answers. My own children will grow up and go to university; I want to know."

"It's hard to give an answer to your question," I said at length, in utter confusion, since I felt that this woman was

65

not to be feared only when she started talking about love, or wanted to feed you to bursting at the dinner table, but on several other occasions too. How was I supposed to answer her? Everything that I wrote above? In Erika's presence I had to say I was a *Korporant* because coursing in my veins were dozens of generations of slaves' blood, and that I too felt like a slave, as do my parents, brothers, sisters, relatives, acquaintances, complete strangers, because why would they otherwise admire me in my coloured cap, which leads me down to Võnnu, but does not call men to arms beyond Narva or near Pskov? And should I perhaps add to that that my present mad love was rooted deeply in slaves' blood and that every glance I cast on that girl in admiration, every word with which I tried to approach her, every movement, every action whereby I tried to please her, every dream of mine in the middle of the day or late at night, was nothing more than a little glow-worm's service of devotion bowing before the moon? Perhaps I should explain in self-defence that just as nothing that is not in the water can rise to the water's surface, nor can anyone who is not in society rise to the top of it? Prophets of a new faith arise every time that society is bursting with a new faith. So why do you hang prophets, but not the society that created the prophets and lifted them up on its shoulders? Only to make things easier for executioners and gravediggers – and for no other reason. Well, pass judgement on me as a *Korporant*, because I and my companions are fewer than the whole Estonian nation that admires us. Was I really supposed to say all this to the landlady? Even now I don't know whether there is an ounce of truth in these words and pronouncements. Maybe my explanations will turn all of society and the Estonian nation on its head, maybe my mad love will thus only become a bit of tomfoolery, which doesn't correspond to any reality. All of this flashed like lightning through my brain as the landlady said with a haughty smile, "You see now what you men are like – Germans or Estonians. It's all fiddle-faddle with you, and then you wonder that history is going that way and not another. You put your cap on without…"

"But why do women do it, if men are just fiddle-faddle?" said the landlord, to support me.

"Girls?" responded the landlady. "They want to please the boys."

"But if the boys want to please the girls as well?" replied the landlord.

"Exactly!" I cried and added, "and that's all." And I was surprised at my own failure to realise that simple answer to the landlady's question in the first place. But as with everything in the world, there had to be a natural reason for my failure to realise it. Now I can guess the reason why: I was afraid of the word "love" and therefore I also refrained from mentioning "liking", because that's how it is with people: loving is never far from liking. This was proven today as well. Hardly had I uttered my happy words than the landlady said, turning to the young lady, "You see, miss, how men make their lives easy: when some foolishness hits them, instantly love is to blame, which is the same as saying we women are to blame."

"But, my lady, maybe that's true," she said.

"There it is: I was seeking support from you, but you go over to the men's side," joked the landlady. "But I warn you, miss, be careful with men. If we trust them too much at a young age, then we'll trust them too little in old age, and both of these will do us harm."

With that wise adage, we rose from the table because we had all finished eating long ago. I went up to my room, but I couldn't find peace there at all. My body was heating up, actually burning, inside and out. Time passed at the pace of a snail feeling its way carefully with its horns. But to me that protracting animal was repulsive, because it forced me to think, and at the moment I didn't have a single beautiful, useful idea. Everything that came into my head worked against me. I couldn't escape the feeling, try as I might, that at today's lunch something wounding and humiliating happened to me. I was wounding and humiliating myself – that was my conclusion, except that there was no way I could collect my thoughts and clarify where my own mistake lay. Finally, I could stand it no longer and left the house. But even on the street I could find no consolation or ease. After about half an hour I came back home, and when I looked at the clock I saw that the young lady would be free in just a couple of hours. To revive myself in time, I threw myself on the sofa, if not to sleep, then to rest a bit. As I closed my eyes I tried to think only of the young lady, not of myself. I remember that all my interest was concentrated on one question: did she lie to her grandfather today for my sake or not? That question was to my mind parallel with another question: does she love me, even a little? And with that last question I woke from my sleep, which had lasted ten whole minutes longer than anyone should be allowed. For the first moment I was senseless. My arm, holding the clock, fell listlessly on to the sofa, and there I was oblivious, until the next moment I jumped to my feet, grabbed my cap and coat, and rushed downstairs as if on fire. But having got to the second floor, I very nearly tumbled on to the reason for my hurry: Erika was coming up the stairs towards me. There must have been something terrifying about my demeanour, because she froze to the spot and asked, "Good Lord! What's wrong?"

"I'm late!" I cried. "Sorry, but –"

"Wait for me outside, I've forgotten something," she replied and carried on up the stairs, while I continued downward. But as soon as the outdoor air struck my face, I asked myself, Did she really forget something, or did she only come back for my sake? And I had to struggle with myself with all my might not to creep back up the stairs and listen to whether she went inside to ask for something, or would come back after me anyway after a while.

When we were at last side by side on the street, she said

with enthusiasm, "It was so interesting at the lunch table today!"

But somehow I couldn't share her enthusiasm, and that was painful to me. For how great could my love for her be if her enthusiasm didn't become mine as well? So I walked almost sadly, my breast full of tingling pain, and not knowing what to say. But she didn't even notice it, she was glad that just for once they had been talking about things that were new to her and could help her to mature. She even wanted to tell her grandfather what had been discussed today at lunch, but she would have to wait a little, because Erika had already spun a great long lie about why she had to stay out longer today.

"I lied in a way that I can use again in the future," she told me. "But I'm not going to explain it to you, I'm keeping it to myself. It's my sin alone, you have no part in it."

"Our first sin, our first crime," I said.

"How terrible that what is beautiful turns straight into a sin!" she cried. "Grandfather is always repeating to me that whatever I do, I shouldn't lie to him, and now it's happened anyway, as if it were meant to."

"If you lied for love, then your sin will be forgiven you," I said, as if taking her confession.

"But if it was for forbidden love?" she asked. "I've heard so often about forbidden love."

"Then you are doubly forgiven, because forbidden love is great love," I explained, without really knowing whether that explanation was right or whether it made any sense at all. But she asked with great interest, "Is forbidden love really great love?" And since I didn't answer straight away, she carried on: "What really is forbidden love? What kind of love is forbidden?"

"For instance, if a king's daughter fell in love with the son of a fisherman or a peasant," I answered.

"But if the fisherman's or peasant's son loved the king's daughter, would that be forbidden?" she enquired.

"No, that wouldn't be," I explained. "A small person may love a greater one, a lower may love a higher, not the other way round. A wolf may howl at the moon, but the moon has to this day never howled at a wolf; that is the order of things."

"That was a joke, about the wolf and the moon, wasn't it?" she said. "You said that because the moon suddenly happened to shine on us."

"That's why," I replied. "I suddenly had a feeling that I'm also a wolf howling at the moon."

"Why?" she wondered. "I don't understand, because..."

"It's best that way," I said, and asked, "shall we go to the seaside?"

"I'm afraid of going there, I might be recognised in the moonlight and grandfather might find out that..."

"... that the moon is walking with a howling wolf," I laughed.

"You mean you thought of me as the moon?" she asked, amazed.

"No, I was thinking of a king's daughter."

"No, you were thinking of me, and I'm so embarrassed."

"Why are you embarrassed, if I thought of you?"

"I can't tell you that," she replied in a voice as if she had to blush.

"But who can you tell it to?" I asked.

"If I had a mother, then to her," she didn't hesitate to reply.

"So what would you tell her?"

"I'd say that someone compared me to the moon, but..."

"But?" I asked, when she stopped.

"Now we come to what I can't say any more," she explained.

"To your mother, you could."

"But I don't have a mother," she said. "I don't even remember my mother, or only something white as if through a fog, and auntie says that must be a memory of my mother, because she loved to dress in white – white silk with a red rose. Last year there was a reception at the German Embassy, and there I saw a lady in white silk with an enormously big red rose, and I asked auntie, might my mother have been like that lady, but auntie said, 'Ah, phooey! Not at all! Your mother was a fine lady.' So I don't know what my mother was really like, I only remember from auntie's answer that that lady there at the embassy was not fine enough, she thought, to be my mother."

She went on talking for a while about the German Embassy reception, her auntie and the lady in white with the big red rose, who she only remembered dimly memory as something white. It was nice that she talked and I could be silent. I too was thinking of my own mother, among other things, I thought that if she had died in my early childhood, what sort of memory would I have of her? At any rate not white, because my mother was one of those, as I recall her, who thought that you can't wear white, because it gets soiled too easily and it always has to be washed. That was the difference between my mother and Erika's, and somehow that difference had been carried over to us, I thought. And as Erika spoke, I was walking silently beside her and imagining her dressed in white, and I felt that I was starting to love that white as a distant memory or enchantment, entirely different to my love up to now. Suddenly it seemed to me that what had gone before was not love at all, but only a sort of mental stupor, which had come over me and everyone of my age who grew up in the period after the Great War and the Revolution. We had heard of love only as desire, nothing more, because anything beyond that belonged in the realm of Platonic ideal, or romance divorced from time and sense, both of them ridiculous. I was taught that by the life around me, I was taught it by the talk I heard about love, I read about it in books. Even in the hands of poets, love became only a tickle or an obscenity, and since hymns didn't contain either the one or the other, it wasn't worth reading them. But what happened with me must have happened with so many youths: when we had tickled ourselves enough or told enough dirty jokes, and satisfied our desires, then little by little the moment would arrive when we were overcome by a strange restlessness. And then we dreamed of some distant white thing that walks, a red rose on its breast, and sings of something great and beautiful, something like our mother in the flesh, who has left us an orphan at an early age. At any rate I have had that feeling so many times – I can't answer for others – but I have never had the courage to admit it either to myself or to others. It's possible that I couldn't have admitted it, because that distant and beautiful dream was only a dim surmise, not a deep feeling giving rise to ideas. Only today in the moonlight, walking like this, did I understand really what for so long I had been longing for: I had been yearning for a great love, one I'd never heard of in all my life, the very thought of which might make a person ridiculous. But today I was no longer afraid of ridicule, not today, while Erika talked about her mother as if she were that great white something.

"Your memory of your mother is like that building there in the moonlight," I said, pointing to the castle, which shimmered vaguely through the foliage thinned by the autumn storms.

"Not like that," she said, when she had surveyed the front of the moonlit castle for a little while, "nothing is like the white memory of my mother."

"Only the memory of a great lost love can be like that," I said, as if to myself, because it didn't matter what I said or did, I was still thinking of my great love and wanted to touch it in words, somehow make it audible.

"So is the memory of a great lost love easy to bear?" she asked.

"So is your memory of your mother easy?" I responded.

"Yes, very easy," she explained. "She descends sometimes like a delicate veil before my eyes, but even the slightest disturbance, mental movement or just exertion makes her rise, to be more clearly seen, back into the air, or glide further away, getting tinier and tinier, until there is nothing left of her but a small dim blot, God knows where, in infinity. Whenever I see it I think that that blotch or speck is nowhere else but in my own eye, my left eye in fact."

"If the speck is in your left eye, how can you see her with both eyes?" I asked.

"Really!" cried Erika, as if she had discovered something new. "How can I see her with my right eye if she is only in my left? That means it isn't after all a black spot in my left eye, but a memory of my mother."

"The memory of a great lost love," I repeated my previous statement, as if it would please me, or should please Erika.

As we chatted we walked back and forth along a narrow road under the trees. To tell the truth, I was drawn by the broader roads and the more open places where the moonlight shone. But when I said that to Erika, she said, "No, please let's not! I like this dimness now, these rustling leaves under our feet and the patches of moonlight here and there." But as if she feared somehow grating me with her words, in the next moment she added, "All the same, if you really want to, we could…"

"I don't want anything," I interrupted, "I thought perhaps you…"

"No, so we'll stay here," she decided.

"This is the best place in the whole world," I said as if to console myself. "The best place and the most beautiful avenue in bright moonlight. What do you think, miss, if we walked here like this until ten o'clock, till twelve, till two, till the morning when it gets light?"

"Good God!" she cried. "What would grandfather and auntie think?"

"Let alone if they found out that you're walking with me, an Estonian boy," I said.

"Then I'd tell them straight away that you're a *Korporant*, so that..."

"Please, not that!" I declared, trying to take her by the hand, but she withdrew her hand, started laughing and said, "Don't take me by the hand, I would get terribly embarrassed."

"Why embarrassed?"

"My gloves are frayed, that's why," she explained.

"So are mine," I laughed back.

"That doesn't count, you're a man."

"What?" I cried. "If it isn't possible for a woman to buy whole gloves in place of frayed ones, it's shameful, but the same situation isn't shameful for a man?"

"Not like that," she countered, "but if a young girl doesn't mend her frayed gloves, that is shameful, that's very shameful, auntie's always assuring me."

"That means a young lass with frayed gloves is lazy and careless, but a young man with frayed gloves is a quite proper and decent gentleman," I concluded.

"Exactly," she affirmed, "a young lass with frayed gloves is lazy and careless, auntie is always telling me."

"So you yourself are lazy and careless, if you come walking in the moonlight with frayed gloves on."

"No, sir, I'm not lazy and careless, although I'm walking in the moonlight wearing frayed gloves," she retorted.

"Why not, if auntie says that?" I asked.

"Because I had a choice of walking with you in the moonlight or doing some darning at home. So why did I lie to my grandfather, if I was going to go home anyway?"

"Then we'll have two sins on our souls: a lie to grandfather and frayed gloves," I laughed.

"Those are only my sins," she said. "You may laugh, of course, but I don't know which causes me more pain on the conscience: the fact that I lied to grandfather, or that my work is waiting undone. Late in the evening I can't manage, because then I go to sleep."

"Poor thing!" I pitied her. "Please give me your hand here, and you won't be embarrassed any more or less, I'm just looking with my own eyes at how big the sin of the gloves is, and what's troubling your heart."

And now, as I took her hand, she let it happen without evasion, even stopped and stood in a pool of moonlight, as if she wanted to give me the opportunity to view how much darning her knitted gloves would need. I raised her hand closer to my eyes, as if I couldn't be certain otherwise, but when I saw the open finger-ends of the gloves, I rapidly pulled them back as sheaths and pressed my mouth on the bare fingers. She squealed, and her hand made an indefinite movement, as if she wanted to free herself, but stayed on my lips.

"Now you've torn my poor glove right open," she said, like a grateful remark, as we walked on a little later.

"If it were up to me, you'd have quite different gloves, not these lousy ones," I said.

"You're right about that, they're simply lousy," she agreed with me about her gloves, "but let me fix them; then you'll see that they're quite decent to put on for the autumn darkness."

Thereupon our talk ended for a little while. Erika looked at my face furtively a couple of times, as if seeking something or finding something beyond understanding. Noticing this, I was happy to carry on in silence, to see where her seeking and considering would end. And it ended with an indefinite, timid question: "Are you always like this?"

"How do you mean?" I asked.

"I don't know how to say it," she replied. "Or if I do, you won't like it."

"Say it boldly, it doesn't matter if I don't like it," I insisted.

"Well – so like a *Korporant*," she said, and elaborated: "Stiffly polite."

"So is it stiffly polite and *Korporant*-like to call your gloves lousy?" I asked.

She replied with a question: "But if you kiss my hand in those lousy gloves?"

"But if I say that if it were up to me, you would wear quite different gloves, is that very polite too?" was my next question.

"Isn't that polite?" she asked in turn.

"How should I take that?" I said, evading an answer.

"Why isn't it polite?" she pursued.

"Maybe it's hard for you to understand this," I said. "I myself only realised what my words meant after I'd said them. I meant one thing by my words, but they might mean something else which is not polite at all."

"But is that polite – what you meant by your words?" she asked.

"In some situations, they might even be impudent," I replied.

"But today?" she enquired.

"Miss, forgive me, but the wolf is howling at the moon," I replied.

She was silent for a while and then said, as if turning aside, "I'm terribly embarrassed. I can't really understand it at all, but I am embarrassed, maybe just because of it. But couldn't you tell me quite clearly what your words really meant? Let me be embarrassed – it doesn't matter, because here under the trees you can't see my face anyway."

"Haven't you ever heard of when a young man gives gifts to a female stranger?" I asked.

She was silent for a while and then cried, "Phooey! So that's what your words meant! But just think, that doesn't embarrass me at all; I don't think I'm even blushing."

"Quite understandable, because it's so very foreign to you," I explained.

"But what did you mean when you wanted quite different gloves for me?" she asked, although I was already hoping that she would forget that question or be happy to leave it.

"Believe me, miss, it isn't good for a person to become overly sophisticated," I responded.

"Why isn't it good?" she asked, quite dismayed.

"Sophistication makes a person unhappy," I said, because I had read somewhere in a book or newspaper about why the number of suicides was increasing. It claimed that the development of civilisation is inevitably accompanied by a higher rate of suicides, because it is much easier to arouse a person's desires than to satisfy them. Civilisation tickles the passions of millions, but satisfaction is available only to thousands, even then only partially, with a certain bitter yeasty residue even at the bottom of a tasty cup.

"Sophistication makes a person unhappy," repeated Erika thoughtfully. "But why then does everybody talk about it, why does everybody want it?"

"I don't know," I replied.

"Well, that's not right," she resolved. "You're only saying it to get out of answering the question. Everybody matures and I want to be more mature: if others become unhappy, why then must I alone be happy – or happier?"

"That's right," I agreed, thinking of how to revolve my own perplexity, "because it's best that everyone is equally happy or unhappy."

"Sir, I'm waiting," she said jokingly, but there was anxiety in her voice, as if she guessed what I meant.

"Spare me today – I'll tell you some other time," I begged her.

"No, tell me today, otherwise I won't sleep tonight."

"There's nothing to say," I said. "When does a man worry for a woman's sake? When he's marrying her. That's all I meant."

I waited for her to say something, but she was silent, only raising her left hand to her breast, as if she had to keep something there, as she leaned forward a little into a curve. Faded leaves rustled under our feet, and through the leafless crowns of the trees the full moon cast shimmering silver beams here and there on our path.

"Forgive me, miss, for thinking like that," I said at length.

"Don't believe that it's like that; I can't help it. It might hurt you, but..."

"You're wrong," she interjected, "it doesn't hurt me at all, but I assumed everything, not that. And how you said it, too! My heart was ready to explode!"

"If you knew how happy I am!" I cried.

"That my heart was ready to explode – is that why?"

"Oh no!" I replied. "And yet, that too! Just to hear that your heart would explode for my sake."

"For the sake of your words," she corrected me.

"It doesn't matter – me or my words. From the beginning I have never, looking at you, thought anything else than about when I would ask you if you'd become my wife. Of course today I wouldn't have done it either, I simply didn't have the heart for it. But from day to day I was more and more afraid that some obstacle would come, so that I wouldn't get to say those words to you. That's why I'm so glad that it turned out like this today. Now, whatever happens, at least you know what I think of you. But I'm not demanding an answer from you – not today. It's enough for me to be able to talk to you like this. If it had depended on me, then I wouldn't have done anything else this evening than repeated to you how I love you, adore you, venerate you. Don't ask why, for I know as little as you do. And if I at first called your gloves lousy, it was only because I wanted, but didn't dare, to say to you, how much I desire to cover and enfold you in everything that is beautiful, precious, sweet and fine in the world. For the first time in my life I feel that I've discovered a totally new world, which is bigger, wider, grander and more beautiful than everything I've seen before, and all because this new world was created by you, that this new world is you. For ages I haven't known what is faith, but thanks to you I could have faith and even start believing in my blessed soul..."

"Please, no more!" she said, touching my arm, and that was the first touch from her side.

"Forgive me," I replied, "of course it was terrible of me to…"

"No, it's too beautiful," she said. "I can't take it, it's too sudden."

"And of course, too sudden, you can't do that, I understand," I agreed, but continued straight away, "but my dear miss, do understand me: I was terrified, I am terrified even now, that I can't say fast enough everything that I have to say and I must say."

"I'm terrified too, when you talk like that," she said. "What eyes will grandfather make when he hears it! And auntie too, God forbid! This should be kept as far as possible from her."

"Right, you have a grandfather and an aunt!" I cried in real amazement, because in speaking of my own terror, those two had not occurred to me at all.

"Not only a grandfather and an aunt, but a whole set of relations and friends," she explained.

"Quite right: whole set of relations and friends," I repeated, and suddenly I was convinced that it was this that caused my secret unexplained terror, that everything could break up before it had even begun.

Now followed a number of days of which I don't really have anything to say, because the same thing was repeated: we met at the lunch table and afterwards on a walk together, or only accompanying her home when Erika had no opportunity for a walk. She could tell some lie to her grandfather to keep away from home longer, but the circumstances, the conditions did not allow anything to be changed with a lie. And for the first time she felt, and perhaps I did too, that there was something inevitable about life, something fateful, that nothing could oppose. You struggle like a fly in a spider's web, which might stretch a little this way and that, but which finally means that you can't get anywhere.

Today, thinking back with a peaceful mind to what then

happened, I'm amazed at how little it takes to feel happy, so happy that the glow of that happiness colours the rest of your life, no matter how monotonous, quotidian, dull and senseless it may be. We two in our happiness did not have anything other than a few shared lunchtimes, where we had to strain to conceal our feelings, and shared walks on the dark autumn evenings, where we couldn't even enjoy the colours of foliage falling from the trees. We didn't even have shelter to escape the rain, be close to each other and exchange silly words that could be forgotten in the next moment, as we looked into each other's eyes, where you can read everything that you have ever dreamed of, or where you read new, unrealised dreams. Even in the rain we walked side by side, our shadows upon each other, which kept us apart at a respectable distance, as if we were complete strangers and we had said nothing to each other that could endear us.

To tell the truth, she didn't say anything endearing to me or about herself; it was only I who talked, as if it were a question of the very warmest friendship, a spiritual affinity. She only listened and did not dispute; she didn't reject my forceful words, as if they were spoken from her heart as well. Now it seems to me more and more that she couldn't have said anything particular, because only I knew what I could not be silent about. For her perhaps my words were only an interesting pastime, my soul's outbursts an amusing experience which could make her more mature, as she had kept emphasising. My actual endearments, which never went beyond hand-squeezing or kissing, must only have enriched her wisdom about life, so that one day it would be easier for her to go her own way.

But every time I analysed our relationship thoroughly to myself and sifted the minutest events through the filter of reason to ascertain that this was without doubt mutual psychic devotion, some ridiculously trivial fact about our exchanges would come to mind and I would renew the work of mentally sifting, choosing and picking through facts which might prove the opposite case. So in the end I'm always going round in circles, and getting nowhere after hours of racking my poor brain. But I don't do this in order to grasp some sort of absolute truth, for what sort of truth could have convinced me that those minute facts and even the most trivial words can be explained and interpreted in one way or its opposite? For ultimately what is the significance of her not coming with me to any place, only a couple of times to the cinema, and even then to a shabby one?

Of course, she may have acted that way because she was ashamed of showing herself in my company, because I mostly spoke Estonian to her, being convinced that she could manage better in my mother tongue than I in hers. Moreover I was used to the fact that poor, ungrammatical Estonian did not shame anybody, and gave them more of a foreign and grandiloquent charm, whereas my bad German would be humiliating to me and to her. I remember her once expressing amazement that I, as a student, a *Korporant* into the bargain, did not have a rich command of the German language. By way of explanation I told her of my own and other people's new orientation, directed toward England, but she immediately asked whether they have corporations and colours in England too. Unfortunately I had to admit, like it or not, that there aren't, just as I should have confessed that despite my new orientation I had no command of English either.

Yes, if I had wanted to be completely honest and open, I should have said, My dear miss, I don't really have command of anything, and maybe I even got into the corporation because I don't have command of anything. Why talk about German or English, when even my Estonian is faulty, because I studied French, which has remained poor because of English, while my English limps along behind my German, and my German is hobbled by

English and French? Everything I have studied I know only to the extent of wanting to be what I am not. If I want to please others – and every young person does – then it is with some foreign mannerism or trick, a foreign language or custom. And I am a little troubled that this is the way I best display my intellectual clumsiness and mental immaturity, and thus I detract from my own and others' respect, because I and my companions don't have much of that. I am proud but have deficient self-confidence, and I am haughty, but low on self-esteem. It's as if I had grown up among upstarts, who would make grand gestures while cringing at the same time, make promises but break their word, and take on obligations but not think of fulfilling them unless they were financially rewarding. I and my contemporaries regarded ourselves as smarter than our fathers, more advanced, more cultured, but we lived with blameless hearts at their expense, and willingly extended and multiplied their mistakes or we ruined what they had created. I don't have any use for becoming myself, being myself and staying that way, as some foreign poet exhorts me to, because I have always seen, heard and read quite the opposite: everyone tries to become, be, and stay something else, not themselves, and I want to be like everyone else. Or should I and my contemporaries really become virtuous – be ourselves?

No, my dears! I come from the country, but I don't know if I would please anybody by doing that, when every boy and girl is rushing to the city. I am an Estonian, but I don't know where I should boast about that. I am a student, but these days that is appealing only when I have my coloured cap on, as if that item itself were the educated Estonian. Take note of that, dear miss, if you don't want to be disappointed in me. For it follows from all that that I don't have much belief in myself: no one can believe in what he doesn't have. Only once in my life have I felt that belief with all my body and soul, all the blood in my heart, and others should have felt it together with me, but about that, dear miss, I cannot tell you, because that would lead us finally down to Võnnu, about which you probably don't want to hear. It would lead us to a completely unknown man, who said to us, "Brothers! Every one of us has been up against two, three, maybe even ten Russians, even a dead Estonian has come up against a Russian – so can't a living Estonian come up against a German, who is mortal?" Never mind that the speaker himself perished – we won because we believed, and even I believed, in ourselves. But that belief has vanished; I don't know why. That is what I should have said if I'd wanted to be open.

And yet, obviously I'm deceiving myself and the reader too. At that time these thoughts scarcely occurred to me, but came to me later and still are as I write about it. Then I would more probably have asked, Isn't it more likely that she wasn't so much ashamed of me as afraid of her own people, who would immediately pass on to her grandfather and auntie, to the whole clan, that our meetings should be eliminated at all costs, although Erika might have to change her position in service or even lose it? And of course I consoled myself then that she was more afraid of her own folk than ashamed of me or my stumbling use of language. She was more ashamed of herself and her own plain raiment than of me and my awkwardness, and therefore she refrained from appearing in places where there were bright lights and eager eyes. For in this world there is nothing more humiliating and shameful than poverty, which is seen in your face, your look, your clothing and your jewellery.

And she didn't want to let me pay with my own money for tickets, as she would recall our conversation about the broken gloves; spending her own pennies more often at the cinema was obviously beyond her means. She seemed to have a different understanding of money to myself and many of my contemporaries. We borrowed without troubling ourselves too much about when and who would pay back the loan for us. We all had some sort of hopeful faith in our futures and our surroundings, while she seemed to live only in the present, where deprivation prevailed.

And so, in the rain, our only natural shelter was those awnings that stood in the park on the ends of posts, but we could use even those only rarely, because under most of them we found others who also seemed to have nowhere to go. The situation was made especially difficult because I didn't even have an umbrella and I had to borrow one in emergencies from the landlady, who was of course very obliging, but looked me in the eye with such an expression that, like it or not, I had to come up with reasons why I needed shelter. But she would always block my excuses and say with a laugh, "Don't do too much terrible explaining, otherwise I'll think you're fibbing – that your conscience isn't clear." That made things embarrassing, and so on many occasions in the autumn I walked in the drizzling rain without an umbrella, just my coat collar pulled up, while Erika, on the spot, carried a little umbrella, which scarcely covered her shoulders and dripped water either on to my head or under my collar, if I didn't walk at a suitably respectful distance.

But all this essential shabbiness did not dampen our spirits at all; in fact, we felt like two orphans who had suddenly stumbled on some fairyland. In the dampness of an autumn evening we dreamed of our shared future. Or rather, I did, and her silence or indirect words indicated her assent. For example, she might suddenly interrupt my plans: "You should practise speaking German more often."

"We should speak German together one day, and Estonian the next day," I said.

"Estonian is terribly difficult," she opined.

"Well, I'll teach you it," I promised, without taking my own promise seriously. Life and circumstances seemed in general to me crazily easy at the time, and I was ready to share out all sorts of promises.

"But then you'll have to learn German properly," said Erika to counterbalance my words.

"I'll be speaking it like my mother tongue," I pledged.

"You really will?" she asked with suspicious pleasure.

"I will," I assured her, adding, "but you will then have to learn to pronounce our ō sound so that when the children..." The words died in my mouth, but that was of no use, because my last utterance made me feel terribly ridiculous. But either she didn't notice the ridiculousness or pretended not to, and said, "Unlucky children! That letter will break their tongues in their mouths. Why does such a ghastly letter exist? Can't you get by without it?"

"That letter is our national pride," I explained. "Through it we're related to the great and small nations of the world."

"Who do you mean?" she asked.

"The Russians and the English, for example," I replied. "A linguist explained to me once that just by tracing our ō sound you can conclude that our future will be great and brilliant or great and brilliant has been our past. I of course preferred the future, but the linguist was content with the past, because he thought a dead ancient Greek to be worth more than some obscure nation that still survives today. So you'll definitely have to change your opinion about our ō, if you want to be happy."

"You're joking of course, aren't you?" she asked.

"No," I replied, "you would learn our language more light-heartedly if you adopted the linguist's attitude, who said that through the ō sound we are related to the English and the Russians."

"I don't want to be related to the Russians," she said.

"But the English?" I enquired.

"Grandfather says the English are cruel," she said.

"I don't know about that," I replied, "but the English and their language rule the world. It would be good to be related to the rulers of the world."

"You mean you don't love the Germans," she seemed to conclude from my words.

"At least one of them I adore," I replied, touching her hand. "I want to keep repeating that to you, so that you'll look on me as a blessing on your soul. And if you don't want to become related to the English or the Russians through our ō, then I'm quite content with that."

"No, no, I want to, if you want to," she said, quickly interrupting, as if she feared my next words.

"You are good, you are good as gold," I said.

"Do you really believe that?" she asked.

"I believe it absolutely," I replied.

"Grandfather is always saying that I have such a good heart, he'll never be afraid that I'll make him sad."

"When could I talk to your grandfather?" I then asked.

"Why would you?" she replied in an alarmed voice.

"I want to decide my own fate and yours," I explained, "because I can't wait any longer, not knowing. You have mentioned your family and relations fearfully so often, that I'd like to see one of them face to face. And since you regard your grandfather as the best of them all, then perhaps it's best to make a start with him."

"Grandfather is of course the best," she said, "but I beg you, not yet, not so quickly."

"You mean you're afraid?" I asked.

"Yes, I suppose I am," she agreed. "I simply don't dare to talk to him about you."

"You don't need to," I went on, "simply tell me when I can find him alone at home, and leave the rest to me."

"No, no, no, for God's sake, not like that! You mustn't do that on any account, otherwise –"

"Otherwise what?"

"I don't know what I'm afraid of, but I'm afraid, afraid," she repeated.

"What will become of us both if you're so afraid?" I said, as if suspecting misfortune.

"I don't know, but I'm really afraid," she affirmed.

"We still have to come to a decision about what is to become of us and our love," I persisted.

"And of course we must," she agreed submissively, "but I'd still like a few more days, for..."

"Maybe you don't want me to even..."

"No, no, I do," she cried to interrupt me, "but grandfather has to be prepared, I have to tell him everything first; it's better that way, I feel."

So that is how things stayed. But they developed much more simply than Erika had feared. Since she was troubling her heart about it and shedding tears, her grandfather was inclined to dry her tears. And that was a natural end to the matter, leading to Erika telling him everything, starting with her lie and ending with me and my visit to her grandfather.

"Well, and what about grandfather?" I was keen to know. "What kind of face did he make? What did he say? Was he angry?"

"Not angry," replied Erika.

"What then – delighted?"

"Not that either."

"You mean – sad," I concluded.

"Yes, exactly," she affirmed, but it was evident that she had trouble explaining the situation.

"But he must have said or done something?" I persisted. "Something happened between you?"

"I cried and grandfather stroked my head," she said in a voice that wanted to cry again.

Of course, now that I recollect our situation, there was reason enough to cry, but at the time I was as if struck by blindness. To continue our discussion undisturbed and confer, we went to the park, but hardly had we got there than it started to rain heavily, after which a wind gusted all day long. Because of the fallen foliage there was really no shelter for us from the wind or rain. Finally I hit on a good idea to seek shelter from the bad weather under the thick spruce trees. It was a happy thought, because the spruces were on the edge of a slope and the wind was blowing from the hill, so we were protected against both wind and rain.

I don't know when I've ever been so grateful to an animate or inanimate object as I was to that thick spruce tree when two of us stood under it. Even now, when I go to the park and walk past it, a warm glow passes through my heart, and if I were religious, I would thank God over and over again for creating that spruce and giving it wide-reaching roots, so that its branches could be just as broad, and what is more, not upright like a pine, but hanging down, so that the rainwater would trickle beautifully to their tips and hit the ground drop by drop, welcomed by the thirsty fibrous roots. At that time my thoughts did not extend so far, and were not concerned at all with such indifferent matters as God and Nature.

In a strange way, even then, a painful surge ran through my heart when we had found shelter from the rain, for I thought to myself, Now we're under a spruce with our love. That was my father's saying for people who had ended with nothing but themselves. That saying was a depressing parallel to the words used in the Bible about the Saviour: the birds have nests, the foxes have holes, but the Son of Man has nowhere to lay his head, but we two were in place of the Son of Man, and our love in place of his head. So scripture would be rewritten to say: the birds have nests, the foxes have holes, but love has nowhere in the world to go.

Yet we were happy sheltering under the spruce, and I asked, "Did grandfather say anything?"

"He did, he did," she replied. "He said, 'Dear child, have you noticed yourself that you're talking about a lie and a love all at once? Doesn't that make you think,' he said. 'Until now, when you didn't have a love, you didn't have lies either, but love came, and so did lies. What will become of love if it drives you to lie like this!' That's what grandfather said."

"Had you never lied to grandfather before?" I asked.

"Never," she affirmed. "To auntie, yes, but not to grandfather, because he was always so good that there was no need to lie to him."

We were silent for a little while, as if saddened that our love had led to lying even to the best person in the world. Then I ventured, "But what did grandfather say about me? Does he want to meet me?"

"When I asked him, he..."

"He gave in," I interjected. "That's what I thought straightaway, because I believed only good about him, from what you've said. But when may I come?"

"Grandfather didn't say that," she replied.

"But that's the same as not letting me," I said, disappointed.

"No, no," she rushed to reassure me, "grandfather definitely promised and he will keep his promise. Grandfather is the sort of person who, once he takes on something, he does it, even if the whole world is against him. So if he is with us, we have nothing to fear. He only said, 'All right, let him come, but not today or tomorrow, not the day after either, because I want to rest. Too much excitement all at once.' We have to understand that about grandfather, because he lives in the past. As for today, that's just a dream to him, and he's too old to talk about the future. He told me the last time, when I wanted to talk about our future, leave him in peace about the future, as he has nothing to do with it. Of course he gave advice to think more about the past than the future. One thing he did promise, though: he promised to keep quiet about our affair, keep it completely to himself; so he did care that much for our future."

"That's good," I said, "now it's the three of us against the whole family."

"Yes, now there are three of us," she repeated in agreement, but in a tone as if she didn't believe at all that we really were three sticking together. Rather I would conclude from her tone of voice that there weren't even two of us any more, but each of us separate – myself, herself and grandfather. We were all enduring the same thing, but each in our own way and with our own thoughts and feelings.

The next day Erika was absent from the lunch table and the landlady said, by way of explanation, "The young lady wrote that yesterday evening she had to go out in the rain, got her feet wet and got a bad cold with a little fever. She'll have to stay in bed for a couple of days, and she begs to be excused."

Since no one apart from the children reacted to these words, she continued, "The young lady has been a bit strange generally recently – terribly absent-minded! She must have started courting."

"There's nothing else for you but love," remarked the landlord.

"What else could there be for a pretty young girl?" replied the landlady.

"Is that the only worry in life?"

"No, but young girls don't feel any other worries," she explained.

"That's how it was when you were young, but nowadays young people are different," countered her husband.

"Yes, nowadays young people are more practical," I said, endorsing the landlord.

"Are you, Mr Studious, so practical?" asked the landlady, turning the tables on me.

"I'm not a young girl, and the talk was of girls," I parried by way of answer.

"So why do you think that girls are more practical than boys?" asked the landlady.

"Women are always more practical than men," I explained.

"Women grasp situations quicker," opined the landlord. "Now is a practical age, so that..."

"... women are practical," continued the landlady

mockingly. "I don't understand where you men get it from. The papers are saying that German girls are staying single because of a shortage of men, but why don't they marry Estonians, if they're so practical?"

"Estonians don't want them," said the landlord.

"Don't imagine it," cried the landlady. "Estonians want them right enough, but German girls don't want them, because they're not practical. They require an Estonian man to be young, educated and rich, but there aren't enough such men even for Estonian girls. A practical girl should be satisfied with much less. Lucky if a man has one of those qualities. If he's rich, he doesn't have much education or youth, and if he's educated, well then, she'd have to give up on the youth and the wealth, while youth sometimes wins over good education and wealth. That's what a practical woman would think. And yet nobody wants to think like that, so don't talk to me about practicality! We were talking recently about corporations, which both boys and girls can join. Is that very practical? You should know, Mr Studious."

"It isn't practical at all," I said.

"So why does everyone try to do it, if it's a practical age and people are becoming practical with the times, as my husband thinks?"

"I don't know," I replied. "Perhaps because of some idea or fashion."

"Well, you see, young people aren't practical at all, if they run around because of an idea or fashion," decided the landlady. "That's what I think of German girls too, including our miss. If I could give her advice, I would tell her, Why fuss uselessly about your emotions; you're better of falling on the neck of some man, and if there are no Germans, find an Estonian."

"According to your advice she would soon have a child on her lap, but she'd have to demand child support from a court," said the landlord.

"No, my dear man, you don't know yourself and your

brothers as well as we women do. There's no need to make men worse than they really are. There are still enough among you to instil love and fidelity in a woman. The only problem is that there's so little fidelity around these days. If I were a young girl now, I wouldn't fear for a moment that I wouldn't find a man in my whole life."

"And we haven't buried each other yet," joked her husband.

"But we will, I don't doubt that for a moment," said the landlady gravely. "Listen, you men, you aren't as wise and strong as you think you are. And as for women's practicality these days, allow me to doubt it. I think that whatever else happens, the most practical thing a woman has is love."

"But if women don't love any more, what then?" asked her husband.

"Don't blame men, at least," replied the landlady. "But of course that's silly! A woman loves as she always did; only foolish school learning, literal book knowledge, has driven them to believe that maybe something could replace love and fidelity."

"My dear lady, do you believe what you're saying?" I asked.

"But of course," she replied unhesitatingly.

"The facts speak against you, though," I opined.

"What facts?" she asked. "Divorce proceedings? Claims for child support? Don't believe what people, especially women, say in front of courts, let alone when they talk about love and alimony. If they often love in order to get alimony, they mostly make claims when they're not in love. But all these are distant things that leave us cold. Don't you want to answer one question from me? But you, old man, don't butt in; the children have left the table, and let me say what I think. So therefore, Mr Studious, if a nice lass like ours, even if she is German, were to lay her hand on your shoulder – of course she'd have to know how to do it – and say that you're the beginning and end of her life, you're a blessing on her soul, her redemption on earth…"

"This sounds like your own declaration of love at the dinner table," remarked the landlord, while I felt a blush coming unbidden to my face.

"I asked you not to butt into our chat," said the landlady, turning back to me: "What do you think – what would you do with a nice girl, such as our young lady, if she said that to you? Could you really just drop her?"

"I really don't know, because my income..." I wanted to explain.

"Ah, what income!" interposed the landlady. "You pull yourself together, start working, worry about your income, when a girl really does know how to put her hand on your neck."

"You should open an introduction agency," remarked her husband.

"Quite surely, a good introduction agency would be much more useful than bad employment agencies, of which we have more than enough," the landlady told her spouse.

"Yes, that's true," he replied, "but have you ever thought that usually every hand that's placed on the neck of a man is heavier than a yoke on a bull?"

"If that were so," she replied, "then why are people killing themselves for love more often than they used to?"

"The growth in suicides isn't only explained by love," said the man, somewhat disdainfully.

"Well, what then?" she asked. "The economy? Well, only you men could believe that. But, young man, answer me frankly, what would drive you most easily to suicide – hunger for food or for love?"

"It would be worst for me, I think, if both hungers came at once," I replied, for I felt that I should easily deal with both together.

"Of course, the two together would be worst, but taken one at a time, hunger for love is more painful than hunger for food, because you can steal food, but not love. Once you start believing that your life's happiness is in somebody's eyes, there's nothing for it but to..."

"… get a bullet in the head, a noose around the neck, dive into the water or under wheels," her husband finished her sentence.

"Exactly," affirmed the landlady, "or you turn the whole world upside down to lure the eyes of happiness into your room."

"For otherwise there'd be no one to divorce a couple of years later," mocked her husband.

"Rubbish!" she shouted. "Let's ask Mr Studious whether he would be thinking of a divorce a couple of years later, if he got those eyes that shine the joy of his life?"

"I don't know any such eyes," I lied.

"And you never have?" she asked.

"I don't think so," I replied hesitantly, as if trying to recall something.

"You don't think so," she repeated. "That's just it! I simply don't believe that there could be any natural young man anywhere who hasn't dreamt of eyes that glow with the joy of life. Those who say so are fibbing or they don't know themselves. It's the same story with you. I've already told you once that if I were a young man of your age, I would have long ago fallen head over heels for our young lady, asked for her hand in marriage and maybe even eloped with her, if there had been no other way out. But you sit with her at the table as if you were made of wood, or you were keeping a bag of ice under your heart."

Things were becoming embarrassing for me, so I had to be extremely much on guard. The only incomprehensible issue was whether the landlady was talking like this intentionally and deliberately to tease me, or was doing it because she hadn't the faintest idea of my relationship with Erika.

"A practical question," said the man, turning to his spouse, "is where would you elope to with a young lady like ours, if you had the same income as this young man?"

"Ah, where?" wondered the lady. "Doesn't matter where. How about Haapsalu or Tapa?"

"And for how long?"

"For a couple of days, for then everything would be facing the inevitable."

"Very good," said her husband. "But meanwhile, what's the situation with your position in service, your only source of income? The gentlemen in a ministry, a bank or an office are of course very concerned about where our precious young man has got to, what unfortunate thing has happened to him, aren't they? No, my dear woman, under those circumstances you wouldn't elope anywhere, and you wouldn't find a single sensible girl who'd want to commit that foolishness with you. For after a couple of days, when you come back, someone else is sitting in your place at the ministry, bank or office, who isn't liable to go off eloping. And the girl in whose eyes the joy of your life recently glowed, will cry her eyes out when she sees how rapidly she has made herself and others face the inevitable."

"If all young people thought like you, there would be half as many marriages," she told her husband.

"Mr Studious can draw only one conclusion from that: he has a long way to the harbour of marriage. He can't elope with any girl worth eloping with, and without eloping he won't get, or won't be allowed near, any girl that he'd want to elope with."

That was the brief outcome of a long discussion, which was a bad prediction for my love. And that prediction came true quite quickly, more quickly that I could ever have guessed.

When Erika appeared a couple of days later at the lunch table, she was paler and sadder than ever before. To the landlady she said the reason was her bad health, excessive tiredness, her grandfather's illness and several other distresses burdening her soul and body.

In the evening, when I met her outdoors, she told me that she had no time at all, but added straight away to console me that grandfather was expecting me the next day between ten and eleven because then her aunt would not be at home. She herself would be going out at that time, she said, so that grandfather and I could be quite alone. I did plead with her to sacrifice half or a quarter of an hour to me, but in answer she only quickened her step, hurrying homeward at a half-run as if her house were on fire.

"What point is there in me coming to chat with grandfather tomorrow if you treat me like this yourself?" I said finally, while trying to keep up with her pace. "For three days I've been waiting for you as the blessing of my soul, and now you run away from me to your grandfather and aunt. I can only draw one conclusion from this: you don't care for me at all or you keep your heart more for your family and relations."

Now she slackened her pace, almost wanted to grasp my hand and cried, with tears in her throat, "Have pity on me, at least you!"

That shut my mouth, because suddenly I had a feeling that I should take her like a little chick and pucker my lips to her, as I had so often done with their down feathers. What else should I say?

"This is terrible," I said at length. "Otherwise today is so beautiful again, after a long time: clear sky, stars shining. See how many there are! The land is dry and frost-covered, but we're running side by side as if we were being chased."

"Don't you remember any more what you once said about love?" she said.

No, I didn't remember anything special, for I had said this and that about it.

"You called it horrible," she said. "I didn't believe you then, but now I'm starting to. You must be a lot cleverer than I am."

"Everything's supposed to be foolish about love," I said.

"I'd like to be a lot more foolish than I am," she sighed after a little while.

"So would I," I said, "only if it rescued the love. If only

we didn't need to run like this, as if love were running away from us."

But we had reached the street corner where she usually stretched out her hand to me. When she did that today, she said, "Tomorrow then, between ten and eleven."

"Tomorrow," I replied. "But when will you have time for me?"

"Tomorrow too," she replied, and left, as if it were hard for her to stay longer in my presence. I stood on the spot like a post, where she had left me, and I didn't move until a couple came along who bumped into me as they passed; then I turned around and went back. Only some while later did I notice that I was walking those streets where we had so often walked together. And I took it upon myself that day to walk through all the places that had been touched by her feet, viewed by her eyes. I did it as a sort of test of whether I could be in one evening in all the places where we had spent time over the weeks.

When I had tramped enough cobblestones I went to the park and to those trails we had measured with our steps countless times. I even went to look at our shelter, and as luck would have it there was no one there that day. Like a wolf in the dead of night I crept finally under that spruce where we had last sought cover from the rain. I supported my back against the trunk and stood there, hands pushed deep into my pockets.

As I started walking back, the grass and moss had frozen, and crunching underfoot. I was content to go on walking on that frozen moss, but on hearing that crunching sound, it brought a painful feeling to my breast, as if, step by step, I were trampling something to pieces.

And as I now think back to that feeling, it seems to me that to this day I've done nothing else than trample something to pieces in myself – step by step, day by day, hour by hour. Writing these lines now is surely nothing other than trampling all that happened to pieces, to get rid of her, because otherwise I couldn't go on living. And if that really were the case, what does it mean to a person that the heavens are broad and high, and millions of stars shine in them, created by God? What are these great and beautiful things for, if we have to crush everything beautiful in ourselves? Or must the heavens and their stars and God the creator exist just for that reason? Yes, maybe just for that reason, for otherwise there would be so many who couldn't stand their own lives. The moon and its quarters, the sun and the clouds, spring and autumn, summer and winter, warmth and cold – perhaps they all exist only for a fool like me to have something to anticipate, hope for and believe in, so that procreation and death will not end.

The next day my main worry was whether I could get free between ten and eleven o'clock. And I decided to do it by hook or by crook, even if it cost me my job.

But that morning there was a rather special excitement at the ministry, the reason for which the secretary had let slip was coming redundancies. Actually this was nothing new, as they had been talking of redundancies even before me, and it had been repeated during my time at the ministry, and yet there was always a reason to take on new staff from time to time. Why the secretary's words had such an effect just that day was at first incomprehensible to me. The secret whisperings of others seemed strange to me, which I hadn't noticed before.

"They talk about it for a while, and then everything stays the same, like today," I said to a colleague who was sitting at the same table with me.

"No, now there's something real behind it," he replied, "and the first ones to get the sack will be the ones who came last and don't have a wife or children."

"So you and I will be among the first to go," I concluded.

"Not I," he contested, and added, jokingly or sarcastically, "Today I registered, and with God's help I might be doing a baptism in a few weeks. So if they can just wait a little, I'll soon be a father."

"Then I'd better hurry too," I tried to parry with a joke, "if that's supposed to help."

"They don't want that," he replied, now quite seriously. "They'd rather sack people from the ministry than have them take a wife."

"What about you?" I asked.

"Me?" he shrugged. "Why would everyone have to do what I do? Believe me, dear friend, our combined salary with my wife is less than ours on our own without a salary." Since I didn't understand this, my colleague went on to explain. "Let's say you lose your job, how much will you be short to live on in a month? It'll only be for a while, I think, as you're bound to find something else. This is how I would calculate it: ten crowns for a room, right? Fifteen crowns for food, would that be enough?"

At the time that sum seemed small to me, but now I would tell my colleague that you can get by on less, as long as you bear in mind that you mustn't walk much, or you won't last. I can say that on the basis of my own experience. But I didn't say anything then, so my colleague was free to carry on: "We'll put five crowns for amusements, you understand: a cheap cinema sometimes, upper back row at the theatre, a couple of times at the café even, a little piece of cheap scented soap, a box of tooth powder, sauna a couple of times a month, on the cheapest day of course – in other words, quite a decent living for people like us, and taken together the shortfall is thirty crowns a month, if you don't end up in some job. But do you know how it is with a wife? You take your salary from the ministry, and if you start living, by the end of the month the shortfall is forty or fifty crowns. Now just calculate which is more profitable – salary with a wife or no salary and no wife. Now believe me, my dear colleague, as far as salary goes, it's not worth running after a wife. But of course, if you have other reasons…

Because there are women who earn on their own, or who have assets – well now! That's quite another matter."

"But how can you be so sure, if you only registered today?" I was keen to know.

"I just told you that I registered today and in a few weeks we'll have a baptism," he replied. "I mean I've been married for quite a while, so why shouldn't I know? You've been getting book learning all the time, I've been learning from life, and what's more I'm quite a few years older than you. I got this job here through my wife."

"Oh I see!" I said, as if amazed.

"Of course," he affirmed. "And through my wife I know about the redundancies at the right time, so we could register at the appropriate moment. For if a man has the right wife, he does everything at the right time – bear that in mind! A woman, if she's the right one and loves properly, is like a boa constrictor round your neck, you can't get rid of her so easily."

"And I don't want to," I said, for my part.

"Quite right: you don't want to, that's the main thing," he assured me, and then asked, "but how do you know all this?"

"Some lady told me recently," I replied. "She assured me that if a woman can get her arm around a man's neck, then –"

"Then it's like jiu-jitsu," laughed my colleague. "Quite right! Just like that!"

"Not just like that, but the idea's the same," I explained.

"Well, what are we talking about, if the idea's the same," he said. "The idea's the main thing."

That was our conversation during the break, while I was itching to go to the boss to get some leave between ten and eleven o'clock. While chatting and itching, though, I was debating with myself: if there really will be redundancies now, as has long been threatened, then I will probably be the first one to get the boot, as my colleague thought. So what am I seeking from Erika's grandfather, what can I tell him, if I am a decent person at all and if I'm not completely senseless? Do I go and tell him that I love his granddaughter madly, or do I go to ask that same granddaughter's hand in marriage? To do the first is stupid, and to do the second is criminal or ridiculous, if today or tomorrow I'm going to lose the job I have.

Yet I had to go and ask permission, because I couldn't fail to go; I had wanted and promised to. But now it all seemed to me downright incomprehensible and senseless. I was being led like a blind man somewhere, as if some woman already had really put her arm around my neck. Or should those words only be understood metaphorically? There was nothing for it: I had to go.

And I did go, although my heart was turning cold within me. Even coming away from my boss, there must have been something unusual about my face, because everyone looked at me quizzically and my colleague joked from his desk, "You mean: register or baptise first?"

"No, just to arrange a loan," I replied.

"A smart man after all!" sighed my colleague. "To borrow and have fun, it's worth it, but to love and then get married, nah...!" He didn't finish, and I left.

On my way my feet took one step forward, two steps back, so to speak. Looking back now, I cannot wonder enough at myself, my state of mind and my understanding. I had dreamt of such a moment in the past, and in my head and heart I had everything wonderfully ready to say to that unknown old gentleman, so that he would grant the hand of his granddaughter whether he liked it or not. So why all this reluctance to go, and why was my state of mind almost sinking to hopelessness? Maybe it was the discussion at the lunch table at home recently? Or my colleague's sarcastic joking chit-chat this morning? Or was my state of mind really depressed by the knowledge of the coming redundancies and the possible loss of my job? But until today I hadn't really appreciated that job anyway, and I'd been thinking of finding a better one, to enable a more decent way of life. So why did I no longer hope for that job? Was it because even the present bad one threatened to vanish? So was I a chancer, driven by nature or love, who believed in greater winnings soon, if he manages to gain smaller ones that vanish with his latest failure and the loss of all other hopes?

At Erika's home she opened she door herself. She was already wearing a coat and hat, as if hurrying off somewhere, but was only awaiting my arrival. Anxiously she whispered to me, along with her greeting, beseeching, "But ask grandfather nicely! Be sweet to him!"

As I took off my overcoat, she went to announce me. Her speech and every and action betrayed her extreme excitement and she appeared to be very pleased when she finally took me to her grandfather, only to disappear.

"Through here, please," she told me, as I composed myself in front of a floor-to-ceiling mirror, framed in mahogany. Grandfather was waiting for me in a smaller, office-like room, after I'd passed through a spacious hall, which was piled high with redwood furniture, as if they didn't want to leave space for any people to live or exist in. A single glance at this wealth and finery – for that is how I appreciated it then, and still do now, with slight adjustments – and my already grim mood immediately changed into one of despair. Certainly I must have loved that fair-haired girl madly at that time, and that love must have been much deeper than I can even explain to myself now, otherwise I would probably have turned on my heels, grabbed my coat and hat from the peg, and run out the door without a word. For what was the point in my appearing before that unknown old gentleman if I had the slightest wit to assess my own situation, past and future? But I didn't have that wit, or if I did have it – for otherwise why did my heart sink so low within me? – then I was driven crazy and completely stupefied by a much stronger force than human wit.

So I carried on through the hall piled with furniture into a smaller room, where a thin, white-haired gentleman sat in a tall armchair, but I couldn't make out the lines on his face clearly, because the blinds on the window cast a dim light and his back was to the window. As I stepped in he continued to sit calmly, but stretched his bony hand out to me kindly, almost joyfully, and that hand seemed to glow in the gloom, like his hair. He said, "A choy to see you, for my dear Erika has tolt me all about this business. Be so goot and take a seat in front of me there, so I can well look at you." And when I, stupid as I was, sat down in the chair he'd indicated, without remembering to introduce myself politely, the old gentleman continued: "I am so glat that I can, after a lonk time, again speak this Estonian lankuach, for I luff this lankuach, but I no lonker haff anyone to speak it with. Now again sits before me one *echt* Estonian man, so that I can speak this dear Estonian country's lankuach, as when was in the old days."

"Herr Baron," I tried to interject, but he cut me off by crying, "Why shoult I be Herr Baron, if Estonian lankuach? Estonian man, if he is real man, says always Sir Baron, not Herr Baron! That way speak one town man and he is not the real Estonian man. And why you say me Herr Baron, if Estonian state and government strictly forbit it? Do you call my dear Erika also Baroness?"

"No, I don't, Herr Baron, but…" I tried to explain.

"Why shoult I be Herr Baron, if my granddaughter not be Baroness and if state and government strictly forbit it? We shoult be oll now that citizen, Estonian Republic citizen, so goes the right name."

"Herr Baron," I said now decisively, "I grew up in the country and in my eyes you will remain Herr Baron until you die."

"Then you is rebel against own Estonian state," he

replied, and so my intended flattery fell like a sling on my own neck, which this white-haired old gentleman battered into a coma with his next words, uttered now in German, the more freely and precisely to express himself: "If you still want to regard me as Herr Baron, then naturally you should honour my grandchild with the same rank. Or don't you think so?"

"Yes it is, Herr Baron," I replied trying to continue, "my honour and respect for your grandchild..." but he couldn't wait for the end of my sentence, interjecting, "I don't understand you properly. You said you grew up in the country and you regard me, as your father does too, as a baron until I die, but why are you honouring me with a visit today, if you regard my grandchild as being of baronial rank?"

"Herr Baron," I tried to say, but he wouldn't give me a chance to continue, and went on, "Allow me, young man, I know what you want to say, because my grandchild has explained it all to me. I'm not accusing you of anything, not making any reproaches. I am old, I am already approaching the smell of the soil, the grave awaits me and I have seen much more of the world than you have, young man. And I tell you: I have seen more of the Estonian people than you have, and God grant that you love it as much as I have. Of course you won't remember the year 1905, but I do, and I was one of those who wouldn't let Russians armed with knouts into the grounds of our estates. What that meant at the time is something for you to ask your older brothers, if you have any. Ask your father, your mother, if they are alive. But the Estonians even burned and plundered my home, though not in the way they did other places, because I, and my father before me, had a different attitude to the people than many others, and so the people on my estate were different to those on others. I'm telling you all this only so that you won't misunderstand or decide wrongly. Times and circumstances have changed in the meantime, yes – what can you do, they've completely changed – but the fact that I'm a baron and will remain one until I die in your and your father's eyes, as you put it, can't be altered by times and circumstances. The same applies to my grandchild, who is in my direct bloodline. Or do you disagree?"

"No, Sir Baron, times and circumstances can't change blood, let alone so quickly," I agreed.

"Quite right!" he cried, "at least not so quickly. Breeding is more permanent than times and circumstances. And I tell you, young man: my pedigree is old and exceptionally pure, if that interests you. The government of the Republic of Estonia is interested in that anyway, because it has learnt to respect the breeding purity of animals, which pleases me very much. Maybe one day they will go so far as to respect human strains too, as I do. And therefore I ask you, young man, what do you have to offer if you marry my grandchild, whose dowry is at least an ancient pedigree, if nothing else under present circumstances?"

"I love her more than anything in the world," I cried, rising from my chair and almost wanting to fall at the feet of this white-haired old man, as if he were venerated by me. But he remained quite calm, asked me to sit down again and said, "Young man, don't be so sure that your love for my grandchild is greater than her love for you. At your age we men don't yet know anything about the greatness of a woman's love; we only get to know and appreciate that much later. At your age we're more interested in our own passions and desires than a woman's love. At least I have reason enough to think that if your love is great, which I'm happy to believe, for otherwise I wouldn't be talking to you like this, then my grandchild's love is at least as great, if not greater. So one love confronts another, but you have still not earned my grandchild's pedigree by any means. What do you have to offer her in return, so that your marriage would be at least a little between equals, so to speak, not a misalliance in every sense?"

"Herr Baron, I really don't know what I can offer," I said in awkward embarrassment.

"Haven't you graduated from university?" he asked.

"Unfortunately not."

"You're a member of a corporation?"

"I am, Herr Baron."

"Then of course you will have debts, as I too incurred debts in my time in a corporation, although my pocket money must have been much greater than yours could have been."

"I haven't ever had pocket money," I said.

"All the worse," he replied, "your debts must be all the greater for that. You're a professional, it's been explained to me; can't you tell me how long you have to work to pay off your debts, if you spend all your money on paying off the debts? An honest and frank answer, please."

"At least a couple of years," I said.

"Well, in that case, things can't be too bad," he said, as if considering, and added, "but how big is your current salary?"

When I had given him an exact answer about that, he said, as if hopelessly, "But how are you proposing to start living when you get married? You won't even get a one-room apartment if you want to liquidate your debts in even ten years?"

"I'm hoping for a pay increase soon, because I have connections and acquaintances," I now said, although I should rather have answered, "I'm afraid of losing even this job I have."

"It's difficult to base such an important decision as marriage merely on hopes," he said. "I am a poor man, but I do have a greater income than you and I am completely free of debt now; yet my grandchild finds it necessary to earn a living. If she were to marry you, then, in order to get by somehow, she would have to start earning twice or three times as much. Firstly, there is nowhere to get such a position, or if there were, then love or health would not sustain you for a long time, quite apart from the fact that my grandchild's health is not of the strongest. You can draw your own conclusions from all that."

"But Herr Baron, you are forgetting the main thing – love," I said.

"Quite the contrary, I was just emphasising that given the circumstances, love would not sustain you for long," he said. "And if you really love my grandchild, and honour her as well, then you shouldn't get her into a situation, with her youth and inexperience, that would be a heavy trial not only for her, but also for yourself. You, as a corporation member, should understand that more easily than anyone else, because you belong to a circle where it is thought that each nationality should have its special and chosen stratum or rank, with a natural right to hope for easier opportunities than the great mass or hoi polloi –"

"Herr Baron, you are wrong there, or at least you're exaggerating," I said.

"Where am I wrong?" he interjected impatiently. "That you don't believe in, desire or want or hope for an elected or higher position? Now listen, young man, you don't have to try to prove anything to me, an old Baltic German. Our corporations were not only for drinking and singing, and you had to keep quite pure from women. The corporations made men into what they had to be in later life, and therein was their main significance. If in your own corporations you have forgotten that single thing, which used to entitle them to drink, then I am very sorry that that fine old institution has slipped to such a low level. But tell me, young man, do you really need corporations in order to drink and sing together? If that is so, then I had better change my decision about you completely and give up, on any account, granting permission to my grandchild to marry you, since at the moment the only major obstacles to it are economic ones."

"Sir Baron, I am in great perplexity," I said, "as your grandchild, Miss Erika, suggested to me at the beginning of our acquaintance that I am too much of a *Korporant,* but you want to accuse me of not being enough of one; I can see no way out of this dilemma, even if I were richer than I am."

"I understand my grandchild very well," said the old gentleman. "In getting to know you she had hoped to find a simple and well-educated young Estonian, but now she has met a *Korporant,* who one way or another was supposed to continue the same thing that has become a stumbling block perhaps even to us. Naturally this disappointed her somewhat. But believe me, Mr Studious, my disappointment is even greater and deeper if I hear from your own lips that you are not continuing anything at all, but you only drink and sing. Or you don't drink, do you?"

"Herr Baron, how am I supposed to take this?" I stammered, a little embarrassed.

"Well, anyway," he said. "Of course, it cannot be otherwise, that is natural. But let me ask you directly and openly: so you don't do anything else when you meet but drink and sing? Forgive me, an old man, but I'm interested in the development and progress of my homeland." And he said in Estonian, "I luff this Estonian nation, that's why I want to know. I understands: you comes together, you drinks and sings, and if you gets enough drink and sing, then you starts this dear Estonian nation to lead and rule, because it be one stronk nation, as I myself with own ear hears. But how lonk you thinks to sing and drink so and to rule this Estonian nation? My heart gets heavy when I so thinks, because I luff this Estonian nation, I vill luff him with own old heart, until it stops." In his big armchair he seemed completely hunched as if from extreme exhaustion; only his shiny white hair and almost identical hands, supported from the elbows on the arms of the chair, glimmered clearly in the gloom. After a little while he continued in his own language: "And my heart is pained for my own dear grandchild, who is the only worry and joy of my old age, because it seems to me that she has given her young love away to a man who doesn't really know the seriousness of life, for he is a member of a society that only drinks and sings."

"For the sake of my love I am ready for anything, even to leave the *Korporation*," I said, trying to save whatever could be saved.

"That only makes the matter worse," he replied.

"Herr Baron, I don't understand you," I exclaimed. "I'm in the *Korporation*, and that's bad; I leave it, and that's even worse."

"Exactly!" he affirmed. "Even worse! For that only goes to prove it: you lack seriousness in life. You take steps and you take on obligations that you are prepared to give up at the drop of a hat. For me and my contemporaries the corporation and its colour were a shrine, and will be until I die; it was the same with my marriage: I intended that to be a lifelong one. But of course, I am old, the former sanctities are vanishing; even wives are exchanged like shirts these days, as if they needed laundering."

"When I came to you, Sir Baron, it was only to ask you for Miss Erika's hand for all her life. And by all that's holy, I swear…"

"But what is actually holy these days?" he asked. "What do you regard as holy? Tell me, for example: do you believe in God, the source of all that's holy? Do you believe in him in any form at all? Do you feel in your heart anything eternal and limitlessly great, before which you want, once a day, a week, a month, even a year to sink to the ground with all your being, repent of your mistakes in all seriousness, trying to become a better person in the future? Don't think I'm asking you for my own sake; I'm not much interested any more in the people of today and their gods and sanctities. Some things that have come from the past are much more alive to me than the people of today and their gods. I am only asking for the sake of her whose hand you are asking me and whom you say you love above all things in the world. So answer me with the voice of your heart's blood, as you would answer her: do you have any basis for holiness, as I explained it to you? Do you ever fall to the ground before it?"

"Not quite that, but..." I made to reply.

"So you don't!" he intervened. "With you and God it's the same story as with you and the corporation: he does exist and he doesn't. But by what holy thing do you want to swear that you're asking for Erika's hand for life? Your parents' god is dead for you, your forefathers' idols have become indifferent and their traditions ridiculous. Of course your forefathers did have traditions, I know that – but what will you have to support you, what do you have to hold on to? How will you convince me that I should entrust you with the fate of the one who's dearest to me?"

"Herr Baron, you're asking more of me for the hand of your grandchild than any young man of today can promise you, if he is as honest and open with you as I am. I'm sure that the same change is going on among your young people, the same development, the same ruination, if you want to call it that, as you tried to find in me, but you wouldn't refuse the hand of your grandchild to a young man in your own circle."

"Of course I wouldn't," he replied with an obvious lack of hesitation.

"So the basic reason for your objection is that I'm an Estonian, then?" I concluded.

"That is so, and yet it isn't," he said. "Your conclusion is off the mark, because, apart from the love that you keep praising, you think more of yourself than of your beloved. Have you ever really tried to imagine what would happen if you married my grandchild? Perhaps you'll forgive me, but now finally I come to things that maybe we should pass over in silence. But the question is important to both you and me, so let us say everything there is to say now. If you marry my grandchild, you can't be unaware that you're marrying a baroness, can you? You love her not only as a young girl, but as a baroness, although that title is forbidden by law. Perhaps you are emphasising to me, an old man, my baronial status not so much for myself as for yourself, because it is not a matter of indifference to you whether you ask for your sweetheart's hand from an old farmer or a former lord of a manor."

"Yes, of course, but…" I wanted to interject, but he said, "Allow me, young man, I haven't finished yet. So then you think you are not marrying a mere girl that you love, but you're marrying a baroness. Well, what about the circle you are taking your young wife away from – how will this affect her? Will they see her only as your young wife? No, first of all they will see her as a baroness, and they will see her as that even when she doesn't want them to. For what does that title mean to her, if she's living with you in a one or two-roomed apartment, washing her own dishes and yours, polishing the floors, because you won't have enough money to get help, just as we don't at the moment. You'll be lucky if it ends there – then the misery won't be so great. But as I've already said, in your circles my grandchild would always remain a baroness, and that would mean that she could never be her own person. In a word, one way or another, she will remain outside of society. Moreover, she might be slightly detrimental to your career, for how could you be trusted completely if your wife, whom you love, cannot be trusted?"

"You're wrong there," I said, "there are plenty of men among us who are in similar positions, whose wives have not even taken the trouble to learn their husband's language."

"No, young man, it's not I who am wrong, it's you, if you think that such men and women can be completely trusted, that society can rely on them. But forgive me, this is probably unnecessary, for I wanted to say something quite different. You see, my grandchild would remain in your society as a more or less alien being. But what would happen in her own circle – the one she comes from? In marrying you she would even lose that, wholly or in part – we can't ignore that. So she would be left completely high and dry, her whole world would be only you. So tell me now – shouldn't I be demanding much greater guarantees from you than from a young German who might ask for my grandchild's hand? In that case, my grandchild would have, apart from a husband, his circle of friends as well, with their interests and traditions, their joys and woes, their hopes and disappointments."

"You're quite right," I said, beaten, and added, "but if you look at it that way, there can be no question of marriage between Estonians and Germans at all; there must be no love affairs between them; they must always remain hostile to each other."

"You're exaggerating, young man, because you're in love," he said quite calmly, as if this question didn't concern him. "I think that if one side loses its social circle without gaining a new one, when it brings with it an old, pure pedigree and name which has not yet lost its power and dignity, then it must receive some sort of recompense from the other side, whether it's a husband, like an 'amen' in church, or a certain economic advantage, which allows the lovers to live even without closer ties with one or the other social circle. That is how I understand it."

"And according to your understanding I won't satisfy you, either in my person or in my financial situation?" I asked.

"I may be wrong, but unfortunately that is so," he replied. "I am old, I don't understand things or people well any more – it's possible, very possible, that judgements about their values should be made by very different yardsticks. But what can be done? I'm getting older by the day, not younger."

"I'm very sorry," I said, getting up, because I saw no point in continuing, "but I can't do anything about the fact that I still love your grandchild. My honour and respect for her, though, has grown considerably now that I know she has such a grandfather."

"Young man," he said, now raising his head to look at me almost pleadingly, which led me to believe that he also loved her, "if you really love my grandchild, then forget that she is a baroness, and give her up; that's the only good you can do her. Be content with love alone; marriage to you would be too heavy a burden for her. In any case I will do everything in my power to see that she does not take on that burden."

I didn't reply, because I didn't dare to promise, and just bowed silently before him, as if in agreement, intending to leave, but he stretched out his hand to me, as if I were supposed to kiss it – as if it were my sweetheart's hand.

"You'll kindly forgive me, but my old limbs won't let me get up from my chair. Please leave the doors open, so I can hear when Erika stirs. If you need to, come and see me. Talking with you is so interesting, but now I'm so tired that I'll have a little nap before Erika comes. Then I'll have to stir my stumps anyway."

Those were the last words I heard from him. Outside, my first thought was, did the old man – that is what I called him, for some reason, as soon as I got outside – really believe everything he told me, or did he only tell me to convince me and thus get me to give up my love? I would still like to know that even now, as I write these lines. Did he really think I was the spineless and shapeless mollusc that he tried to convince me I was, or was it just his stratagem?

When I got back to my workplace, greatly delayed, I had a feeling that the whole world could read in my face what had happened to me in the past hour and a half. And evidently it was not only my feeling, for otherwise why would my colleague, who had previously advised me so personally and sagely, ask me without demur, "No luck, eh?"

"No," I replied.

"Did you want to get a new one or extend an old one?"

"Get a new one," I explained.

"Then things are not too bad," he consoled me. "Loans that aren't agreed are never called in, and bonds that aren't signed cannot be protested against through a notary."

Of course these were very wise words, but they didn't ease my mind. I was going over the same old question: what now? – and could find no answer. When the depressing working hours were over finally, I hurried home impatiently, and I almost wished that I wouldn't meet Erika at the lunch table that day, or better still, that I would never see her again. In my letter box at home I found a letter addressed in an unknown hand, which left me quite indifferent, like everything else. I tossed it carelessly on the table and then clean forgot about it.

But, strangely, my mood evidently had no effect on the world or other people: the landlady was much the same as before at the lunch table, offering food like mad and talking of love, as if there were some secret bond between those two things, while the landlord threw his clumsy jokes into the chatter, and the children seemed like wild creatures who had just been unleashed from their tethers. Even Miss Erika appeared, and sat at the table as if she knew nothing of my visit to her grandfather, or else had not the faintest idea of its outcome. There was something unusual only about me, for otherwise the landlady would hardly have set me to worrying so often about the young lady, as if she wanted to keep me alert with her words.

"The only young lady at the table, and she is left on her own," moaned the landlady on Erika's behalf. "Can your men, I mean the Germans, be so obtuse and impolite?"

"I've eaten so rarely with gentlemen at table that it's hard for me to judge," Erika replied to the landlady's question. "The only gentleman I know well is my grandfather, but what attention or politeness can I expect from him? My aunt and I both look after him."

"Mr Studious would probably like ladies to look after him," said the landlady.

"So it should be, that ladies look after men, not the other way around," said the landlord.

"Why should that be?" countered the landlady.

"Because there are more women than men," explained her husband. "What's more, they're trying to take over all the men's occupations – well, such as serving at table here. At least I would have nothing against it."

"What do you think about it, miss? I don't dare to argue with the young man about it today."

"Perhaps our landlord is right," Erika replied to the landlady.

"Mr Studious, would you tell us what happened to you today?" the landlady now turned to me directly.

"Happened to me? So far, nothing," I answered.

"But later, what will be happening?" the landlady pressed me.

"Who knows? Maybe... There may be redundancies later," I told her.

"I see!" said the landlady, considering, as if she now understood everything. "So that's it!"

And for a little while complete silence reigned at the table, as all eyes turned on me.

"They've been talking about redundancies for years, but so far the number of staff has just kept increasing," said the landlord at length, as if wanting to console and calm not only me, but everyone else sitting at the table.

"See that you don't become redundant too," said the landlady to her husband in a tone that suggested that she wished for it.

"I could use the holiday," he replied.

"Couldn't you two change places?" asked the landlady.

"There would be no profit in that, at least not for your spouse," I explained, "fathers with families are not being laid off."

"Well then, it's quite simple: get married quickly," said the landlady.

"Easy to say!" sighed the gentleman. "But where to get children just as quickly?"

"Where does a poor man even find a wife?" I said, and my words must have come from the heart, because Erika looked at me somewhat reproachfully. The landlady noticed her look – and I felt it.

"This is now spiteful talk against women," said the landlady half-jokingly. "There are so many young girls who would go with a poor man, if he's acceptable in other ways. What do you think, miss – would you go for a poor man if you loved him?"

This question made Erika's ears burn, but she had time to recover, because the landlord commented on his spouse's words: "Well, you see, my dears, all roads lead to Rome: happily we've got around to love again. How nice that everyone's stomach is full; otherwise our appetites might have vanished."

"Leave out the silly jokes now, the young lady wants to answer," said the landlady.

And Miss Erika did answer, looking the landlady in the eye across the table: "My lady, I can't answer your question, because I've never been in love with a man, and no man has wanted me for his wife."

"You know, miss," said the landlady now, "I don't believe that until today you haven't loved anyone, and even less do I believe that no one has wanted you for his wife. Are men blind these days, or what?"

"I suppose they are," replied Erika adding, "at least as far as I'm concerned."

With these words she got up from the table, as if she no longer wanted to continue the conversation, and moved with her young charges to another room. Now the landlord said to his wife, "Why do you embarrass the poor girl?"

"How do I embarrass her?" countered the landlady. "Young girls like it when they're asked about getting married."

"But you always talk as if there was someone here that she loves, and with whom she should get married," declared the landlord.

"Carry on with your own story," contested the landlady, but a red flush did steal across her face. "Our young man is so dumb and passive that... Mr Studious, does it seem to you too that I'm trying to bring you and the young lady together somehow?"

"No, I've never noticed that," I replied. "That would be too wild – me and a baroness!"

"Wouldn't it?" agreed the landlady, adding, as she turned to her husband, "You hear that? You're the only one who reads such wild things and innuendos into my words. Nobody else does!"

When I went up to my room, I wanted to throw myself down on the sofa, but my eye fell first on the forgotten letter. I tore it open and read: *Wait for me today, please, a quarter of an hour before the usual time, and over on the other side, not the usual place. Erika.* I had to read it three times before I realised what the letter said. And then I was seized by an inexplicable terror. Why? I don't know. Perhaps because I thought of what would have happened if I had completely forgotten the letter left on the table today and had gone to meet Erika at the usual time? Or were the words *a quarter of an hour before the usual time, and over on the other side* something to cause anxiety? Did I perhaps detect in the letter a tone that caused fear? Did I feel that the writer of those lines had not yet been made as dull and insensitive as I who was reading them?

And when I had thought about it, I started to consider those blows that had rendered me so dull and senseless that day. Firstly, of course, the redundancy. But after all, this wasn't such a great surprise that it should have left me in a state of shock. The main cause must still be that old man, as I was still consistently calling the white-haired baron. And by that I didn't mean to belittle him or insult him – no, but it was a sign that I no longer saw in him so much as a baron or former lord of the manor as an ordinary mortal – as person who had experienced much more of life than I had, and who had the same feelings as every old person, every old man I had met thitherto, but his understanding was somewhat different.

Yes, one of the blows must have been the fact that I went to talk to the baron, but happened upon a man who only had a past. He was tethered to the present by only one living soul, and even that one I wanted to take from him, to start building a future for myself. That is why he told me everything I'm now trying to understand. But actually I still don't understand what he was accusing me of when he concluded that as a *Korporant* I lacked real seriousness about life. That was his term for it. What was he actually demanding or expecting of me? That same separation from this country and its people that he and his kind had been cultivating for centuries? Or, if he had not been doing that – as he tried to demonstrate – what was my task, then? Only the creation of a so-called upper stratum, rooted in the land and the people? So that I, for example, would claim some sort of privileges, while my kinsfolk – father, mother, brothers, sisters and so on – should be overlooked. But only a baron could think like that, not an ordinary old man, as I was beginning to regard him. That would go against common sense and human feelings. It would be ridiculous.

And yet he was speaking of it in terms of holiness. Actually, afterwards I had a clear feeling that for him the corporation was the dwelling place of this holiness, not only God in any form at all, as he expressed it. Or in his view, did the corporation come first and God second? God was left only when the corporation and its sanctity didn't exist? For he only came to the question of God when he was disappointed in the sanctity of my corporation. That is how it appeared to me in retrospect.

As to the question of God, here at least everything is

clear to me. For an old man like him, with his past, it could not be otherwise if he had to catch hold of God. Formerly, when he sat in his manor house and power enslaved him, it was natural that there had to be some sort of higher power, which gave him superior privileges and benefits, and now, when those privileges and benefits had gone, his great consolation was that there was still God, whom no nation or revolution could take away from him.

My situation was completely different to his, but he, an old man, could not understand that. I didn't have the power to rule or any special benefits, and was not aware of the past either, so I couldn't mourn its passing. I only have the future, which is not forcing me to be anything, so I'm free within myself. For only the past binds you, not the future, I believed at the time. That inner freedom of mine was something he couldn't forgive, for perhaps he wanted to see in me and my contemporaries the real masters of the country, bound by the future perhaps even more than by the past, while the country and people, like a beautiful woman, must be conquered anew every day if you don't want it to slip into someone else's hands. At any rate he would have wanted to bind me to some tradition inherited from the past, which would have allowed him to guess how I would attend to both the past and the future. In other words, he wanted a sort of assurance. But our times are no longer like that – something he couldn't grasp. No one could guaranteed against them harming them, so where was I supposed to find the guarantee he demanded of me?

Of course he was right in that my forefathers and my actual father had something certain, a tradition. But for him things were much easier in that regard than for me. For him it was still important that one season follows another. Every morning and evening his heart got a new assurance that the sun rises in the east and sets in the west. Every warm shower of rain on his spring sowing told him that there is something permanent and certain in the world, so it would be worth sowing and reaping the next spring too. The arrival of the birds in spring and their departure in autumn was for him renewed proof that everything was as before, that a fixed order pays, that tradition lasts, continuing on for many generations, so many that it is quite easy to start believing in eternity.

But what of that is there in me? When the redundancy comes, will someone say to me, It's autumn now, we won't be sending you out for purchases against the winter, or now spring is coming, that most beautiful season, we won't disturb your joy? Would a bank or a shopkeeper say to me, today is the first sleigh-run, we'll discount this bond for you, or today the starlings are singing so joyfully in their boxes, here's a kilogram of sugar for you, young man, a second rye loaf, a third brown loaf, a fourth pat of butter and a tin of sprats? No, nothing like that has ever happened to me. So I'm only sure that everything has to be paid for, without anyone getting any assurance that they can pay for it.

Is there something of eternity in that? Or is there divinity in it – in paying, I mean? Perhaps there is but I don't feel it. I don't feel it yet, for maybe I haven't gone far enough with the payment. Perhaps I have to pay in advance for several generations, before I start to feel the presence of divinity and eternity. So I have become detached from the eternity and divinity of my forefathers' land and its nature, but haven't yet attained a new eternity with its divinity. And will I attain it? That is perhaps what the old man meant when he spoke of the Estonian man who was supposed to be some sort of counterpart to me as a *Korporant*.

But if I had been what he called the Estonian man, would he then have granted me his grandchild, or would he have even come any closer to granting her? And if he had, then I ask – why? Did he believe that that proper Estonian man would have more eternity and divinity in his blood than I had, that he would be less detached from his father's and mother's land than I am? Did he believe that such a person has more seriousness about life than he thought I had, and that he could be trusted more than I am, especially at life's difficult moments? Did he, that mad creature, really think that, since I was prepared to give up the corporation for love, I would also, in a certain case, be prepared to give up my love?

In that case he also doesn't know what an Estonian man's love is. Such a man may be detached from his own forefathers' and mothers' eternity, he may have lost all his sanctities, yet he is left with love, the love of a foreign woman, as happened to wise Solomon, and that enslaves him just as any of the greatest sanctities or deities would. But the old white-haired man didn't understand that; only a proper Estonian man understands it. He knows what the wise Solomon knew: what use are a country and a people, and what use are God and his sanctities, if there is no love, the holiest of all?

Thus I reasoned to myself, my head in my hands, when I had read through Erika's two-line letter. This mental tramping back and forth might have lasted about an hour, without my noticing the time. Only then did it occur to me to look at the clock, and now a new terror seized me: lost in thought like that I might easily have dropped off to sleep, as had already happened to me once, for nothing made me doze off more than thinking did: thinking and sleeping sometimes seemed to me like almost the same thing, for in sleep I solved puzzles that were insoluble when I was awake.

I jumped up from the sofa on to which I had dropped to think, and started pacing around the room – from corner to corner, four steps in one direction, four steps back, as if I were some criminal behind bars. And the longer I walked like that, the more clearly I seemed to feel the old man's words invading my blood, and if not my love, then at least my respect and appreciation for his descendant, that blonde girl, was growing more and more. My feelings in general seemed to be taking a new direction, hard to express in words. Impulses that led to passions, lusts, were receding further away, and into their place, from somewhere deep within myself, came a spiritual tenderness and delicacy, which led only to adoration and veneration. I felt, in thinking of that girl, as if I were becoming purer and better, and as if I sensed a little of what that old man called falling to the ground before something boundlessly great and powerful.

But I didn't stay pacing in that room until the appointed time, because I started to feel cold and warm at the same time. In between all the other thoughts came my immediate main concern: what am I supposed to tell her? What is my decision about the whole situation? Where do I even begin? Am I supposed to tell her today, already, that it would be best if we didn't meet any more? Am I really supposed to accede to grandfather's viewpoint, that our life together would be an unbearable burden for Erika's health and her love? But can't our love survive anyway – a love that doesn't result in marriage? Those were the questions that danced continually in and out among my thoughts, without my finding a single answer.

Answers were not to be found outside either, where I roamed along badly lit streets, looking at my watch under nearly every street lamp. But the more often I did it, the slower the hands moved. And when the moment finally arrived, when Erika came running toward me, a little case on her arm, I was almost taken aback. Without saying a word we rushed onward together, as if we were escaping from evil pursuers or as if we were afraid of being late somewhere. Only after a while did she say, "I was afraid that grandfather might send auntie after me – that's why I invited you earlier."

"Your auntie knows already too?" I asked, taking the bag from her to carry it, to which she readily agreed.

"I'm no longer sure that grandfather hasn't told her," she replied. "But now I'm no longer afraid; here no one we know will find us and nobody will look for us in the dark park. The only trouble is this suitcase I took with me."

"It's so light to carry," I said.

So we headed straight for the park.

"Is it true, what you said at the lunch table today?" Erika asked after a while.

"What exactly?" I countered, because nothing special came immediately to mind.

"How can you even ask!" she cried. "With a couple of words you half-killed me at the table, so that I could hardly stay and sit there – and now you're asking me!"

"Oh, that redundancy!" I now said, because I recalled her look which was caught by the landlady. "For those words I beg you a thousand pardons, but I really didn't know what to answer to the landlady's question."

"So you just said it anyway?" she queried, more happily, and for a moment I hesitated over whether to tell her the truth or conceal it at first. Finally I told her anyway, "No, it is true after all, and that's why I shouldn't have said it at the lunch table."

"So you knew it already when you were visiting grandfather!" she almost screamed.

"Yes, I knew it already," I said, crestfallen.

"You've known it for a long time!" she pressed me further.

"No, I heard it only this morning," I explained. "If I'd known it a few days earlier, I wouldn't ever have appeared before your grandfather."

"But how could you tell grandfather that you're hoping for a pay increase?" she now exclaimed, which was a double blow to me: firstly, they must have taken it seriously after all when they kept such a trifling thing as my pay increase in mind, and secondly, this pay increase revealed me as someone who, one way or another, was untruthful and deceitful, in short a person who can be trusted only guardedly. This was clear to me in a moment. Therefore I shouted, "Oh miss, you can't even imagine my state of mind when I came before your grandfather! When I heard about these redundancies at the ministry in the morning, my only wish was not to go anywhere. But what was I supposed to do? Tell you that I wouldn't be coming today, that I wouldn't come at all until it was clear whether I have a job or not? But the decision might take weeks, even months. What would you want me to tell your grandfather? He would not have understood? No, I had no choice, I had to got and see him, because that seemed the only reasonable thing to do. Once I got talking with your grandfather, though, I liked him right from the start so much that…"

"You really liked him?" Erika asked happily.

"Believe me, I liked him so much that through him I started to love and honour you much more ardently. And I wanted so much to win his support and trust that I forgot the real or likely situation completely and came out with hopes that were aroused by my love for you. Because I had earlier assured myself so many times that if I managed to win your trust and love, then I would also achieve a salary increase, which would be insignificant compared with the first thing. So that was how I talked about it to your grandfather. But as soon as I had done it, my heart began to hurt within me, because I felt it wasn't decent or proper to talk like that."

"But if grandfather had changed his mind because of it, what then?" she persisted, as if enjoying my embarrassment.

"Oh Lord!" I cried, almost distracted. "I don't know what then! It was so terrible that I had to talk like that to the one I least wanted to tell it!"

"But just think what I had to go through when I lied to my grandfather," she said, as if in consolation. "For me it's even harder. But thank God, my heart is so pure, and I'm glad that you lied too, for now you have your own sin of love staining your heart."

And as if she felt closer to me because of that, and as if a particular wave of tenderness were rising within her toward me, I came closer so that her hand touched mine, and her shoulder touched mine, so as to almost support herself on me. But when my fingers closed tightly around hers, she seemed to awaken from a stupor, shifted away from me and slipped her fingers from my grasp, albeit gradually, as if regretting it or fearful of upsetting me.

Having reached the park, we sought out our old familiar avenue where we had walked when Erika had lied to her grandfather the first time. Today I was the liar. There were still plenty of leaves on the trees; today they dappled the light on to the road. Showers, storms and night frosts had done their work. Underfoot in the dark it felt like a thick, soft, scarcely rustling carpet. It smelt of damp and incipient mould, awaiting everything that was vital. This was the usual late autumn weather, neither warm nor cold, but sharply cool, as if a whiff of approaching winter could be felt. The wind had spent itself. The cloudy cover of the sky remained in place and no star penetrated it. Nor was the moon in sight, but from a faint glimmer of light through the clouds one could guess that the moon was moving unseen across the canopy.

Along the road people were moving; occasionally talk and laughter could be heard, sometimes it was peaceful and silent, as if everything had died. We were alone.

"Grandfather told you?" I said at length, when we had been silent long enough.

"He did," she replied.

I wanted to say something else, for the silence emphasised that I couldn't find the words. So the moments stretched into eternities.

"What now?" she finally asked.

"I don't know – I don't know anything any more," I replied.

"You must know, you must decide," she said oppressively.

"Of course I must," I agreed, "and yet I don't know. I'm desperate, I've been going crazy all day. Everything's dark, everything's confused, everything's incomprehensible, only one thing is certain: I love you more and more, more madly, and that seems to rob me of my power to decide, because I'm terrified of losing you."

"But you must do something so as not to lose me," she said, as if wanting to entice me.

"I can't find any way out," I said hopelessly, at length. "Or if there were a way out, I couldn't use it, not any more."

"What way out would that be?" she asked with a slight tremble in her voice.

"I don't want to talk about it," I said.

"But I want you to," she said insistently, almost angrily. "I want to know what way out it is."

"It's what our landlady recommended," I explained instead of answering.

"So she knows about our affair."

"Probably not," I replied, "she was just talking, as usual."

"What did she say?"

"She said we should elope."

"I'm ready for anything," she said unhesitatingly.

"Are you even thinking about what you're saying?" I asked, almost in terror, for somewhere deep in my being something seemed to emerge that wanted to postpone his insane step.

"No! What for? I'll do whatever you want," replied Erika just as unhesitatingly.

This moved me so much that I grabbed both her hands and kissed them almost tearfully on the gloves; in the meantime we had reached a solitary bench and wordlessly sat down on it. And when I had kissed her hands enough, I left them in my own, as if wanting to warm them.

"Our elopement would mean compromising you," I told her.

"Yes, of course," she replied, "but what's to be done if there's nothing else, if grandfather doesn't really believe that we love each other?"

"Aren't you really thinking of what will happen afterwards?" I exclaimed.

"Of course I am, if you are too, but if you aren't, then I won't either," she explained.

"Then I have to think for the two of us," I said. "Our landlord said that in the present circumstances elopement would be completely mad. For if I arbitrarily didn't turn up at work today or tomorrow –"

"Why arbitrarily?" she interjected. "Can't you ask for a few days off?"

"Now, when they're all taking about redundancies?" I exclaimed. "Asking for days off at the moment would be like asking to be dismissed from service. So, one way or another, eloping would mean me losing my job. And what would we have gained by that?"

"I would be compromised," she replied.

"And I would be forced to leave you on the spot, because I would have nowhere to put you, I wouldn't have anywhere left to lay my own head, I might have to move to my parents' in the country."

"And I would go back to my grandfather, because he, no matter what is said and done, will take me back anyway."

"And how would I look appearing before your grandfather, when I'd previously lied through my teeth to him about my salary increase and then fully consciously compromised you, when I knew that I was about to lose my job and had no other? If I hadn't talked to your grandfather today, or if I respected him less, honoured him less, then maybe I could stand being such a swinish cad, but now..."

"... you love grandfather more than you love me," Erika finished my sentence and started crying loudly. This was so unexpected for me that I completely lost my head. I simply didn't understand what could upset her so much. I could do no more than kiss her hands, which I had gradually released from their gloves while talking. And when kissing her hands couldn't silence her crying, I sank before her on my knees and beseeched her to calm down and listen to my explanation. And I summoned up all my wit to make her understand what sort of unhappiness, distraction, madness it would be to elope at this moment and compromise her. Gradually the weeping stopped and she started to realise how things stood, so that I could sit beside her again on the bench and warm her hands in mine and kiss them occasionally. She hardly uttered a word, as though she had become indifferent to everything. When I finally asked her whether she appreciated that I was acting this way out of love, she said submissively, while still convulsing with the last spasms of tears, "I understand you very well and I can respect all this. Of course you're right, when you think about it, but at first I didn't want to think, only love."

"You are simply terrible in your directness!" I cried. "And I feel ashamed before you."

"No, no, it's I who am ashamed before you," she said. "I'm terribly ashamed."

While still holding her hands and with our knees together, I felt her body convulse with shaking, which extended to my fingers and ran down past my knees.

"You're getting cold; we should walk," I said.

"Yes, I got cold from crying," she said by way of excuse, grasped her suitcase and got up from the bench. I tried to take hold of the case several times, but she wouldn't relinquish it and claimed that carrying the case kept her warm. But I still had the feeling that she didn't care whether she was cold or warm. She walked with downcast head; her pliant, sure and light step somehow became stunted, fumbling, as if her thoughts and attention were not where she was; her voice, words and movements betrayed a dullness that I had never noticed before. But when I approached her and tried to touch her anywhere, she jumped every time as if frightened, and I understood that now she needed peace, because her internal shock as she sat on the bench must have been somehow terribly great and deep. That consciousness, together with her continuing mood and behaviour, had an ever more depressing effect on me, and I came close now to starting to blubber, which would have made me utterly ridiculous in her eyes, which I feared dreadfully. In my depressed state I was aware of an increasing notion that if we had until today been speaking about the sins or crimes of our love, we had done it like children, but I committed my first real sin of love today, and perhaps that was the cause of everything that happened between Erika and me. A hot wave of pain passed through my heart each time I tried repeatedly to release her suitcase from her hand and she repelled my attempts with the same firmness. Finally I was seized by a sort of mad conception that everything would turn out well between us, nothing would have happened between us, if she had not had with her that annoying accidental case – it was I who called it accidental. And ever more persistently and with greater effort and new pretexts I tried to seize that bewitched object into my own hands, and no one could say how long I would go on trying to get that suitcase if Erika hadn't said that now she had to go home, now she definitely had to go home. There was nothing left for me but to give in to the inevitable. Of course now I know that she didn't have to go, and that only her aunt would be surprised at her staying any longer, while her grandfather would have awaited her arrival quite calmly. But with me life has always been such that I get to know the most important facts either too late or not at all. At school I got to know most of those things least needed for getting things done, while not a single person told me about the most necessary things, because they all evidently thought that people learn these things by themselves. All teachers and trainers are quite right about that, as surely that's what happens with the majority, but not everyone. There are those like me who learn the most necessary things too late.

Erika was missing again for a couple of days from lessons and from the lunch table.

"The girl is getting out of hand," declared the landlady, while the landlord tried to excuse her, explaining, "With the first chilly weather, everyone complains of colds and headaches."

"How do you know that she's absent because of illness?" she challenged her husband.

"Well, why then?" he countered.

"How would I know today's young people so well that I'd know why they're absent," said the landlady. "Here's our young gentleman, sort of half-dead for the past two or three days – why don't you ask him what's wrong? Of course you think that he's affected by the first chilly weather too."

"No, he has things of his own, we know that," he replied.

"My lady thinks of course that today's young people don't care whether they're in service or not," I said in self-defence.

"Oh, what's this!" cried the lady. "Now you have to hang your head because of a silly job! Will you hold your head up if I promise you half a year's lunches on credit? I make my promise having seen the first shoots of the crop, as they say, because you will find a new position, if you lose this one – and what's more, you haven't even lost it yet."

"New debts won't make anyone lift their head," I said, declining the kind offer, "especially when I don't know when I can pay you back."

"Why are you worrying about paying if I'm saying you're the first shoots?" asked the landlady. "Believe me, it means very little to me whether I set the table for six to seven or seven to eight."

"And to me it would mean very little whether I started paying for six to seven, instead of seven to eight," I explained, "but since I'm only paying for one and I can't even do that, it's easier for me to go without lunch than to eat and not pay."

"Well then, I can't help you," said the landlady, "but you

must have special reasons why you don't accept the offer I'm making."

"No, my lady, I don't have any special reasons apart from personal ones – that is, it's the way I'm made."

"And you can't re-educate yourself?" asked the landlady.

"So far I haven't been able to," I replied.

"Well, we'll try it in the future," said the landlady somewhat threateningly.

"You'd always like to re-educate everyone as if other people were children beside you," the man told his spouse.

"What are you men beside women other than overgrown children?" she replied to him.

"Do all women have to suffer delusions of grandeur like you?" ventured her husband now.

"So this is delusions of grandeur, is it?" asked the woman. "In this world it has always been so that women lead and men run, women command and men obey."

"Be sure of being the best!" cried the man.

"My lady, you ascribe to women very dangerous qualities," I said.

"Leading and commanding are always dangerous," opined the landlady.

"One thing is sure, anyway: wherever or whenever anything goes wrong, there's always a woman in the picture," declared the landlord.

"Yes, revolutions are all made by women," I said.

"You think so?" queried the landlady, as if tickled by it.

"No, I don't think anything, but I've read it somewhere," I said. "Women's jewellery, fine style and precious stones wreck any kind of social order much more quickly than even inflammatory speeches by the fiercest of male rebels. There are dresses, coats and diadems in the world that have a much greater effect than dynamite, pyroxyline or any other explosive. They can only be compared with poisonous gases."

"You must be unhappily in love at the moment, or you

131

were in love earlier, otherwise you wouldn't be finding things so topsy-turvy," cried the landlady enthusiastically. "The French state, the royal court and the brilliance of its whole society were once created by women, not men. Frenchmen even today live on what women created."

"No, my lady," I contested, "to my mind it's as I've suggested: not my idea, but one I once read when I was young and revolutionary."

"Young and revolutionary, eh?" smirked the landlady mockingly. "Now, of course, you're old and conservative."

"At any rate much older and more conservative than when I read that French women, with their jewels and dances, did away with their king and after that themselves and many of their best men, by chopping off their heads."

"Didn't Nikolai the Strangler turn out to be a woman?" asked the landlord.

"Are you still on about your Nikolai?" said the landlady to her husband sneeringly. "You'd be better off giving us your opinion on this: if a man's neck is twisted somewhere, it's always done by a woman. Have I understood this correctly?"

"Well roughly," concurred her husband.

"You, *Herr Korporant*, are of course of the same opinion?" the landlady turned to me.

"I don't know women so well yet that I could express an opinion," I replied.

"Just you wait, you'll get to know them and then you'll definitely share my husband's opinion," the landlady consoled me. "One day you're neck will be twisted too."

"May God grant that it happens as soon as possible, because it definitely will happen," I said, laughing, though for me it was almost serious.

"It usually happens faster than anyone would expect," explained the landlady. "There are men whose necks were twisted long ago, without them having the faintest idea of it."

"I'd like a twisted neck like that for myself," I laughed in response to the landlady's words.

It was as if some god were sitting with us at the lunch table listening to our wishes, to fulfil them! At any rate I, on seeing Erika for the first time since the last evening, felt from the beginning that my neck was going to be twisted. I looked, almost amazed, into the face of the woman I adored, and found it altered and unfamiliar. Something bold and challenging had appeared in her, but her gaze avoided catching my eye. I got the feeling that I was not at the table at all. Even when I offered Erika something – and on this day I was trying harder than usual to do that – she somehow managed to remain very polite and yet did not grant me a single glance.

"Miss, don't you want to tell us who is right, I or my husband? He thinks you've been gone because of illness; I think because of courtship."

"Oh yes, my lady!" cried Erika "I am very sorry that I didn't inform you. But my aunt and I have been at our wits' end, so that I forgot everything: grandfather was mortally ill, and I was afraid that he wouldn't recover. I have cried so terribly these past days, almost cried my eyes out."

"I can see that even now," remarked the landlady.

I looked at Erika's face too, but couldn't find anything that confirmed what the two of them agreed: it was only a little paler than usual, and her lips were convulsively pressed together.

"Grandfather got ill the evening when I was last here," continued Erika. "I didn't go home directly from here, but to visit an acquaintance, because I had in my case some things that I had to take away – my aunt sent them – and when I finally got there after a couple of hours' delay, my aunt was running frantically through the rooms while grandfather lay in bed. But the doctor had left shortly before I arrived. This has been going on for a long time, as he has a weak heart, but every time it happens I completely lose my mind, because grandfather is the dearest person in the world to me."

I had never heard such a volley of words from Erika at the lunch table before. The landlady was also surprised by it, as I gathered from her look.

"Then I did you a grave injustice, blaming your absence on courting," the landlady apologised.

"Staying away from work for courtship even once is not worthwhile," Erika explained.

"Oh yes it is," opined the landlady. "It's worth doing even worse things for courtship, if it's the right one."

"Well, then I suppose I haven't met the right one yet," laughed Erika a little nervously, glancing at me for the first time.

In the evening, when I was waiting for her in the street – I'd been doing that for half an hour before she came – she told me that she wouldn't have time today, because the previous evening she'd received the worst dressing-down she'd ever had in her life.

"Just think about it," she told me confidentially, "my aunt went out to meet me; she almost came in to ask if I was still here. Of course, in the end she went home with her nose out of joint. You can guess from that what was awaiting me at home. With great trouble I got grandfather around to allowing me an extra hour to come. At first I thought it was all over, and that's why I didn't tell the landlady anything."

"Ah, so it wasn't really grandfather's heart trouble?" I asked.

"No, you're wrong. Grandfather really was seriously ill," she explained. "Of course it began with the terrible upset of my not coming home at the right time; God knows what was going through grandfather's head. He must have feared that you really would compromise me, because he doesn't know you so well. That 's to do with his ailing heart. He made me swear by all the saints about whether anything had really happened to me, and today he said, 'Bear in mind, my girl, that if anything fateful happens to you, that will be the end of my life. So then, if you don't want to be a nail in my coffin, come home every evening at the right time.' So that is what I had to swear to do, and that way he allowed me to turn up for lessons again."

That is how she explained her situation, and that would all have been fine were it not that she had become so talkative. She had always been in the habit of thinking through everything she said, but now her words somehow came easily and superficially as if gliding indifferently over everything. Even about her grandfather's illness she spoke as if it didn't move her at all, and when she mentioned the coffin nail I didn't doubt that it was mere empty words. I would have liked to tell her that, or at least ask her to explain why I might get that impression, but I didn't dare. She spoke almost incessantly about her grandfather, her aunt, other relatives and acquaintances, but I got to hear only the most trifling things: who had seen whom, who had been where, who had said what, who had sent regards to whom, who had received a letter or card from whom, who had greeted whom, who had wished whom luck on what occasion, and so on *ad infinitum*. There was no longer any chatting or discussion, and none of what a young man and woman like to talk about most. And if I did try to say something that might have had any sense in my opinion, she glided over it quite easily, as if it didn't interest her or she didn't understand it. This happened not only on this day, but also on the days that followed, when I, despite all this, went to meet her every evening to accompany her home. The only relevant question that interested her at all was the redundancies for numbers of staff that hung in the air. Almost every day the conversation led one way or another to that, and if she was told that still nothing definite had been heard, she would repeat, "How silly that pointless fear lasts so long! Maybe it will come to nothing."

"Don't worry, something will come," I replied. "The matter is being sifted and weighed."

"I'm not worried," she said, and suddenly in her voice there was a long-dead nuance – something that had been there once and I had had time to forget. "You obviously think that I'm expecting and wishing for you to lose your job."

"No, I don't, but…"

"But you have changed your opinion of me quite a lot," she continued.

"Yes, sometimes I don't believe my eyes and ears," I remarked.

"But my opinion of you hasn't changed," she said, "except that I have tried to get sense into my head as grandfather wishes, and you also wished once, there on the park bench. That's all."

"Then I am the most ungrateful creature in the world," I said, suddenly feeling tears in my throat. She must have sensed my change of heart, or even sympathised with it, because as we walked she shifted closer to me and was silent for a while.

But then finally came the day when I could tell her that redundancies in the ranks had had their effect on me. She gave me a frightened look, turned her eyes aside and said, "And yet!"

"And yet!" I replied just as tersely, and that was all we had to say on the subject. But both I and probably she, both of us, felt that the last reed of our future hopes had been broken. Of course that reed was more imaginary than real, but it was still something, because at least I had not tired of believing that I might miraculously be spared redundancy, then I would have a little spark of hope for a salary increase which I had been weighing up for a long time. So now everything had vanished, we knew it and we didn't want to waste a single word or look each other in the eyes. It was made easier by the fact that our meetings still took place in the evenings and on poorly lit roads. One evening she said to me, "Oh, this evening we have to be quick, I'm expected." She said it as if I were expected with her, so we both had to hurry. But obviously that concept only flashed into my head, as her next words clearly proved: "Do you remember my distant relative who used to say it was interesting to be with Estonian girls, but boring with me? I told you about him once. He's back here; we're supposed to go to the cinema together today."

"Oh yes," I said rather indifferently, "I do remember." But behind this apparent indifference was a heart which was writhing in pain, especially as Erika carried on.

"He told me that he wouldn't even recognise me, I'm supposed to have changed so much. They say my mind has opened up and I talk like a developed person. You see! He says I've been developing in the meantime. But you're not listening to me, you don't like me talking about him. Did you hear what I said?"

"Of course I did," I replied with the same indifference. "I heard that you've developed in the meantime."

"Well, good!" she said, relieved. "They say I have the eyes of an adult woman. Have you noticed that my eyes have changed?"

"Not your eyes," I replied, "but your look, your gaze, maybe that has."

"Ah, really!" she cried in joyful amazement. "You see, he's right after all! I thought he was just telling me that, to get grandfather or auntie to say that."

"Why would grandfather or auntie be made to say that?"

"To get them to – well, they might give a sign that Ervin should try to amuse me, interest me in something – and he'll start from the assumption that I've developed in the meantime. But if you also think that a different look has come into my eyes, then maybe Ervin isn't for grandfather, but simply for himself."

"I still don't understand why grandfather or auntie should..." I wanted to say.

"Ah, you know, lately I've been terribly melancholy, and they're afraid that..."

She didn't finish, and just as well, because even without that, I realised how silly it was on my part to force her to answer.

"When did you first notice that about my look, or my gaze?" she asked after a short pause.

"After you'd been gone for two days last time and then came back," I explained, trying to make good my previous clumsy question. "Not only had your look changed, but your whole bearing, your appearance even."

"So that was it," she said slowly, as if to herself.

"Yes, that was it," I repeated, as if I understood what she was thinking.

"But you don't know what's behind those words," she said.

"My visit to your grandfather and the evening on the bench in the park," I said.

"There's something quite different, that you have no idea of," she explained. "Only grandfather and I know about it."

"And you can't tell me?" I asked.

"Not at the moment," she replied.

"Then when?"

"Some time maybe, maybe never," she said, as if far away with her own thoughts.

"But just now you said you feel the same towards me as ever," I declared.

"Of course I do, but I didn't say that before," she explained.

"Then I'll repeat your words that distressed me greatly: 'You love grandfather more than me.'"

"Did those words really distress you?" she asked.

"Terribly!" I assured her.

"I was in terrible pain myself, that's why I hurt you too," she explained. "But those words don't affect me, because we're talking about what I haven't confided to grandfather, but what he knew from the start. Without him this couldn't have come about. This is something between him and me, not between me and anyone else. You understand: this matter only concerns me and grandfather."

"Then I don't understand anything at all," I said, as if satisfied with her explanation, but deep in my heart a worm of doubt was gnawing away. This didn't concern only her and her grandfather; it couldn't, as I too must be involved. Finally I felt obliged to ask, "So I have nothing to do with this business?"

"Not a bit," she affirmed, and added as if in passing, "or if you did, the only explanation I could give is there wouldn't be anything worth talking about."

"Can't you tell me which part of this trifling thing involves me?" I asked.

"Of course I could, very well, but…"

"But … go on and say it!" I cried.

"But that's just it … I can't talk about your part in it without explaining my own and grandfather's, and I can't do that now on any account," she concluded, and that didn't satisfy my curiosity at all, rather it increased it.

In the ensuing days too, whenever I steered the conversation to this secret business, she stayed firm in her resolve: she couldn't tell me, because it was her own and grandfather's affair, nothing to do with me. And it was the sort of thing, she said, she wouldn't tell anyone at all, even if it happened – which it wouldn't – and if it did happen that she would marry one day, then she wouldn't tell her husband either, because it would be no concern of his.

"But if your mother were alive and asked you?"

"Yes, I might tell my mother, if she was like I imagine she was," she replied.

"So you would love your mother more than me," I concluded, to get her to talk somehow.

"That isn't love, it's understanding," she explained. "Maybe you wouldn't understand me, but mother would, if she's the sort of person I imagine she was."

"Grandfather is for you a substitute for mother then," I said.

"Exactly," she affirmed, "for me grandfather often stands in for mother, because auntie is busy with social affairs, she's never at home and doesn't love children."

"You're no longer a child."

"In her opinion I'll always be a child; both of us, grandfather and I, are for her a little like children, and so she keeps her distance, though we all live together."

"You said before that you wouldn't tell even your own husband about this thing," I began again after a while, "but if the two of us could have been…" I didn't quite dare to express in words what we two had once dreamt of marriage – yes, it seemed to me then, terribly long ago – when we saw in each other a husband and a wife.

"Then you would have known everything anyway, I wouldn't have needed to say or explain anything. Or if I had done it, then…" She didn't finish her sentence either.

"What then?" I asked.

"I don't know what then," she replied. "Then it might have been so, it might have been good to talk about it, but now it wouldn't."

Even now I think I feel how I was burning with curiosity then and how, along with that, there was sprouting within me a desire to stand close to her, so close that I would know everything, for I was convinced that standing close to her would make me omniscient. At the same time I felt that something beautiful and great had passed me by, never to return.

When we discussed this subject, she was thrown into a strangely sad or melancholy state, and that day we parted as if we had made each other sad or at least upset. At any rate this secrecy had affected me as if, for the first time in our acquaintance, I had left her for a day and not accompanied her home, as if I wanted thereby to loosen her heart and tongue or punish her a little. But when I turned up the next day she smiled at me most innocently, as she had done at the lunch table, and said in her usual happy and superficial tone, as if she were dealing with the most trifling thing, "Well, where did you get to yesterday? I looked and looked, I stopped a couple of times, I looked and waited and wondered to myself whether you'd fallen asleep again, like that other time, you remember, when you bumped into me on the stairs. Just think: what would have happened if I'd fallen down those high steep stairs that time!"

"Things might be easier for me now," I said cruelly and grimly.

But she acted as if she didn't understand my words, or as if she saw in them only a silly overblown joke, as she replied with a smile, "Oh Lord, these Estonian men are certainly comical, when they go to sleep rather than meeting! I thought you wouldn't come and keep me company any more, but you've been spoiling me with your company. I didn't want to walk all that way alone, so I asked Ervin to come and meet me today. Do you want me to introduce you? He has also been in a *Korporation* and knows other Estonian *Korporanten*. Very nice boys, he says."

"Thank you," I said, "but at the moment I'm not in the mood for new acquaintances." Even as I said those words I felt that I should have given some other answer or at least spoken in a different tone, but what could be done. It had happened. I had acted as if I were insulted or as if I were burning with petty jealousy or lacked the courage to make contact with this young German, so that Erika could compare us side by side.

"Don't get annoyed," she said with the same lightness, "I was just joking. And Ervin isn't an acquaintance of yours."

If her first words only jarred me, then these words of hers actually irritated me. Had I, compared with her Ervin, become a figure of fun already, to be mocked and teased? It's quite likely that today would have seen the first squabble between us, which might have grown into a real argument and quarrel, if she hadn't been more tactful than I. Instead of waiting for me to speak, she let her own words soar with butterfly lightness, hitting me like a sledgehammer: "So I really must apologise if you're not in the mood for new acquaintances, and I wish you a good evening right now, because Ervin's waiting for me at the next corner. I didn't let him come here, because I was afraid you wouldn't want to meet him. But thank you very much for coming today and not forgetting me."

At the end of the sentence all the lightness was suddenly gone, at least so it seemed at that moment. Suddenly my ears sensed that something had snapped, something had frozen in her throat, something she was struggling to hold in, so that it didn't gush from her eyes. But for me it was not frozen and therefore filled my eyes. Half-blinded, I reached for her extended hand and began to kiss it crazily. I don't know whether the odd tear also fell on it, but her hand shook. Suddenly Erika pulled her hand from mine, and hurried away.

"Can I come tomorrow evening?" I cried after her.

"If you don't sleep in again," she laughed to me over her shoulder, as if nothing had just happened between us. But it's very possible that nothing had happened, everything was just my demented imagination, so I rambled on to myself as I gradually started walking after her, as if I wanted to accompany her despite everything. I'll walk alone, but I'll still accompany her, for if she weren't there I might turn to someone else. So I thought, as if to console myself.

As I later thought over that parting – to tell the truth, on the following days I did nothing else but think about that parting as if it were a new challenge in life – I was firmly convinced that the strange world of dreams, in which I'd spent such happy hours, was coming to an end. Love had remained, might remain forever, but the dreams had returned whence they came – into oblivion. I only wanted to know one thing: when she went with another, did our love remain with her, the memory of that love? Was she also burying her dreams and leaving for herself just mere love without any egotism, for dreams do have a bit of that? What will happen to me if at some time I go with someone else, as she is doing now, while our dreams are so present and fresh?

These were irrelevant and pointless questions, but at the time they gave me a reason to live. When I recall that time now, I feel that my questions indicated one major thing: my love at the time was still far from free of egotism, as if my dreams had not had time to die. For what was the point in wanting to know whether your love is returned or not, when you have no more hopes? It is enough to know that you are in love, and in love you burn like a candle which will soon go out. Love free of egotism is only a glimmering sadness, a flickering hopelessness. It is born of death and gives birth to death. Or in a few cases, the lover becomes a saint, a hero, a sage whose wisdom is of no use to anyone, even to their own kind of sage.

That's what I say now, as I write these lines, but at the time I was trying to suppress emotions, to throttle irrelevant questions even momentarily, and submit to impulses which now make me smile sympathetically. To begin with, that evening of our parting I decided not to appear at the lunch table the next day, because I was afraid I wouldn't be able to endure the landlady's knowing banter and Erika's light-hearted laughter. And to make sure I didn't go back on my decision, I didn't go back home before the time Erika finished teaching. Coming home, I went from the street corner where Ervin was due to be waiting, as Erika had been thinking of introducing us. I wanted to see whether anyone was waiting there today, because if they weren't, I could reasonably assume that no one had been there yesterday either – by fibbing, Erika had got rid of me more easily. My suspicion was actually confirmed: there was nobody on the street corner or anywhere near it. I hurried home at great speed, my heart blending pleasure and alarm, and in front of my house door I bumped into some young man, so that we both saw the need to apologise to each other. Only as I stepped in the door did it occur to me that this must be the Ervin I'd been looking for: taller than I, in a jacket, leggings and long socks. Definitely him! On the stairs I encountered Erika coming towards me, and today she was the one who practically ran me down in her hurry to get down the stairs.

"Good evening!" she cried when she noticed me. "Today I don't have any time, grandfather is waiting."

"Your grandfather has rather light feet," I would have liked to reply to her, but before I had time to, she was out of the front door. It was true: yesterday's goodbye had really been forever. If I had not taken the hints, they would soon have been followed by other, clearer ones.

Actually it had already happened, only I didn't know it yet; I heard about it only the next day when I appeared at the lunch table, where the landlady said to me, "Where did you go yesterday? Firstly I knocked with a stick on the ceiling, and when that didn't help, then my husband did, and I tried again, but you still didn't come. Then I sent the girl up to look and she brought the news that your room was quite empty. And we were nearly bringing the ceiling down!"

"They kept me back at the ministry yesterday, I only came in the evening when the young lady went out; we met on the stairs," I replied as indifferently as possible.

"You're playing some game with the young lady," said the landlady, "when she doesn't come, you don't either."

This surprised me so much that I quite forgot my pretended indifference and asked anxiously, "Was she out as well?"

"Of course she was!" cried the landlady. "Don't you know yet?"

"No! How could I know that?" I replied, trying to return to my former indifference. "I haven't exchanged a single word with the young lady in the meantime. Yesterday on the stairs she just shouted good evening to me over her shoulder, that's all."

"And I was joking to the old man: look, our young folks have got to a state where they don't even want to see each other at lunch. Because the young lady only turned up after lunch and wanted to give up her lessons completely. Only after a lot of palaver did I get her to promise to come every afternoon for a couple of hours until Christmas. She says her grandfather's health has suddenly got worse; the young lady can't be away from home for so long. Of course that's what she says, but what's behind it, who knows? More likely she's going out with a man. It's understandable, for what's the point in such a nice girl waiting any longer – her most beautiful years are passing her by."

"You'd make everyone go out with men, whether they're Estonian or German girls," said her husband.

"Of course!" cried the landlady with assurance. "Girls to husbands and boys to wives. If it were up to me, I'd even look for a partner for our Mr Studious. Don't you want me to take you in hand?" she appealed to me.

"No, thank you," I replied, trying to joke, "soon I won't have anything to put in my own mouth, let alone a wife's."

"I'm thinking of someone who has enough to put in her own mouth, and enough for yours as well," explained the landlady.

"That would be the worst of all – to live at a wife's expense," I said.

"I think so too," agreed the landlord.

"You have experience of that, to be so sure about it?" she asked her spouse.

"A little bit," replied the man, "because you're rich and I'm poor."

"But you've always had your position and your income."

"Of course I have, but it's always been a beggar's kopeck compared with your income."

"But has my income made you unhappy?" the landlady asked.

"Isn't it enough that it isn't my income?" countered her husband.

"Well, if our young gentleman looks at it the same way, he'll have a long time to perish alone and maybe even starve," said the landlady.

"It's easier to starve than eat from a woman's hand," I said.

"But if you love that woman?" she asked.

"Where would you come by love so easily," I said to myself, while the landlord rushed to support me, saying, "A starving man's love is like a homeless dog's howling in front of the house where it's beaten."

"Listen – don't upset the young man with your silly jokes," the landlady told her spouse.

"I'm not joking at all," he said.

"But a rich woman can fall in love with a poor man?" she asked.

"A rich old woman can, with a poor young man," opined the landlord.

"But not a rich young girl with a poor young man?"

"I've never seen or heard of it," said the landlord, "or unless the young man is from a great family, exceptionally handsome, gifted, famous or something like that, which is the same as rich."

"That's definitely right," I said, turning to the landlord.

"You have experience of it, to say it with such conviction?" the landlady asked me.

"Not personally," I replied, "but I've never seen it, heard of it or read of it. That some man, especially a young one, rich and of good family, would fall in love with a poor girl and then, so to speak, renounce the throne, is possible, but a woman – she is very practical in love as in other things, much more practical than we men."

I felt a real enjoyment in saying these words, obviously influenced by the events of the past few days.

"You men don't know anything about a woman's love, you only love yourselves," retorted the landlady. "For us women, love is a question of life, for you it's a question of fun."

"That's possible," agreed the landlord, "but we give our souls over to fun more lightly than you give yours to life."

"Just so," confirmed the landlady, "you don't seek love, only fun. We women are the only ones who love."

"And the more seriously you love, the more practical is the purpose of your love," the man replied.

"Ever more practical, more practical!" cried the landlady, now agitated, as if her spouse's words concerned her personally. "A person wants to live, a person must live! Don't you think so?"

"I've no idea what a person must do in the world."

"But somebody has to know, and you men don't!" cried the landlady.

"There is only one conclusion to our conversation: a person must love," I said.

"But if a woman loves so much that she is ready to cut her ties with her previous life, you'll immediately say, 'A woman's love always has a practical purpose, she wants to live or die. Only we men love rightly, because we don't have a purpose, we only have fun.'"

While she spoke, the landlady looked at me intently, as if her words were intended just for me. And though at the time I couldn't accept those words, they still affected me painfully, for, I don't know why, I was reminded of Erika sitting and crying on the bench because I was supposed to love grandfather more than her, and afterwards, of her carrying her little bag and keeping it away from me.

When the landlady started talking about men and women and their love, it affected all that was most sensitive in my nature and evoked my most painful memories. I would gladly have given up her lunches, but was hindered by various circumstances. Primarily the fact that the young lady had withdrawn, which on no account was due to grandfather's health, but only her conversations with me and with Ervin. If I left the lunch table immediately, I thought that I would reveal my own conversations with the young lady, and I wanted avoid that for my own sake and, until much later, for hers as well. However things stood, it seems to me that despite everything I was still hoping for I knew not what. And revealing what I was hoping for was beyond my powers, although I suffered day after day at the hands of the chattering landlady, let alone the fact that, like it or not, I had to take part in that myself. Another reason why I was forced to continue my lunches was that they enabled me, for a little while each day, to occupy the spaces she moved in, breathe the same air as she did, accept her greetings along with the others, and afterwards hear her voice through the door as the lunch continued. This was painful, but at the same time calming. The last link between us was not yet broken, I thought. I could still see her white curls, her evasive eyes, her disfiguring pimples, which in recent times had given her an especially hostile appearance, as though warning me, You see what happens to a young lass when she abandons one young man and goes with another.

Those two main reasons were accompanied by others. We had earlier talked about how I would give up the lunches when I lost my position, but my position was continuing, so why shouldn't I come to lunch? Both my position and Erika's lessons would soon be coming to an end, so what was the point of prematurely losing the chance of the last contact: on Christmas Eve she wouldn't be coming any more, and on the same day I wanted to travel to the country.

In the run-up to Christmas I was struggling like a fly in a spiderweb. Work got out of hand and I made mistakes that bordered on madness. Everyone must have come to the conclusion that management would have been quite right to dismiss a colleague of my calibre. So be it! That didn't interest me in the least. But my colleague, who was definitely going to continue sitting at his desk either because of his wife and newborn child or for some other reason I didn't know of, told me once, "You really are off your head! What amazes me is that so far not a single woman has snapped you up. Really unbelievable!"

"Do women love people who are off their heads?" I asked.

"They don't, but you can get hold of them more easily," replied the colleague. "Because a man like you can hang around any street corner, and if your chance comes, you'll go through fire and water for it."

"So I'm not mad enough then?" I exclaimed.

"No, you are, otherwise you wouldn't make serious mistakes so often, which is a great shame for you, if you'll allow a comrade to point it out. In this way you're spoiling your chances of getting a new job, believe me," my colleague told me almost heartily. And when I didn't answer his words, he continued, "But perhaps you're the same sort of man as a distant relative of mine, who also wore the colours. Women didn't sink their teeth into him either, for he was already so highly regarded that he always said – joking, of course, but still with a bit of truth in it – he said that he'd get married only to the daughter of a king or a prince, nothing less would satisfy him, because plenty of them were available. And you know how it ended?"

"He got himself an emperor's daughter," I said.

"No, he fell so completely in love with his father's shepherdess that, believe it or not, he married her and they've been together for over two years. Everyone predicted that the boy would leave the girl after a couple of months or at least a couple of years definitely, but to this day he hasn't, and there's no sign of him planning to. I'm sure you're going to do the same."

"I'm holding back," I explained, "I'll fall in love with the shepherdess and marry the emperor's daughter, to win her father's throne back for her."

149

"The wolf howling at the moon!" he cried, and that was a harder blow than anything else he'd said, because I'd once used those words about myself, when my dreams took hold of me. Then I had perhaps spoken in part to titillate my "king's daughter" – to move her and awaken her love for me, while in reality I had changed into a wolf howling at the moon.

That was how I lived through the whole pre-Christmas period, like a howling wolf. Not that anyone heard my howling, for two-legged wolves only howl in their hearts. A few times a day I would go and look at my letter box, as if some message were supposed to come that would end my howling, but the box was always empty, or I mostly found messages in it that made me howl even more madly if they didn't leave me indifferent. Very often, if not every day, I found myself wandering close to home as Erika was leaving her lessons, as if I wanted to find out whether Ervin was coming to call every day. And he did. At least there wasn't a day when a tall male figure was not waiting for her, and at that distance on a poorly lit street I couldn't see any more.

For some reason I got interested in whether Erika and he were keeping away from any kind of premises or places of amusement, and in this way I wasted my last pitiful cents on cinemas, cafés, theatres, concerts and dancing to find out whether the couple were there or not. But not a single time did I find them anywhere, as if they had disappeared into thin air, except Erika turned up for lessons at the right time and the tall male form was there to meet her after her lessons. So the holidays came without anything special happening, although day after day I had some strange presentiment of something happening, I didn't know what. For the last couple of weeks I hadn't seen Erika at all, or if I did, at a distance, recognising her form, her gait, posture or bearing. I had only heard her when she talked to the children or read aloud by the piano: *eine, zweie, eine, zweie*... On Christmas Eve I met her in the street when she hurrying by with holding some packages. Yet she did stop straightaway, when I took my hat off to her.

"You're attracting people's attention," she said to me with a sad smile, reminding me of my bare head.

"I don't care," I replied, but I did put it back on.

"You still only think of yourself," she said as a mild rebuke or snub.

"No, miss, I only think of you," I replied so loudly that passers-by could have heard it. "All these days and nights my thoughts have been about you."

"Do you have to say it so loudly?" she asked with a smile.

"I could say it even louder," I replied.

"Then I must run, otherwise you'll compromise me in broad daylight in the middle of the street," she laughed with affected lightness, but the word "compromise" was a strange reference to our past which sounded like a scream to me.

"How are you, dear miss, if I may ask?" I said when she stretched out her arm. "Shall we go for a stroll once more down the Avenue of Lies?"

"Don't talk so cruelly," she appealed to me directly.

"I'm not," I said as if excusing myself, and added, "So you won't come to see us any more?"

"No, I won't have any time," she explained.

"I'm going away to the country today," I said.

"Have a good journey then!"

"Have a good stay here!" I replied. "Or may I help you carry your packages home?"

"No, thanks, I'm not going home yet," she said.

I had intended to stay longer in the country, but at first I kept my room in the town just in case, to have somewhere to lay my head should there be a change in my luck while I was in the country. And so it came about: in the country I was in for more than I could have imagined, for everything was different to what I'd believed. Perhaps this was influenced by the fact that I'd brought my notification of dismissal with me, although I added as a consolation that in a couple of months I would definitely get a much better job. That may have consoled others but not me, and because of this I concluded that everything was not different at home; I was the one who was different. I had changed under the influence of recent events, but home perhaps had not. My mother, father, sister and brother did not feel things the same way I did. Perhaps they didn't have anything against my staying at home for a while, as a so-called freeloader. When I went to bring in the hay or the wood, not what you would call urgent work, I went with my brother instead of my father; my father didn't have any pressing business at home, but an old person could take a little rest. Once my mother said to my father in everyone's hearing, "Look, old man, isn't it good that you have two sons to bring in the hay from the forest to the hayloft!"

But my father answered my mother quite simply, "If they were just going to carry the hay into the hayloft, they didn't need to rub their arses so long on a school bench, they could have done with much less. Or is the school bench only good for wearing out trousers?"

"Why do you bring that up now?" mother upbraided him. "Of course it's just that you're a hard man to please, even when you have an educated son and the hay is coming home with his hard work."

"That's another thing: he hasn't forgotten haymaking at school," said father, "but I would have liked to take more pleasure in my own work and effort, that's the thing. Why trouble your head so much and bring debts on yourself and others, if you still have to earn your crust by working with your own hands?"

"The papers say that haymaking is easier and you can do it better if you've been properly educated at school," said my brother.

"Do you believe the papers and everything they carry on

about?" father said sarcastically. "In the summer the paper announced lovely weather, so why was the rain soaking your skin? Best to ask Oskar himself if it's easier now for him to carry the hay."

"What is there to ask?" I interjected. "It's obvious that it's harder."

"I think it's harder too," said father. "And you went to school to quit the hardships of farm work. But there you are – where do you get it, when everyone wants to get it? The world is that way – there isn't enough to go round for everybody. They barge into the countryside, then there are shortages there, so they all head back to the town, then that gets crowded, so there isn't enough room for everyone. We might have more space in the countryside, but I'm afraid everyone will soon be so educated that no one will want to live in the country any more. Things are so crazy now that there's a school for everything. You want to be a housewife, there's a housewives' school, you want to be a lady, there's a school for young ladies, and for cooks there's a cookery school. But as for potatoes, nobody knows how or can be bothered to peel them any more; it's best to cut them up for the pigs. There's nothing for it but to open a potato-peeling school."

"One has already been opened," laughed my brother.

"Well of course, what can you do," opined father, "when people have got so blind that they won't turn up their trousers any more and won't learn to stop up the pigsty door without schooling in it, as old people used to say in my boyhood. But what's mad is that as soon as a person's gone through housewives' school or school for young ladies, they don't want to be a housewife or a young lady any more. And as soon as a man has learnt at school to turn up his trousers and stop up the pigsty door, he's only good enough to be a master in the town."

"Things are not as bad as you make out, father," said my brother. "You see, the farmer at the farm on the church road is an educated man, and he makes a terrible fuss and bother of things."

"Of course he makes a fuss and bother – with other people's money. Take notice, son, we have to pay for that educated farmer's fuss and bother," warned father.

"Why?" asked my brother. "We don't have anything to do with him."

"But what if the debts caused by all that fuss, bother and new-fangled ideas are written on the chimney?" responded father.

"Who would come and write those on our chimney?" contested my brother, defending his view of the supposed mortgage on the neighbour's house.

"My dear child, where would they write, then?" cried father. "In the end they write debts on the chimneys of those who still have a chimney. And he doesn't have his own chimney any more, that's surer than sure, and he and his little wife can sell his place to the highest bidder, but he'll never see the money back that he's put into it."

"Of course that is surer than sure, that he'll never see that money," agreed my brother.

"Well, but whose money was it that will never be seen?" asked father. "According to my stupid reasoning, it belonged to all of us who live on our own money and not in debt."

"But we have debts too," said my brother, and now all eyes turned on me, for they all knew that those debts were incurred by me.

"Of course we have debts," agreed father, "and they're connected to the school too, but our place is worth more than them many times over. Or don't you think so?"

"I do," said my brother.

"You see!" cried father triumphantly. "So we can pay off our debts and help to pay off that educated farmer's debts at the same time when he goes bankrupt; after all, the money is supposed to come from somebody's pocket."

"But if it's given away?" asked my brother.

"No, son, in this world nothing is given away," replied father, "or if it is, it's taken from others' pockets. You know what I tell you, children, and you, Oskar, don't take offence that your father tells you this: it's the same story with the educated farmer and his fussing as with your fussing about your coloured cap – that's the conclusion I've come to, when I think about your education and everything else. Other people, who are more decent and modest, have to pay for it."

"Old man, you're spoiling what little pleasure we have with your talk, when we're together rarely enough as it is," said mother, and you could feel from her voice that the tears were not far from her eyes.

"Father, I've told you once already that I'm voluntarily giving up my right of inheritance in favour of Enn and Mall – isn't that enough?" I said, as if emboldened by Mother's words.

"No, son, it isn't enough," replied father, "your schooling costs more than either Enn or Mall will inherit."

"So then, I'm in debt to Enn and Mall," I concluded.

"You don't owe me a thing, Oskar," said my brother with a heavy heart at the embarrassing turn the conversation had taken.

"Nor me either!" cried Mall, getting up from her chair and going into the other room, no doubt to hide her tears.

"I didn't mean that either," explained father, "but I only said it so that you'd know how things really are. I don't believe Enn would ever regard you as her debtor, Oskar, when I'm not –"

"Father, why are you even bringing up this subject?" shouted my brother. "Do what you think is right, and let Oskar and me do what we think is right. But since this subject has come up, then I'll tell you one thing straight from the heart, Oskar, that if you come home now, or whenever you do come home, I'm always pleased, if only because my educated brother hasn't forgotten us. Of course

I'd be even more pleased if you were doing well, and not just to get something from you."

Those words made me wipe my own eyes and blow my nose, so the family atmosphere was perfect. But we menfolk don't weep; we just sat silently, each by himself.

So then, everyone was pleased when I came home, but would they also have been pleased if I'd stayed at home longer? That question went unanswered, and it didn't occur to anyone to ask it. Yet it was the main question that came to my mind only later – together with another, even more important one: am I also pleased to come home, let alone think of staying longer? For what help is others' pleasure, if I'm sad myself? And that last question became increasingly pertinent with every passing day.

I thought of my situation as somehow unnatural. It was hard to bear the knowledge that we all – father and mother, brother and sister, myself, had once had other hopes for my future than what I had achieved, and others still had hope and belief in me that I wasn't able to realise. There was such a big gulf between everyone's dreams and realities, especially other people's, that life became hard for me. What could I do about the gulf between us clearly conveyed not only by people's faces, words, looks, but also by the bony backs and flanks and sagging necks of horses, the bleating of lambs and the lowing of cows in the byre, and the cluster of stumps where the forest had been, when I went walking, a gun on my back and a dog by my side?

Walking as a hunter used to be one of my favourite pastimes. The mere sight of a sniffing and tail-wagging dog or the sound of his barking would make my heart beat faster. A hunting dog's pleasure pleased me as well. Now I was going in search of that pleasure, but I didn't get very far on the snowy fields, meadows, pastures or forests, with the same white covering everywhere, which deadened the sound of steps and voices before I forgot all about the joyful dog and his barking. Or if I noticed them at all, it was something confusing, disturbing. It was painful to see a dark spot passing across the silent, bright white surface and making a noise. Why this, when all around everything had sunk into slumber, when all around was nothing but a white dream, as if someone were remembering their long-dead mother, who loved whiteness! Yes, white with a red rose! Why that joyful barking, when all around, as far as the eye could see, was a silent sadness, as if someone were mourning hopelessly! The dog should run its snout deep into the snowy plain under a cloudy sky and howl, its tail between its legs.

But of course the dog didn't do that, for he didn't know that there's a gulf between belief, hope and dreaming on the one side, and reality on the other, or that I lacked the luck or power to bridge that gulf, whether I was living in the country or in the town. That may be the same gulf that the old man meant when I sat before him like a poor sinner and failed to take life seriously enough. He was probably right about that, and today even the dog could have confirmed that, if anybody had asked him. But since there was nobody to ask, he looked at me almost tearfully and whimpered, for what else should he do? When he drove his hunted prey towards me, I either didn't notice it, or if I did, I didn't shoot at it, and if I did shoot, I didn't hit it. Thus the dog learnt to know the gulf between belief and reality, for I was looking more at the hare's tracks than the hare itself, more the length of the hare's leaps than the leaping of the hare. It had a long stride too, I thought as I measured the tracks with my eyes, knowing exactly who it represented. And how could I shoot that same hare who reminded me of that other one who didn't have long legs or ears, but is tall, who doesn't fear the barking of a dog, but might also bark, if there were no gulf between belief and reality in the world.

Nobody at home could understand how I failed to bag a single animal after firing so many shots. Only my sister seemed to realise something, for she looked at me with an alert gaze and asked, when we were alone, "Have you forgotten how to shoot, or are you thinking hard about someone?"

"I was thinking about myself and my situation," I replied.

"You were thinking about yourself and you let the hare run away," she smiled brightly. "But I thought you were thinking of someone else when you let it go."

"Why did you think that?" I asked with interest.

"But you're a bit strange anyway. You used to be like that once, and then you changed, but now you're back to who you were before. Then you went hunting for a young bird and you let that go too, but not quite like today. That's why I thought that if you can't catch them, your mind's on other things."

"Of course," I agreed, "my thoughts are in town."

"So she's in town," said my sister, while a blush rose to my own face.

"Who's she?" I asked, as if I didn't understand.

"She's the one you didn't kill the hare for!" laughed my sister, as brightly as before. "She's beautiful, terribly proud, wouldn't even talk to my sort! Can't you tell me then?"

"Only on one condition," I replied, approaching her, "you mustn't breathe a word to anyone."

"All right, just tell me," she replied happily.

"I don't have a hope of a position in town, that's why I couldn't catch the hare," I said, and I must have done it very hopelessly, because my sister burst into tears. But my own eyes were getting wet too, because in saying it I wasn't thinking of my job, but of her, the only "her" who hadn't gone from my mind for a moment.

"And I was stupid enough to think you're again with some...," she was going to say when she had throttled her tears.

"We think too much, dear sister," I interjected, as if afraid of what she was going to say. "We think, and the hares and life run past us."

"Hares and life run past us," she repeated tearfully, as if

some wisdom lay in those words. "Yes, you've reached full manhood and you still haven't caught anything. Mother once said, when we were talking together, that our Oskar could take a really rich wife if nothing else helps."

So my mother in the country was just as wise as town mothers are, at least our landlady, who thought that the easiest solution for the problems of life is for poor boys to take rich wives and poor girls to take rich husbands. Women generally seemed to think that life takes a turn for the better if you take a wife or a husband. But instead of that, my father asked me before I left the country, "Are you thinking of graduating from university or have you given it up?"

"For the time being I'm only thinking of supporting myself," I replied.

"Well, but are you hoping to get ahead in your career with your half-finished education?"

"I'll manage, if there's a position," I said.

"You say that as if you had no hope of it," my father pointed out. "Yesterday I read in the paper about the heavy redundancies and I thought, Look, they'll shut the door in your face."

"I don't think they will," I explained with an indifferent air, "because a higher education is an advantage."

"But you haven't finished anything," he protested. "That's why I sometimes think that you should just try to get it finished. If you can't get by otherwise, I might try to help you, though things are tight with me too. I was talking about it with Enn, and she doesn't seem to have anything against it either. She said, 'Well, he'd have to get a roof over his head,' and added, 'if there's someone to take him.' So you see, it's up to you. Just don't start thinking that I can give you everything, no, I could only help you out. You'll have to be a man, bear that in mind, you're old enough for that. For when does a person get any sense, if not at your age? I even wanted to say to you that if you'd try to give up your old life, that cap and all that other German stuff, then maybe you'd get rid of your old friends and start doing a better job. What the Germans had has been messed up; their estates and everything have been taken over, and now they're ruined. It's not right. Of course, you'll know best about that, but I thought I'd better say it anyway – maybe it's your own way of life and habits that are to blame, that you somehow can't get a roof over your head, as Enn says."

Father said all of this quietly and calmly, as if just in passing, and as if he'd planned it well in advance, so I started to wonder whether these were his own ideas or someone else's, and I said cautiously, "You haven't talked about this before."

"Look, son, I haven't had to think about it before, but if you've come away from the university, then... Enn mentioned once that men tend to play the German, riding on the shoulders of power, sort of. But we only have mums and dads, brothers and sisters, and they're poor. That's what she once said, and I've started thinking too, that if you really..."

Those were the lessons I was fed at home to turn me into a man, as they said, if a "man" meant a person who had a decent income and a reasonable life. In a nutshell, I was assured at every step that I didn't have that in their opinion, although they didn't know yet that I had nothing at all.

But the more I was lectured and the more they worried about my past and future, the more I was being driven back to the town, although I didn't really know what to do there. Nevertheless I did know one thing: I wanted to be closer to her, to the one I compared to a snowfield, to a running hare, to its tracks and its ears, with everything I saw and heard. I no longer hoped for anything, but a piece of my past was buried in her – a large piece, I felt – and for the first time in my life I seemed to realise why people, estates, whole nations, cling so much to their pasts.

But it was one thing to think about going to the town, another to go there; one thing to dream, another to act. I wanted to get to town to escape the annoying talk, the embarrassing looks, and the general feeling that I was a bother, a trouble to someone. But in town that is what I became. For when I tried to carry out my intention of no longer taking lunch with the family, I was given no peace, day or night, until finally the landlady caught me in the middle of the street, because evidently that was a politer place for our conversation than up in my room. Out of stubbornness I had refused to set foot in the family's rooms, and she told me she wanted to have a serious talk with me. So we walked and looked for quieter places, as if we were a couple of lovers, drawing aside from people, and we talked about my lunchtimes and the future, for the landlady was able to easily link those two subjects, saying, "When a person can't eat a proper lunch, he can't become a proper person and has no future."

"But why should a person have a future?" I asked, merely to ask and to draw the conversation into some impersonal realm.

"You're talking like a child!" cried the landlady. "Really, you men are children!" she continued almost in rapture, for nothing moved her mind so easily as the thought of children. "So is a person a butterfly or a midge, to be without a future?"

"People don't have a greater future than any midge," I said sagely. "They're merely born, they live and die, nothing more."

"Nothing more!" cried the landlady in amazement.

"What else then?" I asked. "Perhaps a person leaves behind bigger piles of rubbish than a midge."

"Something, anyway!" cried the landlady as if in triumph. "Bigger piles of rubbish! If anyone who doesn't know you heard that, they would definitely think you're either a halfwit or unhappily in love."

"Thank God!" I mentally repeated the landlord's words, "at last we've got around to love."

"Believe me, Mr Studious, men always start talking like that when they're unhappy in love. Unhappy love only changes your own life and other people's into a pile of rubbish."

"Then people are only unhappy in love," I tried to wisecrack, "for just think about it, my good lady, what have we got from the ancient Greeks and Romans? A pile of rubbish!"

"What about the pyramids?" she asked. "What about the pharaohs' tombs? They've lasted thousands of years and they're not rubbish yet!"

"What's the significance of a few thousand years, when the age of the earth is counted in millions?" I retorted.

"But what's the point of you going to school, if you talk like that?" said the landlady.

"I wouldn't have talked otherwise – it was just an idea," I replied.

"So now out of hunger, a noose around the neck or a bullet to the head, eh?"

"Why those?" I asked back.

"Because that's how you'll end up anyway, if you go God knows where to eat your lunch, just to get it a few cents cheaper. How long will your health stand it?"

"Half the world goes God knows where to eat lunch these days, and if so-called culture carries on developing at the same rate, soon everybody will be going God knows where to eat lunch, especially in towns," I explained in self-defence. "Even you, my dear lady, used to talk about it."

"And I recommended it, did I?" she asked. "I mentioned it as a warning. I don't believe in any culture where you don't get fed properly. If every last thing is changed into a factory business, then all culture will come to an end. Strange that they haven't made or invented machines that play football or lawn tennis!"

"That's a slightly cleaner activity than preparing food, that's why."

"And you think people love cleanliness? I don't think so. Why do people smear themselves with grease and oil so terribly? As if they were some kind of machine? Believe me, I have a feeling that a person doesn't want to be anything other than a machine."

"Well, you see," I said, "you must agree that if a person is a machine, you can shove any old food or fuel into it at any factory or office."

"Phew, shocking!" she cried in English, and asked, "So you don't care what sort of can or hose it's done from, then?"

"Almost," I said, adding, "Please, madam, you said 'shocking'. But where do all these cans and ready-made sauces and condensed milks come from? The place where they say 'shocking'. I read in some book about an Englishman who complained about his wife's carelessness and laziness in preparing food. But is there culture in England? Or isn't there?"

"Listen, you're arguing with me about nothing," she said. "You're arguing so as not to come to the point. An Englishman has a place to live, where he can get God knows what to enrich his stomach, with plenty of preserves and sauces and our bacon, but you don't have a place to live. You don't have factories and plants to make the food for your stomach in droplets and powders, when you're exhausted from working. That's why you have to eat differently from an Englishman."

"I do eat differently." I replied. "I don't put our bacon in my mouth, and tinned food and all sorts of sauces are priced out of my reach."

"Ah, let's leave off this useless chat," she said impatiently, "and talk sensibly. You say you can get by more cheaply without a proper lunch. All right, I believe you. But you do eat lunch, don't you?"

"Sometimes I do, sometimes I don't," I replied. "As my pocket demands or denies."

"Ah, so even going completely without lunch?" she exclaimed.

"As it happens, sometimes without lunch, sometimes without breakfast or dinner," I said.

"Is that really so?" she enquired, as if she didn't believe me.

"Just so, my dear lady," I confirmed.

"And you don't want to eat lunch at my place even on the most favourable terms any more?"

"No, thank you," I replied.

"Then you know what I think, and forgive me for expressing my opinion: you're not refusing the offer of lunch just for reasons of economy; you must have some other reasons."

"What others?" I asked, starting to laugh, but I felt that my laugh betrayed what the landlady was guessing. My laughter clearly gave me away.

"I don't know what others," she said. "There must be something in us or our lunches that you don't like. But I will tell you one thing: as long as you won't eat a proper lunch, I won't take the rent for the room from you either."

"Then I'll pay it into your current account at your bank or I'll look for another room," I replied.

"Look, tell me what's wrong with you!" she now cried in surprise. "I'd like to help you and it won't cause me any difficulty – why don't you want my help?"

"My dear lady, I don't need help at the moment," I replied, "and that's that."

"How can you not need it, when you can't even eat lunch any more?"

"Oh Lord! There are more people like this in the world than there are who do eat a proper lunch," I replied, as if indifferent. "And as I said before, if culture carries on developing at this rate, there soon won't be any more proper lunches made."

"Forget your culture and your development! I don't want

164

to hear any more about them!" she cried, getting agitated. "Your culture is only good for poisoners!"

"My dear lady, real culture might be at the point where it makes people immune to poisons. You know that anaemic people are given rat poison. I had a school friend who was regularly fed on rat poison, which they used to call arsenic. Just think, that if a tiny droplet of rat poison is fed to a person, what would happen if he could ingest a large amount of it. Perhaps a person might live only on rat poison and that would be the real culture."

"You turn everything into a silly joke," said the landlady, "but I'm no longer so young that I'm interested in men's silliness. I only wanted to talk directly and openly with you."

"Not much has come of that for me with younger ladies," I explained. "These days a woman can rarely find a relationship with a poor man."

"Yes, I'm very sorry," she said, "that I wasn't able to make my proposal more attractive to you."

"No, madam, don't be sorry," I consoled her. "You did all you possibly could, but it's not a matter of you or your lovely proposal; only of me, believe me. I have undertaken to try and stand on my own feet for once, but, permit me, my attempt won't remain just an intention. However, if the day ever comes when I really need help, then you, my dear lady, will be the first one I turn to."

"Do you promise?" she asked, almost moved.

"I promise," I said.

"Then I forgive you all your sins," said the lady, with a lightened heart.

And so we parted to meet again very rarely and fleetingly, although we lived in the same house, and heard each other's footsteps on the stairs or elsewhere. But if I believed that the matter was now settled and peace would prevail in the house, I was soon to discover my error. It was no time before a new emergency occurred: the trouble with a servant I described earlier. And what the landlady failed to achieve was achieved by her maid, and one might say that she did it almost with ease, only because she was in my opinion so shabby and pitiful – even shabbier and more pitiful than I was myself in my own opinion at the time. Yet that secret bringing of food for me became more embarrassing and repellent every day, partly because I thought that sooner or later the landlady would find the servant out, and how could I then show my face or move about the house! So one day I said to the maid, let today be the last time, I wouldn't eat her stolen food any more, because I no longer needed it.

"So, sir, you'll start coming down to lunch again?" asked the maid.

"Why would I come down?" I responded, astonished because I was struck by the thought that it didn't matter whether I ate with the others downstairs or alone upstairs. "How can you even ask?"

"Why can't you then, if you say I shouldn't bring you any more food?" replied the girl.

"I'll eat elsewhere," I said.

"How come elsewhere, all of a sudden?" asked the girl, uncomprehending. "But where am I supposed to put this food? Who'll eat it up?"

"But you said you have a cat or a dog," I exclaimed.

"The cat has run away God knows where, or some dog has killed it, and I don't dare to give any more to the dog, the lady strongly forbade it. She said the dog will get fat and sleepy, won't hear anything or bother to bark when it needs to."

"Well, then eat it yourself, but don't bring me any more," I said.

"No, I won't eat such fatty food as our landlady makes," said the girl.

"Then throw the food in the rubbish bin, but leave me in peace!" I finally shouted, because the girl was like an annoying fly or mosquito, buzzing around my ear.

"Fatty food like our landlady makes can't be thrown in

the bin," exclaimed the girl, standing by the door. "And they'll soon find the chunks of meat, and it'll finally come out that I've been taking them."

"But for pity's sake, what's it got to do with me?" I turned on the maid.

"How can it not have, when up until today you've been eating up everything I brought you?" the girl replied with a very naive expression.

"I told you – I won't eat any more, and that's that!"

"But what am I supposed to do?" asked the girl in desperation.

"Do whatever you like," I replied. "The simplest thing would be to tell the lady that you can't eat such fatty food, and ask for something leaner instead."

"I can't do that," exclaimed the girl, "because then she'll ask straight away, 'How have you been able to eat until now?' And I can't answer, 'I didn't eat it, I gave it to the dog.' Sir, you don't know our landlady. If I told her that I'd given the roast chops, beefsteaks, cutlets and meatloaves she's been cooking to the dog, first she would knock me to the floor and then she would drive me out the door with my rags. Nor can I say that I've been secretly bringing food up to you and you've been eating it."

"Well I never!" I shouted. "If you really do, Loona, I'll wring your neck, remember that. Crying and begging me like a heap of misery, and when I finally accept, then…"

"No, sir, when you accept, as you did until today, then I don't say anything, but then I don't need to, but if you don't accept any more, then I don't know what…"

"I don't, that is as certain as an 'amen' in church," I interrupted her.

"Then I really don't know what to do. I'll have to look for a new position, I suppose, I have no other choice," said the girl, and started to cry.

"Loona, you've gone crazy!" I shouted, getting up from my chair and stepping over to her. "Because the mistress makes such fatty food, you have to look for a new job, is that it? Come to your senses, for goodness sake."

"You won't eat the food because I bring you it; if someone else did..." she snuffled.

"Believe me, Loona, I wouldn't take that food from anyone," I consoled her.

"So you want me to go away from here," she went on crying.

"No, I only want you to leave me alone ... stop bringing this food."

"But I can't do that anyway if I have to look for a new job," sniffled the girl. "I'll have nothing else to say to the lady but that you won't accept food any more."

"Devil take you – look for a new job!" I shouted.

"But there are no jobs like this to be found anywhere!" whined the girl. "There are no jobs to be had if I go looking, because no one will have me."

"What the devil can I do about it?" I said forcefully, because the business was starting to annoy me. "In the end, if you have no other way out, go and tell madam that you stole food from her and brought it secretly to me. And so that it would be more believable and likely, you can add that you've been coming up here to sleep or that I encourage you steal the food."

Now the girl's heart was full, and she suddenly turned to me, looked straight at me angrily with wet eyes and said, "I'm not a liar and a cheat, as you think, that I should say such things about myself and others. And I haven't been stealing either. If I have lied, it was only on madam's orders and from what she taught me."

Suddenly I felt my heart going cold in my chest, as if something icy had been put around it. Only after a little while did I dare to ask, "So what was your lie about from the lady's instructions?"

"Do you really believe, sir, that it was my idea to start bringing up food for you?" she responded in amazement.

I looked at her like a pillar of salt, then turned around and sat down in a chair.

"What a swine!" I finally blurted out through clenched teeth. "What wretchedness!"

"That's what I say too," the girl agreed. "It's simply a sin to lie and cheat like that!"

"But why did you do it then, the devil take you?" I shouted, turning around in my chair and looking angrily at the girl.

"The lady told me to," she replied. "First of all the lady asked me if I liked you at all, sir, and when I answered that I do – for what was I supposed to say? – she went on and asked if I wanted you to stay alive, sir, and when I answered that I did – for why would I wish you dead? – the lady said that you had had two big misfortunes, sir, that might kill you if the two of us, meaning the lady and me, didn't come to your aid."

"What misfortunes were those supposed to be?" I asked, feeling ice around my heart again.

"You lost your job, sir, and your girlfriend left you," replied the girl.

"I did lose my job, but I don't know anything about a girlfriend," I exclaimed.

"No, madam said that your girlfriend had left you, sir," affirmed the girl, "and by girlfriend she meant our miss, who came here before Christmas. Madam also said she was a baroness."

"Wonderful!" I cried, trying to turn the matter into a joke. "Well, go on!"

"Well, and madam said that you loved the baroness terribly, sir, so terribly that, well, you'd do yourself in if you didn't get her. And you didn't, because miss went to another man, a German of course. And that's why the two of us, madam and I, had to save your life, sir. Because madam said

169

that if you're unhappily in love, sir, and starting to starve as well, then you'll definitely do yourself in. But that's shameful, when a young Estonian gentleman kills himself over a German lass, she said. And since you wouldn't accept food from the lady's own hands, sir, she taught me how to come and talk, and what to do to make you accept food. If nothing else helped, I was supposed to say or give you to understand that I love you, sir, and therefore want to feed you, because if you love someone, then you want to feed them, as birds feed their young. And when you started talking of that love today, sir, I couldn't bear the lying and cheating any more. Of course you can't love me or anyone else, sir, if you love that beautiful baroness. So it's all a lie, what I've been telling you here, all of it, everything, everything. I haven't stolen anything or lied, I only said what the lady told me to, and I brought you what the lady put on the plate. She even made me put on a black apron while I was bringing it, because then you'd believe me more easily, sir, she said. I had to be very stupid and dirty, for then you'd accept the most food, sir. That's what our landlady is like. And so when I started to cry, it was only because I had to lie. I had to say that my stomach can't take fatty food. But that's a complete lie, because I have a good stomach and good health: I could even eat wooden pegs and granite, and still my stomach would be fine. And the kind of chops that I was bringing you, sir, I could easily put away two of them, and it wouldn't do me any harm. At Easter sometimes at home I'd eat six or seven hard-boiled eggs at a sitting, that was nothing for me. That's the kind of good stomach and health I have."

"But you know, Loona," I said, "you may have a good stomach and health, but you're the same sort of bitch as the lady is. To lie like that, to pull my leg, that's damn nasty work!"

"Yes sir, you're quite right about that, it is damn nasty work," agreed the girl. "But madam said to me, 'Loona, I've made a person out of you and I'll make you a better person, in the end I'll introduce you to a good husband, if you help me save the life of the young gentleman you love.' That's what she said: *you love*, as if she was going to introduce me to you, sir."

"But that's enough now, dear Loona," I said, "go, so I don't see or hear you ever again!"

"Yes, but what about the food? I can bring it tomorrow, because now, when…"

"Now, when everything's settled – go to hell, you and your madam!" I thundered. "I don't want to hear or see you ever again, do you understand for once?"

"Then I'll have to leave this job and go away," said the girl, starting to cry again.

"Good riddance!" I shouted, "So the air will be clean again!"

"So why must I lose my job just because you lost yours, sir, and your girlfriend left you," whined the girl, "because if there hadn't been the two big misfortunes, madam wouldn't have forced me to lie so terribly. Who will feed my old mother, if I'm without a job? And it's certain that I will be, because madam told me that if I dared to even breathe a word about this to you, sir, she'd beat me within an inch of my life, kick me out the door and give me such a reference for other landladies that they wouldn't even want to spit on me."

"Then go and die with your mother!" I said with the same brutality, and yet I was starting to feel sorry for the girl, because obviously she wasn't guilty of anything, or only insofar as she obeyed the lady's commands and believed her dire predictions.

"Anyway, what's wrong with gentlefolk," the girl concluded, drying her tears, as if she had already submitted to her fate, "is that one forces you to lie and cheat, another stuffs his belly with all the best stuff, but a poor servant has to suffer. For when I say that you won't accept food any

171

more, it's clear straight away to her that I've blurted it out to you. What's more, she's bound to believe that I've done it out of love – for what other reason could there be – and then it'll all be over, a noose around my neck. I believed everything, but I didn't believe that you, sir, were like this."

"So what do you think I'm really like?" I asked.

"One who won't accept food any more," said the girl.

"And you think that after you've told me everything…"

"Sir, now it will be easier to carry on eating, because there's no more lying and cheating, or if there is, then it is for us in front of madam, but not for me and madam in front of you."

"Who knows, you wretch, if as soon as you get downstairs, you'll tell madam everything we've been saying here," I said.

"I'd sooner have my tongue shrivel in my mouth than breathe about this to madam!" yelled the girl. "For the sake of my own skin, I can't. Besides, I've been on your side from the start, and I told madam that if your girlfriend let you down…"

"She wasn't my girlfriend," I pointed out.

"Oh, really, wasn't she?" queried the girl. "So that's a lie too! It's all a lie! But madam assured me that she was, and that's why you couldn't stand the sight of miss's face. On the other hand I liked her a lot and I'd have liked so much for you, sir, to have a girlfriend like her. But she shouldn't have let you down. And when she did let you down, I said to madam that when a girlfriend cheats, what are we doing it for, we aren't girlfriends and we don't love anyone else. But madam said that cheating must have been involved, because you weren't eating, sir, and if you don't eat, that's the end. 'Loona,' she said, 'she cheated because she didn't love him, so we have to cheat because we do love him,' because we were loving when we wanted to save your life, sir."

"I think that's a lie too," I said. "You didn't even feel a whiff of love for me, you only wanted to feed me your chops and cutlets, come what may, and when you couldn't do it otherwise, you used lies and trickery to help you, madam first and then you. But would you please tell me why you've come to tell me this to my face? Do you really think I'm going to carry on eating now?"

"Yes, I really thought that you would, once you knew everything," replied the girl. "And I had nothing more to lose, when you said you wouldn't eat any more. Because madam said, when you accepted the first portion from me, you remember, when I cried and begged – that's when she said to me in the kitchen, 'So, Loona, now things are all right, but just bear in mind, girl, that if the young gentleman doesn't eat any more, it will be your fault, because you've blabbed or let it be understood by him, then I'll box your ears and drive you by the tail out the door, because shitbags like you are for me to kick out.' Well, when you suddenly said today, sir, that you wouldn't eat any more, it was clear to me at once: now they'll kick me out. And then I thought at the last extreme, that maybe it would help somehow if I talked it all out nicely, how your girlfriend cheated you, madam cheated you and I cheated you. But if that doesn't help either, then my heart's clear of the filth anyway, I thought, because I'm an honest girl, I don't steal, lie or cheat. And now it's up to you, sir, whether madam kicks me out as a shitbag or not."

At these last words the girl started crying again. I sat thinking, reasoning out the whole thing. Now everything appeared in a new light. Even the landlady's lectures at the lunch table contained a new substance and a kernel of truth. But how could she know it all so well? Were the sparrows on the roof also chirruping about lovers? Did she read our secrets in our behaviour, words, looks, smiles, blushes, clumsiness and even silences? Or was there something behind it when the girl talked about a girlfriend who cheated? Or was that really just a ruse? I didn't want to believe it, but I was starting to, and at the same time I felt infinitely naive and stupid. "Men are big children," I recalled the landlady's favourite expression.

"So is this really the end then?" asked the girl at length, rousing me from my thoughts.

"For me it is, yes, Loona," I replied.

"So there's no use in a person being honest and fair?" she complained.

"Do you really think I could accept your food and put it down my throat?" I asked at last, seriously and pragmatically, for this bundle of misery was beginning to arouse my pity, as she had the first time, when she stood on the same spot, a plate under her shabby apron.

"Yes, sir, I believed that if I told you everything and you saw that I'm completely innocent and honest, not cheating or lying, then you'd take pity on me and start eating again. Or if you didn't pity me, why did you pity me the first time? Why did you accept my food at all? If you hadn't taken it, madam wouldn't have made me do anything. It's all because you started eating then. You ate, and madam made me lie, that's why I'm suffering for nothing. Please, sir, I'm begging you, keep on eating – spit it out, once it has been around your mouth a couple of time, but eat, I'll do anything in the world you want me to. If you say I have to keep quiet, I'll keep quiet; if you order me to talk, I'll talk, and if you even order me to come up in the night, like you said at first, then..."

"Loona, are you thinking about what you're saying?" I asked her. "You said you're an honest, decent girl."

"And I really am," she assured me, "but what am I supposed to do if you won't start eating?"

For a moment I had a feeling that I was in a madhouse. People, their faces, movements, the spaces and lines around them – everything shifted and became somehow strangely angular, misshapen, unfamiliar, unimaginable and incredible, as if appearing to me in a funhouse mirror. Along with this I felt my heart beating more weakly in front of this girl, particularly as a new thought occurred to me: what if I do carry on eating? Things can't get any worse than they are, more likely better. Let the landlady believe that with her deceptions she's getting me to eat and taking no payment, but I will make a note of the lunches I have eaten, and if I ever get any money, then I'll pay off my debts, and then let's see who's pulling whose leg, who gets the last laugh. So I said, "Loona, all right then, I'll save your skin this time, but first you have to answer a few questions."

"Ask away – I'll answer them all, I'll do everything you want," she asserted.

"Would you tell me where you and madam got this story of the cheating girlfriend from?" I asked.

"Madam got that one on her own, it wasn't me," she explained. "She started complaining that you weren't eating anything any more, sir. Well, that meant you'd fallen in love. Then she'd seen you and the young lady outside; I don't know where. And to make quite sure, she sent me out into the street a couple of evenings to watch the young lady leaving her lessons; well then it was all clear. Afterwards I didn't need to do anything more than come upstairs each evening to see if your room was empty or not, sir. But it was always empty when the young lady had left us. In the end I simply listened to whether you came before the young lady went downstairs or not, sir. Sometimes madam and I listened together. She would make out as if she had something to do in the hall, but I knew for sure that she came to listen for your steps. I'm not fooled by her tricks. And that's how we got to know as well that you weren't going out with the young lady any more, because there was someone else, taller and smarter, with a jacket and socks on."

"You went outside to look?" I asked.

"Of course I did that too," she replied. "But after that I didn't, because madam said it was clear anyway: a gentleman going with a German lady, and the bumpkin's left drooling."

"So that was the dirty, puny laundry of my great and pure love," I said to myself, thinking over everything I had heard that day. But to tease a little more out of it, I carried on asking, "The landlord was the third player in your game, of course?"

"No, madam kept everything secret from him, because she kept assuring me, 'Bear in mind, Loona, if you have a golden husband, then poke one of his eyes out, if he's good, then both eyes, but if he's bad, make him blind and deaf, for only then can we women get a little life in this world.' Those were madam's words then, and they still are. And all I'm telling you is quite true, because I'm talking as if I were standing before the preacher at communion. In future I won't lie to you any more, if madam tells me to – I promise you that – but when I come to you, I'll tell you everything straight, like it is, as long as you start eating that food of lies and cheating."

"All right, Loona, I will, for your sake," I said.

"How good you are!" she cried in quiet ecstasy, came a couple of steps closer and looked me in the eyes, moved, and I felt that even the most wretched being, the most unhappy face, can sometimes reveal beauty which is captivating. I was aroused from my meditation, as she continued, "I really don't know what I can do or give you in return!"

Like it or not, I had to admit that I was, one way or another, completely beaten by women. Erika had left me, madam had arranged things so that despite refusing, I was still forced to eat her lunches, and Loona had played with me like a cat with a mouse. I should have asked myself whether I was the only one she was playing with. She could have been talking about me to madam, just as she talked about her to me. Perhaps both madam and I didn't believe her when she deceived us? Perhaps both of us were convinced that we were pulling each other's legs, while actually we were both being duped by Loona?

But never mind – why worry about something that was in the past and couldn't affect the present? One thing was certain anyway: the revelation of lies and deceptions and all sorts of behind-the-scenes tricks and schemes ultimately had an enlivening and energising effect on me. My failed love affair, which warmed my breast and drained my body, took on a slightly clownish air which gradually came to make me smile. Perhaps it was all just an empty delusion best forgotten – sooner rather than later.

And there's nothing better to encourage mind games than work and activity, I thought then. A certain obstinacy added to that conviction, as if something primeval within me was rising up against my surroundings. Ah, so everyone thinks they can play with me, and twist me whichever way they want, I said to myself. When the mood comes, they take away my job, when another man comes along, then love takes flight, someone else's whim has me eating food I don't want, and still another twists my resolution hither and thither. But I wanted to show everyone that it wasn't as easy to play with me as they thought.

I started looking for employment because I understood that everything revolves around that, and only an income can make you independent. Day after day I did nothing but run around the town visiting old friends and acquaintances and acquiring new ones, and everywhere the conversation ended the same way: how do I get hold of a job? Through personal contacts, or despite them, I wore out the doors of public and private enterprises, for I was convinced that a man like me is suitable for every trade. Apart from that, I wrote letters, because I wanted to know whether in the whole country there was a place for a man who's ready to work his fingers to the bone.

But there were none – no places for me, at least not for a long time. Occasionally I got some smaller positions, but they didn't last long. Yet day after day, month after month, they helped me onward, and I also sought extra sources. I did what so many young people try to do: I started to write, "to create" something and "to rush off" the odd translation. As we have so many newspapers and journals in this country, I thought that I would have to be a complete fool if I couldn't cobble together some vaguely suitable lines of prose.

In those days I smeared a lot of expensive paper with foreign ink, because I wanted to do things properly and soundly at least as far as my raw materials were concerned. The result was that in some quarters I was regarded as an upstart or even a rich young man who wanted to make a name for himself in literature – there were such people in this country – and they were very surprised when I talked of payment. What the hell are you wasting expensive paper for, if you're writing for money? I was asked – and I was stuck for an answer.

It took some time before I could get a foot in the door with my "creations", and even then perhaps not on my own merits but through the old-boy network. But who cares! The main thing was to make a breakthrough, as I called my partial advantage. At any rate, work and activity, effort and bustle, gave me faith in myself, and no longer did I go around with the hangdog air I had when I went to the country and then returned. I even had enough faith in myself to write this book.

And so perhaps I would have waded through thick and thin, if something had not happened that flung me back to square one, in terms of my state of mind. Suddenly I was again the plaything of forces whose existence I didn't want to believe in. It all appeared to be just a game, a tease, a deception and an illusion whose origins were unclear. Maybe it was too, but then illusions meant more to me than facts.

Coming home one day I found a letter in the box whose address made my heart tremble so that I could feel it in my hands. For a moment, I felt that for a long time I'd done nothing but wait for this letter and this handwriting, as though my life were a dream.

It was pure coincidence that I came home so early that day; I often stayed out until late evening, if only to show the landlady how little I valued the lunches that she forced on me with lies and deceptions. But my "bohemian ways" were promoted by a conviction, acquired I don't know from where or how, that if you want to become a writer – and I did at the time – you have to be homeless. In other words, you mustn't go home, but spend your time anywhere else.

Why I came home early that day I don't know. Was it pure chance or was I led by some presentiment? Who knows? If I had somehow been delayed, it would have been hard to imagine what would have happened to me. The mere thought of it made my heart, all my blood, run cold. But now I ran upstairs, locked the door and ripped the letter open, to find only a few words:

I will wait for you this evening
at eight o'clock on the Avenue of Lies. E.

That was the whole letter, but I read it and read it as if I couldn't read it to the end. Every word seemed a mystery with some ominous significance. Why would we meet at all? And why so late? Why did she call the walk we loved so much the Avenue of Lies? Or did she mean some other place by that name? What sort of place? No, it must be that place! The place where she had spoken of lying to her grandfather, and where I confessed to my own lie. Or were other lies connected to that walk? Did she want to speak of them, or was this the start of something new?

I was wondering about that when there was a knock at the door. Of course it was Loona with her food – the food that was stolen and the source of so much mendacity – for only she would creep up the stairs like a cat. Gladly I would have shoved her and her "stolen goods" down the stairs, but what could I do, I had to let her in.

"Today I don't have the slightest appetite," I complained while the girl placed her plate on the table and I felt the hidden letter burning a hole in my pocket.

"You have a new sweetheart again, sir?" observed the girl with a bashful smile.

"I might have a secret one that I don't know of," I replied.

"There are no such sweethearts," she said. "See that you don't get sick."

"My head is so groggy," I remarked.

"If the trouble's in your head, then eating will help," she explained.

"But if it's in the heart, what am I supposed to do?" I asked.

"I don't know," she replied, "but if it's in the stomach, pepper and ashes will help."

"I think my trouble is more in the heart or the head than the stomach, so I don't need to eat pepper or ashes," I told her.

"You're making a joke, sir – you haven't done that for ages," she said, stopping by the door and holding on to the lock. "Madam did say that lately you've been happier than before."

"Where did madam get such a good look at my face?" I asked.

"On the street, I suppose; she would say, 'Thank God, sir seems to be getting over that German lass,'" she explained.

"Did she call the young lady a lass?" I asked, scarcely able to control myself at the girl's use of the word about Erika. When I looked her in the face and let my eyes wander all over her, it seemed incomprehensible to me that I had felt pity for her and let myself be twisted this way and that inwardly.

"Madam has been calling her that to me right from the beginning; only at the lunch table would she say 'miss' and 'my young lady', because you and the children were there," she said.

"I and the children," I repeated. "So the young lady was a 'lass' and I was counted as one of the children?"

"Didn't you know that already, sir?" she cried in amazement. "Madam is always saying, if a woman doesn't have children, she remains a 'lass' till her death, even if she marries ten times. Childless women run after men like young lasses, so madam says. But men, she says, always remain children, because they don't bring children into the world. An adult person has to have given birth, madam says."

"So make sure you don't remain a lass until you die," I said.

"Madam is always saying that. She says, 'Listen, Loona, you have the sort of face that'll keep you a lass until you die, because love won't come to you.' But she always comforts me and says, 'Happy are the people who don't know what love is, because love is a terrible thing' – that's what madam says. And to get children you don't really need love terribly much; it's enough if you just like a man a little."

"Perhaps the children would come even without liking him," I observed.

"You're joking again, sir," she smiled bashfully, "but madam is talking seriously when she says, 'Loona, look what a terrible thing love is – a person doesn't want to accept food any more, or anyone, then you have to feed him on lies and deceptions like some animal.' That's what she says about you, of course, sir. But about the young lady she says, 'If she falls head over heels for a man, there's no other cure for her love than marriage.'"

Those words dumbfounded me, so that soon Loona had to end her tale, of course in the hope that she could continue it next time, because she was obviously trying to keep the pledge she had given: not to deceive me any more, and tell me truthfully everything she heard madam say about me. But perhaps madam really was right, that I had declined her kind offer regarding the lunches because of love? And did Erika really fall head over heels for a man to find a cure for her love? Might a solution be sought here to today's letter, inviting me to a meeting? Did the words "Avenue of Lies" indicate that everything was somehow deception and lies?

My brain and my heart were torn by endless, maddening questions. I almost went crazy from reading the terse letter over and over again. The food lay where the girl had left it, and when I finally noticed it, it was completely cold and congealed, especially since it was roast lamb with potatoes. I took a couple of pieces, but my mouth became lined with cold fat and I left the rest untouched.

I had to decide how to spend the several hours I had left until I went to meet her. Visit some friend? Impossible! I wouldn't have been able to say a word to anyone, listen to anyone's words or endure anyone's presence. I recalled how once I had gone to sleep to pass the time and been ten minutes late. A whole ten minutes, and nowadays time is measured in seconds, as I keep reading in the newspaper's sports pages.

Nevertheless I didn't want to read the sports news now, though I felt obliged by circumstance to compete with someone – try my strength, jump higher or longer than someone, smash someone's nose, deal him a knockout blow or have that done to myself, so that my sense of time would vanish from my consciousness for a moment. While sports news was boring me, so was everything else I could read, though I had done more reading in recent times than ever before. This resulted from my attempts to write. It seemed to me that my personal life, personal experiences and skills were so feeble, superficial, vulgar and ordinary that it was not worth putting them down on paper. Life had passed me by, and I had passed it with neither of us leaving a trace on the other, as though we had run in opposite directions on carefully oiled bearings.

It's strange and funny to think that this could be the case. Perhaps I was in such a state that I started to think others must have had the same experience, or at least many of them. Why else would writers read so much? I mean writers who digest dusty tomes instead of experiencing the freshness of real, uncharted life. Intellectually we are doing the same as we do physically. Instead of feeding ourselves on green grass, we kill and eat the animals that eat the grass. And if a genius were to suddenly appear who would write a book that was utterly true to life, with nothing to do with other books, then probably no one would read it, just as eating green grass has been left to ruminants. Life is too hard to ruminate and digest, so books are for ruminating. Life is for living.

But what's even easier to digest than a book written from other books is the cinema, because it's a book that has been chewed and digested several times over. On the whole it's as easy as going the pub, café, church or chapel. Right now I needed the easiest option of all, because my mind was sick and my heart heavy. I needed oblivion. So I decided to go to the cinema, where I could doze by myself in the darkness, while familiar, almost indifferent events passed before my eyes and rehashed platitudes caressed my auditory nerves. But even there I had to change places several times, because each time I ended up next to people who were continually whispering, reading the subtitles aloud, humming and whistling along with the songs or tirelessly munching, as if they were being fed by the kilogram. That day I was even disturbed by people laughing heartily in my presence or searching in their pockets and handbags for handkerchiefs to wipe their tears or blow their noses. This was done solely to annoy me.

Eventually I found a quiet, peaceful place by the wall, where there was no one in front of me or behind me. There I could have thanked God with all my heart that he had enlightened people and let them erect a building where they come together as if in church and spend their time as if they were in the pub.

As I left the cinema, the sun was already going down, but the glow of the evening sky still showed that approaching spring was already being hinted at. You could feel it in the air, in the shining stars and in the eyes and voices of people. Because a sudden thaw had recently occurred, the pavements were decorated with scattered piles of snow and shards of ice, and their ugly and filthy black appearance had been covered by fresh, bright white snow which pedestrians were now sweeping aside. A light chill pinched as if teasingly at the tip of one's nose or earlobes, forcing people unconsciously to quicken their step. I too hurried, although I could have dawdled with all the time I had. I wanted solitude, as if I had to prepare my heart for the coming meeting.

This year's meagre snow had, with the thaw, turned into to water or slush on the pathways, and then hardened with the cold mostly into rough ice, which didn't hinder walkers. Where skis had once slid along and left their endless tracks, people could now stride freely on their own legs. The bright fresh snow was fading in the twilight, and further darkened by the shadows of the trees. The ground surface felt untouched and pure. Here and there the old porous snow gave way under the weight of my footsteps and seemed to crackle in warning, but the fresh white carpet in its softness had a muffling effect and I only heard a light crunching and scratching sound which barely made an impression. A strange drowsy silence and peace prevailed, broken only by bright headlights on the highway, which sent blinding shafts of light between the coal-black tree trunks, piercing the pedestrians' eyes, as if screaming in pain.

As the clock approached eight, I no longer had the patience to use the whole pavement for walking, but almost shuffled on the spot at the point I hoped to see Erika appear from. Once again I was mistaken: Erika came not from the direction of town but from the park, and thus had to traverse the entire Avenue of Lies before she could reach me. I was so taken aback by this that I didn't know what to do or say. That familiar form also seemed terribly foreign and new to me, and the greatest impression on me was surely made by Erika wearing a fur jacket instead of a coat, and a fur cap instead of a hat.

"I was beginning to think you wouldn't be here," said Erika after our greeting.

"And I was afraid you wouldn't come," I replied, because I wanted to say something and couldn't think of anything better.

"I came punctually," she defended herself.

"But I'd been here at least half an hour beforehand," I said.

"I noticed that in the darkness – so many footprints – and I wondered whether they were yours or a stranger's,"

"They're all mine," I assured her, "before me it was pure, untouched snow. I walked and walked and finally came to a stop, thinking that you'd come from over here."

"But you see, I came from the other direction," she said playfully and obstinately.

"I was really surprised that you came from the other side," I explained.

"Why?" she asked, as if startled.

"I don't even know," I replied. "With you I never know what will happen to me. If I believe one thing, it turns to be another. I thought I saw you from far away and recognised you despite the darkness, but now…"

"…now you don't know at all," she finished my sentence.

"That's it, I don't know at all," I affirmed.

"You see how quickly everything is forgotten," she said somewhat instructively and sadly.

"No, miss, quite the opposite: I see that it's not forgotten, and can't be."

"But why didn't you recognise me then?" she asked, affecting a light tone, while her voice was trembling with excitement.

"You're quite different to what I imagined, and there's more within you than I can guess, that's why. I feel downright afraid when I see what you really are like. If you were like

I'd imagined, then forgetting would be easy, but you aren't, you're quite different, so how could I forget you?"

"You shouldn't talk to me like that," she said quietly and pleadingly, but in a way that provoked me to go on: "Forgive me, miss, for not being able to say better what I want to say, but firstly, while walking here alone, I decided that, for whatever reason you invited me here today, I want to assure you of one thing: I love you as I always did, I love you as never before. I didn't even believe that I would still be in love like this; your letter proved it to me. Every word in it made my heart tremble. It hardly mattered to me what you wrote; the main thing was that you wrote, and that I could hold in my hand the same piece of paper that you'd recently touched, for that had made it precious and holy. Of course it's silly and ridiculous of me to talk like this, but it's the truth. I dare to tell you this, because I believe that anyone else would laugh at me, but you wouldn't. You'll forgive my madness and stupidity, because you understand me. Although I don't know why we're here today…"

"Don't you remember how, when we last met on the street, you expressed a wish to come walking one more time together on the Avenue of Lies?" she interjected, as if wanting to stop my words.

"Did I ever call this pathway the Avenue of Lies?" I asked in surprise.

"That is what you called it, and that's why I did too in my letter…" she explained, trailing off.

I was confused. All the time I had believed that she invented that name; she thought I did. Which of us was wrong? Or were we both wrong?

"I'd completely forgotten that," I said at length.

"I hadn't," she said. "Your wish stayed in my mind all the time. And since I'll now have to leave town for a long time, I wanted to fulfil your wish before that."

"Are you going to the country, if I may ask?"

"To the country," she said softly, as if she didn't want to

speak of it. So I said, "I went to the country too."

"Was it nice?" she asked.

"Snow, nothing but snow," I replied. "Everywhere was white. And do you know what it reminded me of? Someone who was white all over."

"Do you mean my mother?" she asked, as if alarmed.

"Yes, her," I affirmed. "In the middle of the snowy plain I even thought I saw her, as you once described her, but there was no red rose, there was nowhere to take one."

We both suddenly fell silent, as if afraid to make a sound. Only a while later did she say, "It's terrible, you telling me that today."

"Why so terrible?" I asked.

"My mother is dead," she said.

"She was already dead when you talked about her," I said.

"Things were different then, quite different," she responded. "Now I've come here to fulfil your last wish before I go away."

She said this as if she had appeared by my deathbed, or so it seemed to me. Now suddenly I had the feeling that something white was moving among the trees ahead of us, creeping closer and closer, until it stood unnoticed between us.

"Because I'm leaving, I'm in a terrible rush today," she continued, arousing me from my daydreaming. "No one knows that I'm here. I didn't even tell grandfather. I was visiting a relative and took a short detour; that's why I came from the other direction. If it weren't for that visit, I wouldn't have been able to come. That's what I was afraid of when I wrote that letter, but I've managed it as luck would have it."

"So do you have to go straight away?" I asked. "You don't have any more time at all?"

"I should have been gone already," she replied.

I didn't know what to do or say, for such a rapid departure made every word senseless, every action futile. She too stood in perplexed silence, as if some dumb white being

187

really stood between us. Finally she extended her hand and said, almost in a whisper, "So, live well, and many thanks…"

Her words were broken off, for I had grasped her hand, pressed it to my lips and fallen to my knees in the snow. And when she withdrew her hand in fright, I grabbed madly at her clothes, and in the next moment, around her legs, pressing my face against her knees, which tried to escape or turn aside, but stayed on the spot.

I had suddenly been overtaken by an instinctive terror that I could lose her forever, which would mean losing myself. I was ready to do anything and swear any oath, if only she would stay. At that moment I could have given up my own sister and brother, father and mother, land and nation, language and faith – of which I had none anyway – if she had wanted it. A single word from her mouth and I would have even left my corporation, with its colours, which I had once venerated so much, and "become that real Estonian man", as her grandfather put it, although my father and mother, sister and brother, relatives and friends, even the whole Estonian nation, would have opposed it. At that moment I wouldn't have cared about anyone or anything that came to mind, if she had asked it of me. But she didn't ask anything of me, she just stood there, with me down on the ground, clutching her knees as if terrified of death. She stood and tried to disengage herself, without really knowing how to do it. I felt her hand touching my hair once, for my cap had fallen into the snow, but momentarily she drew back, as if scorched, and uttered these words of pleading: "You ought to have mercy on me, for just think what would happen if my fiancé got to know that you had held me like that."

That had an effect – more of an effect than who knows what else. My hands dropped loosely into the snow and she took a couple of steps backwards. She was silent. At least I don't remember hearing a word or a sound from her. I got up, seeking support from a nearby tree, which seemed terribly big and black to me.

"Your cap is on the ground," she said finally and made to go and fetch it, but I got there first.

We were silent. Then she said, "Forgive me that I had to tell you that, but I couldn't have done otherwise, I didn't know how, believe me."

"You forgive me too, for what I did," I replied, "but I too couldn't have done otherwise, believe me."

I felt those words coming from my heart, from the depths of my soul.

She hesitated about what to do. Finally, though, she stretched out her hand to me again, which I held for a moment in both of mine, without daring to raise it to my lips again. Then she went, leaving at a run along the Avenue of Lies toward the castle, as if her home were there. I watched her leave without averting my eyes once, until there was nothing left of her to see or hear. And as I stood there, black myself amid the bright white snow and the black trunks, it seemed to me for a moment that there had been nothing, only illusions in a yearning heart, chimeras in a scorching soul. Ah, if only one could take an aching heart, if one could catch a pining soul, and send them to their natural home – the land of illusions!

I sat down in the snow, resting my back against the tree that had at first seemed so terribly big and black to me, and started to cry. I did that quite simply and pragmatically, as if I wanted to be myself for once.

That was the end of my love, and that was how I wanted to end my book, for I am not making it up, I am only describing facts. But he whose face is at once birth and death, love and oblivion, did not want my book to have an ending like that, so I've no choice but to continue writing. The following lines have little to do with my love, and in that sense they add nothing to my book, and I could have left them unwritten. Instead they tell of her love – the love of the woman who invited my heart and soul into the land of illusions.

The fact that I really intended to end my book with the foregoing passage is demonstrated to myself and others by my having carefully read through what I had written, corrected it in places where I found deviations from the truth, rewritten several parts of some pages, made interpolations which belong to another time than that of the actual event described, and even submitted it to a couple of publishers, without receiving a reply. One day, however, I read a death announcement in the newspaper, which read: Erika V., née K. I hadn't known her married name, for it had never interested me, but I do remember her maiden name, and that was the one in the death announcement. Likewise it showed the age of the deceased, the name of the home that was mourning her. Thus there was no doubt – Erika was dead! There was no more Erika! The world had become a poor and empty place! The world had become an absolute void, where no organic being could live! That is what my heart cried out. What would I have given now, sacrificed, for that announcement to be an illusion, a mere sickly ghost, a deception!

But no, it was a fact, and I had to do something, go somewhere; I couldn't just sit in my garret, staring at the newspaper, as though my redemption and my blessing were to be found there. But what should I do, where should I go? That was the question. After long hesitation I decided to appear before the grandfather of the deceased once again, or at least make an attempt to. It was crazy, I appreciated that, but I did it anyway, because I couldn't do otherwise.

This was the only time in the course of my love that I was really happy, and no doubt that was only because she was already dead. When I appeared at the house of mourning, everything was empty and silent, as the deceased had yet to be brought home from the hospital. The old gentleman was quite alone among his ancestral inherited furniture, and opened the door for me when I rang the bell. Whether he had become even whiter I don't know, but he certainly was even more stooped, his face more sunken and the skin on his face and hands had taken on a waxy tinge.

At first he didn't recognise me, or pretended not to, but when I told him who I was, and reminded him of my previous visit, he didn't let me continue, but invited me into the back room, taking me through the hall, where as before the piles of things from the dead past were on view, and into the smaller room, where he sat once again in his high-backed armchair and asked me to take a seat before him. I should have spoken, but my mouth, my tongue and my throat became painful and tight, when I saw how tears coursed over his now wrinkled and yellowed face, and his drooping moustache, one after the other, and dripped on to the soft dressing gown that covered his thin, wizened body. Thus we sat in silence for a while. Finally I managed to say, "I beg your pardon so very much that I've come to trouble you at this moment, but I could not do otherwise, I had to know why and how, so quickly, so suddenly, so incredibly unexpectedly..."

"What is there to tell you," he replied quietly, without raising his eyes, as if it concerned a trifling matter. "Quite natural that it came like this, but if it had come otherwise, it might perhaps have been more natural. "A first birth, some sort of premature failure, a lack of the necessary help and skill for something which is just as natural as death in the countryside, a long distance to town, and who knows what else. I am old, I am of the soil, but death doesn't want me, as if my sort of soil were of more use to someone in this world than a young and thriving life."

"I too, grandfather, would have been ready to offer my life for hers, if I'd been asked to," I said.

He raised his head a little, as if he wanted to see better who was calling him grandfather, let his head fall again and said, moving his tired hands, which had acquired a waxy sheen, "Perhaps you should have said that to me better when you were sitting the first time in that chair and talking about her; then she might still be alive today."

"Ah, grandfather!" I cried covering my eyes with my hand. "Then I was so unhappy and frantic that I haven't dared talk to you properly until today, because they were threatening to take away my job, as they did do later."

"I know that, I know everything and I understand you. I am not going to reproach you, rather I blame myself that I, so old, with the smell of the soil about me, am trying to command life and love. But as you see, nothing good can come of that, when the soil takes command over love. Soil only turns everything to soil, even love, no matter how great and self-denying. Then I believed more in your words than in you. But young people's words cannot be taken seriously, for they are bad at knowing people, especially when it concerns themselves. I should have known that you are a true Estonian man after all, with the heart of a true Estonian man, the kind of whom I'd seen plenty in my own life. Let me tell you a little story about that loyal Estonian heart. It must have been in the sixth year of this century when the Baltic lands lost the quit-rent by the command of his blessed majesty the Tsar. Of course you won't remember it, you will have only heard or read about it. I was living at my country estate then. That was a golden age, but nobody wanted to believe then what a golden age it was. A person is never old or wise enough to really judge his times. Just this last year, when you were sitting right here in front of me, I complained in my heart about the bad times, because it was you asking for my grandchild's hand, not someone else. But I do the same again today, because the only joy of my old eyes and ears is no longer among the living. In those days, in the sixth year of the century, when that order came from his blessed majesty the Tsar, I said, Must my manure not be carried and my rye not be reaped because of a decree from the Tsar of Russia? Where can I get so many working hands overnight so that I can give up the quit-rent system without a loss? And despite the Tsar's order I sent a messenger to the distant parts of the forest among the tenants who worked in lieu of rent, and I made him tell them that they should carry on doing their work, because not even his powerful majesty the Tsar could do anything against voluntary quit-rent labourers, particularly as we were working the matter out between ourselves; for a tenant it was easier to do work than pay money, and it's better for me to receive work than money. And believe it or not, the answer came from tenants everywhere that they would do as their baron wished, not according to the decree from his majesty the Tsar. Only one owner of a big place in a far corner of the estate lands, who had about twenty versts to travel to his work – in those days we didn't know kilometres yet in this country – said that he would hold to the Tsar's command, that is, he would start paying his rent in money, because he didn't want to rattle so far over the land with a group of people and tools to the estate. Well, do you understand the people? For several generations in a row the estate has got by on quit-rent, and now suddenly it doesn't. Moreover, if this tenant did take part in the labour-intensive tasks, others will follow him, because everywhere the messenger had been told that if others take part in the quick-rent work, then we will too, and if others drop out, then we will be too. There was nothing else for me to do but get the master of the big place invited to the manor. He didn't come. He didn't come because he didn't have time and his mind was made up. The farmer said that he would act according to the law, so why should he go to the manor? And do you know, young man, what I did then? I had a horse hitched to a little sprung cart, because that was the easiest way to get to the distant parts of the forest, I took a coachman's boy beside me and I drove to the farmer's home. I hadn't been there for a very long time and I didn't recognise my own lands and people, or know how they were living. Whether it was theft of timber and secret distilling, as I had been told, or a lot of work and economies, as the people themselves claimed, it was clear that one way or another the farmer by the forest lands had become a wealthy man. He was living like a powerful and respected farmer behind my back, nobody interfered in his activities. The forester was the only check on him, but he was a law unto himself. I hadn't raised the rent for ages, as they did on neighbouring estates every few years. And a farmer like that didn't want to do quit-rent for me. The only explanation: he had got rich, proud and even pretentious. It turned out that there were two farmers on that farm, father and son. When I talked to the father, he claimed that the matter didn't concern him, because he'd handed everything over to his son, but when I turned to the son, he laughed at me and said, 'Why is the baron wasting his breath, when it was father who decided? So then I went – I, the baron and landlord – from Herod to Pontius Pilate out there in the distant forests. And since I didn't get a definite answer even when father and son were both standing in front of me, I told them, 'If you cannot do this quit-rent, you can look for a new place for yourself!' But to that the son – a man of about fifty, stout and strong, so a pleasure and a joy to look at, hair and beard all over like his father, who was way over seventy, but not half as white as I am now – replied quite simply: 'All right, baron, we will look for a new place for ourselves, a bit of open country, there's plenty of it out in the backwoods. We've already been casting an eye in that direction, because we thought, isn't this matter going to end the way these things always do, so we can go before the spring if you wish, Baron. We've lived well without squabbling, so we'll leave the same way.' That's what the son said. And you won't believe me when I tell you that those words brought tears to my eyes. Do you understand a person who is prepared to leave his forefathers' home for the sake of the silly quit-rent? I didn't at the time. I just sat down next to the grey-haired father on a block of wood and told him in his language: 'Don't you feels shame and pity that you are leaving your forefathers' and my forefathers' land, where everyone has lived a beautiful and heppy life, over the lousy qvit-rent? Do you really luff that great and stronk Russian kaiser and his precious decree more than your forefathers' and my forefathers' land? You wants with a light heart to abendon your own home place and your baron, when he comes tventy versts alonk these pine roots, alonk these stones and stumps? Do we luff each other so liddle that when comes the stronk Russian kaiser's decree, we starts to sqvabble and leave our own homeland? Am I beink to you a bad baron landlord, a bad person? Is my forefathers been to your forefathers a bad landlord and bad person? You open your mouth and say with your grey head to my grey head, I am beink a bad baron landlord, a bad person?' Now the father replied to me, 'No, baron, you are a good person and your forefathers were all golden people.' 'So then why won't you do quit-rent any more, when I ask you to? So is it unjust and bad that I want to die as I lived? Do the work until one or other of us dies.' 'I would of course do it,' said the father now, 'but my son doesn't want to.' But the son was standing there listening to our talk, with women and children nearby. 'Kaarel, won't you just give in, since the baron has come so far and talked so nicely to you?' said a woman's voice behind my back. 'Yes, Kaarel, let it be as it was while you're alive,' said the father too. Eventually Kaarel uttered these words: 'All right, baron, if the others agree, so do I, or else I'd be alone in breaking relations with the manor.' And so they carried on doing the labour with a pure loyal heart, and maybe they would be doing it to this day, if the new times hadn't come. This story came to mind when I thought about your first visit and our conversation. I told you at the time that your *Korporation* and colours, your singing and drinking were empty stuff, eating away at the spirit, that you didn't have the right spirit, the right Baltic spirit. Spirit is what brings life to singing and gives a sense to drinking. You argued then against that right spirit, you said that you sing and drink without spirit or that you drink with a new spirit, as far as I understood you. I believed you then and that was my mistake. I believed your explanation of the new spirit or of singing and drinking without spirit, but I should have been wiser than you in your youth and known that it is not from spirit that singing and drinking come, but spirit comes from singing and drinking. And if you drink and sing properly, as they did in the good old days in the Baltic lands, then you should acquire the right Baltic spirit, the right Baltic spiritual disposition, which drives you to distinction in every sense. And that is what gives a special beauty, brilliance, glow and glory to things, socially, economically, racially, and in class terms, and raises even the greatest follies of youth to an ideal light, an admirable elevation. Seen from that viewpoint the conversation with you has been a real pleasure and consolation, because not all is lost in our dear homeland when the younger student generation cultivates the right spirit. The old generation, the alien substance that arose from Russification in the Baltic lands, wanted to trim everything down to one level, which is completely foreign to us all in terms of history and development, tradition and culture, but the young generation is heading back on to the right Baltic track. Instead of manors there are settlers, but the spirit and soul of the manors, their high ideals, are coming into bloom again. They who bind themselves to earthly things or destroy the spirit, that everlasting and elusive thing, are mistaken in their materialistic blind faith. If the powerful Russian Tsar was unable with his decrees to force a loyal and just Estonian man to give up quit-rent for the sake of his merciful baron, who could demand of youthful students that they had to give up the true spirit of their homeland? That is how I have reasoned to myself about the future of our dear homeland, and I have come to the joyful conclusion that the past is not completely dead yet, that the past is the only living, vital, and life-giving period in the destiny of people and nations, for only the past enables development, and the spirit of the golden past is only now perhaps starting to spread and take root in our homeland, becoming the treasure of the masses, whereas until today it was the private property of individuals. My only fear," he continued in Estonian, "is that they cripples the right Baltic past and spirit, as they don't understand the real drinkink and singink. You says to them, when you goes to them, they must understand that really true drinkink and singink, then comes that really true spirit, that loyal Estonian spirit, which sits on that grey old man, when he says to his son, "You goes does that qvit-rent for your dear baron landlord, until he dies. I talked about this with my grandchild when she was still at home," he continued in his own language, after a little silence, "but she was still too young to be interested in spirit. Moreover, spirit isn't a woman's affair; they seek the soul and love. Yet she did tell me that your young women seek, like your men, the true spirit of the homeland in drinking and singing. But how is it with your soul and love? Who cares for it when everyone is seeking the spirit in singing? Spirit does not love, it assesses. Or is there no longer a need for soul and love? That is the only thing that makes me think, makes me worry about the beloved and loyal Estonian people. But I am old, I am of the soil, I no longer understand well how…"

I got up to leave, because I thought I perceived that the old white-haired man was talking only about immediate inconsequential things to prevent me from leading the conversation to what our thoughts dwelt on all the time, he as he talked, I as I listened.

"You're going already," he said on seeing me stand up, as if he had been expecting me to go for a long time. "It's better that way, because the others will soon get home. But do forgive me for not letting you get a word in at all; I only talked myself. Ever since my grandchild left her home, there's no one left to talk to, and that's why…"

We had got to the door and I was about to open it.

"How are you doing now? You have a job?" he asked.

"I don't have a secure job, just casual work," I replied.

"That's how it is nowadays, there's nothing secure any more, everything is casual, and that's why, the first time with you…"

I was already halfway through the door, ready to close it behind me.

"Once everything was different in this world, quite different," he said. "When my grandchild was still at home there was…"

I hurried to go, for once again I saw tears welling up under the yellowed, creased and thin face, while his mouth made movements as if it were that of a little child. Nor could I hold back the tears any longer. But hardly had I walked a few steps when he called me back, as if he still had something important to tell me, yet he no longer said a word, and merely thrust a letter into my hand in the doorway, and only when I had turned it over between my fingers, looking for the address, without finding one, did he say, emphatically and as if afraid of someone, "That is for you, I almost forgot… an old man's head. Take it, put it in your pocket and go."

I obeyed his order and left. The door shut behind me. I hid the envelope in my pocket and didn't dare to take it out even to look at it, as if it were the trace of a serious crime, hunted by snooping noses, hidden curious eyes. But I turned it constantly between my fingers, as if I wanted to caress and fondle it endlessly or discover its secret. Why did grandfather pass this little packet to me like that? I pondered to myself. Had he really forgotten? Or did he never reach the decision, the whole time, whether to give the packet to me or not, and only at the last moment was he moved to do it?

As I debated this, I didn't once call to mind the name of

the only person who could have wanted me to have this envelope. I kept it from me like we keep the fear of death. I tried to remove it from mind the way even as I fondled it deep in my pocket. I tried instead to recall the words of the white-haired old man, but it was all forgotten except one thing: "The past is the only living, vital and life-giving period in the destiny of people and nations." And I muttered to myself, "Only for the sake of the past should people live and die. Only for the past can and should one sacrifice everything." All the way home I repeated these ideas in endless variations, as if I had nothing else to think about in the world. Actually I was repeating the ideas because they indirectly expressed what I had not yet dared to make explicit: Why am I still alive, when my past is dead? Why am I still myself, when she is not herself? Why do I move and think, while she is lying motionless and her mind is petrified? Why do I still have a present and a future, when she has only a past, or not even that – a mere emptiness, only what does not exist and which hitherto no human tongue has been able to name? Why? Why? That was what I really wanted to think on the way home, yet I didn't dare to – not yet.

At home I found that the envelope contained a letter written on thin silk paper – no doubt silk paper because it would take up less space and could thus be hidden or forwarded more easily. The letter was in German and evidently written at intervals, as I could tell from the ink and from the fact that at the end it was written in pencil and the handwriting was so bad as to be almost illegible. There were no signs of a date, as if the author of the letter were thinking of eternity – no date, year or mention of a night, evening or morning. I reproduce the letter unchanged, although it may be that I have misinterpreted the end of the letter in translating it. Here it is as it was in my trembling hand.

"I'm writing these lines because I feel death approaching.

But don't think that I'm sick, that there is anything wrong with me or that I'm suffering. No, my fragile health is good and there is nothing wrong with my state of mind either, considering my mental and physical condition. And yet I feel the approach of death, maybe because the doctor told me last time in town that my condition is not quite normal, but possibly also because at our last meeting you talked about my mother, which somehow had a horrible effect on me. I know that sometimes a person can live with a horrible feeling in abnormal conditions much longer than in normal conditions without such a feeling, and yet I cannot get rid of my premonition, and therefore I thought of writing these lines to you. But they will reach your hand only when my premonition has become a fact. If it doesn't, I will destroy them because what I want to write seems to me so terrible and unbelievable that for a quite some time it was beyond my powers to put it down on paper and keep it hidden somewhere. You too, if you ever read these lines, must destroy them when you have read through them. I'm writing them only to you, so that you will know how I have loved you and how I still do – that is the only purpose of these lines.

"But I don't really know where to start, because at the moment it seems to me that it's not at all easy for me to say where the beginning of love is, and where it ends. In writing these lines I believe quite firmly that I loved you even before we got acquainted, but I didn't yet know then that it was you that I loved. I suspected it even in the first days of our friendship. But when you came to keep me company, to ask forgiveness for the landlady's behaviour, I didn't doubt it any more. And the next evening – it must really have been the next evening – when you were late and ran into me on the stairs, because I came back for something I'd forgotten – yes, if you hadn't come at all then, I might well have managed to come up and knock on your door. At least I believe that now, because at the time I had not forgotten anything, but I wanted simply to see what was keeping you so long. And how my heart was trembling! Simply terrible!

"Do you still remember how once in the park you called yourself a wolf howling at the moon? And I was supposed to be the moon or a king's daughter. At the time I felt so ashamed that I could say that only to my mother – those were my words then. But now I can tell you too, because what comes next is much worse. When you called me a king's daughter or the moon come down to earth from the heavens, it reminded me that I have around my body something broken and torn, and I thought, what would you think of me and what would you say to me if you suddenly saw or found out what is torn in me and where. It was so terrible to think that you regard me as a king's daughter or a bright moon, while around my body I carry something cracked and torn. I was also missing a button somewhere, in the place of which that morning I hurriedly put a tiny little safety pin. So, now you know why I was ashamed: a lousy king's daughter and a white moon with a safety pin.

"There was one thing about you that I didn't like at all: your great politeness and respect toward me. You behaved with me as if I was – I don't know what. But I didn't feel anything special about myself, only love. That is what I wanted and expected. I came with you into the dark park only so that something would happen to me that would develop me, as I said at the time, but nothing happened. Sometimes I had a desire that you would be shameless and carefree towards me, that you would treat me as a thing and handle me, but you didn't, and I was disappointed. Now that I have been handled, I am even more disappointed. And I haven't developed either, for there is only one thing that develops me, and that is love. Now I know that, and I reproach you no more.

"But I did at the time. I did even when you visited grandfather and we met afterwards, and you told me in the park about your first lie told for love – do you still remember that? But both your lies and mine, up to that day, had been to protect our love, and therefore they were right, and not a sin or an injustice, as we thought at the time, first yours and then mine too. But what I did that evening went against our love and was an outright crime, and that's perhaps the reason I 'm now suffering this premonition of death, for a person can be forgiven all crimes, but not a crime against love. I at least will never forgive myself.

"Of course, to this day you don't know what happened between me and grandfather after your visit. I didn't talk about it because I had vowed not to, and others were unable to talk about it. And the fact that I kept my pledge to grandfather was itself a great crime I cannot forgive myself for. Of course I should have vowed to grandfather, but even more I should have broken that vow for the sake of myself and our love – told you everything there on the park bench, when you were kneeling before me; then I probably wouldn't have needed to write this letter.

"When you'd left grandfather and I came home and heard what you had talked about and what answer you received, I got down in front of grandfather, kissed his hand, clutched him around the legs, just as you did with me later in the park, so that I thought at the time that you were imitating me, except that I comforted myself that my legs are perhaps not as bony and hard as grandfather's. And as I held him, so that he couldn't get away from me, I cried and I begged him, because I thought you hadn't pleaded well enough, although I'd impressed it upon you before I went out. But my tears and pleas helped as little as your talking did, for grandfather remained deaf and dumb. He only said, 'Dear child, it's wiser this way, as I'm doing it, and one day you'll thank me for my present refusal. Young love comes and goes, and no one knows where it comes from and where it goes. They cry who have to give it up, but those who get it often have to cry much more. I am keeping you from that excess, which is no consolation.' Those were his words.

"But I wasn't reconciled to grandfather; finally I jumped up and shouted at him: 'All right, grandfather, if you won't allow it, I'll go without permission! I'll elope, I'll compromise myself, I'll make a scandal for you, for auntie, our relatives, our acquaintances, so bear it in mind, grandfather, I'll be compromising myself with an Estonian.' But even then grandfather remained calm, and said, 'No, dear child, no, you won't compromise yourself with an Estonian. You can't compromise yourself.' 'You and auntie will have to watch over me then!' I cried. 'I'm going to my lesson and I won't come back, then your strength will be tried, grandfather. And I am quite sure that you will take me back when I come, because you love me more than you believe.' 'Of course I'll take you back, no matter how and where you come from, you're right about that, dear child, but that is why you won't be compromising yourself, because you too love me more than you believe, ' replied grandfather. But I shouted at him: 'No matter how much I love you, grandfather, I love him even more, much more. Because you won't agree, I have no choice but to compromise myself.' Yet grandfather stuck firmly to his decision: he wouldn't agree and I wouldn't compromise myself, I couldn't compromise myself. And when I challenged him about what could prevent me from compromising myself, he was lost for an answer. Finally I said to him, 'Grandfather, if you're so sure that I won't compromise myself, that I can't compromise myself, then promise that when I still do compromise myself, you will happily take me back if you need to, and defend me against auntie and the others. Dear, dear grandfather, leave me just this crumb of hope!' – I begged him and once again fell at his feet. Grandfather was silent for a while, as if thinking it over. Then he said, 'Dear child, do you really understand what you're asking of me?' 'I'm asking you for love, grandfather,' I wept, screaming at him, 'only a bit of love, grandfather; my life is wretched and poor anyway, as you keep repeating to me every day.' But grandfather put his hand on my head, which was always his greatest sign of tenderness, and then said, 'Perhaps you're not asking me for love, but for your own life, that's what you're asking for.' At the time I didn't understand those words, and so I could say light-heartedly: 'Grandfather, what is life without love? If I have to give my life for love, then I'll do it happily. Just promise me, dear grandfather, that you won't push me out, no matter what happens to me!' Grandfather was silent again and I awaited my fate crouching at his knees. At last he said, 'But child, will you give me your word, you understand? Your solemn oath, that you will never breathe a word of what we have been talking about now to a single person, even the one you want to go to? Can you swear that to me and can you keep your pledge? For if you don't keep it, then I don't agree to your ever going.' And as if he already regretted the conditional promise, he added as he withdrew, 'You really must understand me, dear child, I am not giving consent on clear conditions, but I am forgiving you for your action, if you keep your pledge. It is terrible that I have to make you promise, and I do it with a bleeding heart and will never forgive myself. People are probably right when they hint to you that old age has robbed me of some of my sense.' 'Right now I see and believe that you are fully in your right mind,' I shouted back to grandfather and vowed to him everything he had asked of me. And my heart was filled with such great joy and happiness that I kissed grandfather's eyes, hands, knees, even feet in great gratitude to him. But he remained silent, austere and sad, trying to restrain my endearments and said, 'Dear child, you'll lose your own sense – what will become of you afterwards?' 'Afterwards I'll come singing and flying, I promise you, grandfather,' I said, but he remained gloomy: 'Child, better not to promise that; promises given lightly are hard to keep.' That was the last thing he said to me, and I left home warbling, suitcase in hand, which later you got to carry. Whether grandfather saw me leaving with a case I don't know, but certainly he noticed when I came back home with it.

"Do you still remember exactly what happened between us that evening? For me it is all as if burned with a hot iron on my heart. And not only my heart, but my whole body and soul. And even if I live for thousands of years, it will not be extinguished; I have the feeling now. You obviously didn't have the faintest idea at the time who or what was walking beside you, just as you didn't realise why I had a little suitcase in my hand. You could carry it quite indifferently, because you wanted to be polite. Your failure to guess, your failure to realise, proved to me best of all how terribly mad my action was going to be. But now I see in your incomprehension only a consolation, because if you had been able to guess even a scintilla of my real intention that evening and still act the way you did, then at least God might have had mercy on me and killed me with a thunderbolt when I thought of starting to write these lines.

"I had put in the little suitcase my glory box, because I was leaving home to spend my first wedding night with you, wasn't I? I haven't really understood that to this day. But if you had said to me that evening that you had no money to go anywhere or elope, or you were hindered by some other circumstance, and you had added that the only way out was if I came up to your room, then I would have done that without a word, unhesitatingly. All the time I was intoxicated with the happiness and pleasure that I could give myself to you, and I had to use all my strength to behave myself, not to start screaming from sheer joy. I suppose you can never imagine how close I felt to you, to your soul, when you took that suitcase from me containing my few things, which were already destined for your touch. I was overjoyed at the thought of what you would do if you knew or guessed what you were carrying in the case. For me too those little things became more precious in the belief that you would love and admire them simply because they belonged to me, had been close to me.

"But you know as well as I do how that great joy and intoxication ended: with my own great sobbing on the park bench, where you consoled me with common sense. Your sense may have been right from your own viewpoint, I didn't dispute that then, nor do I do so now. But what help was my own, your, even the whole world's sense, human and divine, when I had tearfully begged my grandfather on my knees to forgive me for coming to you? Could anyone's sense bring about such a miracle, that I would suddenly no longer know how, with what feeling, with what trembling of the heart I had chosen my own little things and put them in my case? Could any sense at all undo it as if you had never carried my things in that case? No, my darling, no sense was needed any more, but rather the loss of sense. Oblivion was needed, because oblivion is sometimes the only thing that is merciful, oblivion and death, which is surely only a great oblivion.

"Are you still amazed that later I carried my own case, and would not hand it over to you under any conditions? And if you are still wondering, then we can no longer understand each other and our love has run empty. I had come with everything that I had, and I had brought with me my own shabby things, but you didn't want me. Not even my belongings, whose shabbiness I really acknowledge only now. You had carried perhaps only because you saw the case, not knowing that you were carrying things that were destined to cover my body.

"On coming home from some friend's place I would often tell my aunt about my amazement at the beautiful objects and jewels I'd seen there, and ask her whether I would ever get any such things, or when I would get them, but she always said to me, 'Make do with what you have; you won't be taking a husband yet.' Now I wanted to go to my husband and I took with me my best and prettiest things, but my husband wouldn't accept me, as if he were of the same opinion as my aunt. You can't take a husband with those things.

"I don't know if there has ever been a more pitiable creature in the world than I was that evening with my suitcase. At the mere recall of what I was carrying in my case and with what feelings, assumptions, hopes and dreams I had put them in there, a deadly shame burned in my heart, my whole body and my every movement so terribly painfully that to repress a loud scream I had to clench my teeth, which made a crack as they came together. You know that my body trembled all over at the time, and you thought that it was the cold, but I was shaking from the terrible shame and terror. It was about what I was supposed to do with my case and my things now, and where would I go. I was ashamed of myself, particularly because you were there, and the only good fortune was that the park was so dark, otherwise I don't know what would have happened. In the light I would not have dared to get up from the bench, I wouldn't have dared to take a step, make a movement, for I felt thoroughly humiliated, desecrated. I wanted to go straight home to grandfather, but I didn't even dare do that. I didn't have the courage to tell you that I no longer could, and I had to escape, so terrible was my shame and so thoroughly wretched did I feel.

"And how was I to appear before grandfather? How was I going to look him in the eye? Where could I put the suitcase so that he couldn't see it when he came to open the door? How could I move about in full view of him? Believe me, at that time I had the feeling that I would rather compromise myself with anyone than return home in the same state as I had left it. And if some shameless scoundrel had encountered me on the road, I would have gone off with him and then done away with myself. But of course nothing of the kind happened, for who would disturb a badly dressed lady when she is walking with a worn suitcase in her hand? Who would even cast a glance at her? So I reached home safely.

"I was really lucky when I reached home, for grandfather

was alone and opened the door himself. But from his first glance I realised immediately that he understood the extent of my shame. This robbed me of my self-control so that I threw down my case with a bang, and without taking off my outer clothes rushed past grandfather, ran to my room, collapsed on the spot and burst into tears.

"I didn't notice when grandfather followed me, nor did I know that he had picked up my case and brought it to my room. I only felt someone taking off my overshoes, as if I were a little baby who couldn't manage it herself. After that he somehow pulled off my coat, removed my cap and took them to the peg in the hall. Only then did he sit down with me and start to gently stroke me, as if this were the only remedy for my frantic crying.

"Finally he spoke, very quietly and sadly, as if asking my pardon: 'I told you before, dear child, that I can't permit it, I mustn't agree to it, you mustn't go...' 'Now at least I know that he doesn't love me,' I sobbed, almost angrily. 'No, dear child, now even I believe that he does love you,' said grandfather, adding, 'He loves you more than you actually like at the moment.' 'He has shamed me for my whole life!' I screamed. But grandfather stroked my hair and said, 'Ah, child, child, if you only understood what an injustice you're doing him!'

"To that I could no longer give any reply, I only wept to wash my soul of shame with tears, my body of the dishonour, humiliation, defilement. I went on weeping until I feel asleep. When I awoke in the night, I found myself under a rug, but I didn't remember how I got there. Seeing grandfather in the dim lamplight still sitting by my bed, as if I were gravely ill and had to be watched over, I suddenly remembered everything again and once more burst into tears, though with less force than in the evening, for I began to feel a terrible pity not just for myself but for grandfather too, who was trying to calm me, saying, 'Child, what's wrong with you, that you can't conquer yourself! The main thing is that your aunt can't hear you in her room, for you don't want her to know as well. It's easier for two people to handle this than three.' 'There are already three of us,' I said, to which grandfather readily agreed, saying, 'And of course three of us, dear child; my old head is forgetting the third.' 'Do you really believe now, grandfather, that he loves me?' I asked, trying to look questioningly at his face in the dim light. 'And of course, child, now I do believe it,' replied grandfather, adding, 'Sleep until the morning, then you'll understand it yourself without asking.' 'But why did he shame me so much then?' I queried. 'He saved you from shame, dear child,' replied grandfather. 'To shame a young lady is a very easy thing to do, but to keep her from shame, few men have enough manliness and love for that.'

"That is what he said to me that night, when I just couldn't overcome my pain and shame. But in the morning it really was a little easier, as grandfather had predicted, although I didn't get out of bed at all that day. I couldn't move my limbs, because it reminded me of the humiliation and defilement they had endured the previous day. My aunt came to see me, felt my head and pulse, and said that my face was paler than theirs were. At any rate I would be wise not to move from the spot until the next morning. Thus she too approved of my staying in bed to recuperate. But when she was in my room, I suddenly remembered my suitcase and I became fearful that she might happen for some reason to touch it and feel that it was heavier than usual and ask what I had in it and why I had it. At the same time I was afraid she might open the drawer in the bureau to take something from it, and her practised eyes would immediately see that some of my things were missing. But neither one nor the other happened: grandfather had put the case aside and the bureau drawer remained unopened. I had no luck in love, but I did have some in shielding my shame.

"Lying on my own I started to gradually realise what had happened to me and my love the previous day, and soon

I was blaming not you but only myself. Only myself, and I will until I die. I had come to you with the greatest thing that a poor young girl has in this world – love, and I had wanted to pawn myself and my shabby little things for it, but at the same time I had made a vow to a third person, though he was my grandfather, the only good person in the world, and I had kept that vow, as though it were greater, more important, dearer and more sacred than my love. I wanted to come to you with pure love, but I came with a pledge which changed my love to a lie and a deception. For I now believe firmly that, as you kneeled before me in the park and tried to put sense into my head with pleas and explanations, I could have happily and directly told you what grandfather and I had talked about and what we had both agreed, then you would have either taken me upstairs to your room and I would not have felt the shame and humiliation that burnt within me then and will probably burn within me till my dying hour. That scorching sensation is perhaps the principal reason why I'm writing, making a sort of testament to my love, which I have never been able to speak about.

"That I regarded the pledge I made to my grandfather as holier than my love, and thus forced you to confirm the decision you had taken, which in your situation was the only right and honest one, was the crime which I cannot forgive myself for. The traces of that crime, no tears, regrets, consolations or explanations can flush from my soul. When I had decided to come to you, as I did that time, no third party should have stood between us any more with a pledge or a vow, not even God or Jesus Christ. And when I gave that pledge to grandfather, I should have completely forgotten it at your place, or I should have broken it with a light and pure heart, and in the full knowledge that I was doing it for our love. But I didn't have the self-abandonment or the heart to break my pledge, and thus everything that followed could not be avoided. You could not have done otherwise if you really loved me; in that grandfather was right; I could have done otherwise, but I chose not to.

"And the strangest thing of all to me, the most incomprehensible and therefore perhaps the most painful: I didn't know you as well as grandfather did. Just to think that you love someone as I loved you and still do, and at the same time you can be mistaken about them and left groping around in the dark about who they are, whereas someone else who is standing alongside and looking indifferently, sees everything, understands everything – ah! even now I could lose my mind thinking about it. For grandfather, when he assured me that time that I couldn't compromise myself, was thinking of nothing else than that. No, you wouldn't compromise me; you wouldn't do it, because you have a loyal and honest Estonian heart, as he would put it. Grandfather foresaw how I would come back from my honeymoon, and he feared that I might not survive it. He was wrong about me there, and he feared needlessly, but in the end he may be right in that, as in everything else.

"The only thing that consoles me is that you knew me just as little as I knew you. Even today you probably have no idea that I came to you in full knowledge of the consequences. I packed my little things in the suitcase with deliberation and took it with me. Then you believed the silliest lie about the suitcase instead of guessing the truth. The truth then was the most unbelievable thing in the world to you; what I did was so improbable, and you dared to assume so terribly little of me. You carried in the case in your hand all my body and soul, but had no idea of it. You had a whole world of love to carry, but didn't notice a thing. You didn't even understand my madness when I cried out to you in the greatest anguish there on the park bench that you loved my grandfather more than you did me. That was so strikingly stupid on your part, and to this day I wonder why you didn't kiss me even once, or why I didn't do that to you, for when I walked beside you, suitcase in hand, I had plenty of time to kiss you, if you didn't kiss me.

"By the way, Ervin will probably not believe to his dying hour that we didn't ever kiss each other; all my assurances to the contrary can't convince him of the truth. To get him to believe it, I also told him how at our last meeting you clutched me around the legs, and what I said to you then, explaining that, if I can tell such a thing, then I would say I say that we didn't kiss if we had. But even that didn't help; I could see from his face that he didn't believe me, and that now he believed me even less. I'll never forgive him for that, nor that he once said about you, 'Either he kissed you or he didn't feel himself man enough to need you as a woman.' Those two things have perhaps also helped me to write these lines.

"But you mustn't conclude that Ervin was bad to me – no, certainly not. Likewise you mustn't think that we had a bad life. We didn't. He is decent and good to me, and he probably even loves me in his own way, and looks after me as far as it is in his power. As for me, I appreciate him and I can respect him, but to my mind he is a little childish, even childlike sometimes, for he thinks it's enough to be good to someone and take care of them. He has probably never known what love is. I don't think he has ever really loved Estonian girls either, although even now he keeps recalling them. But a man who has not really loved is not a real man, for only love is the measure of a man. But he seems to have the understanding of a child.

"Oh yes! Living next door to us is a little boy, Oskar by name, but they call him Ossa. I really like that! I make it my business to go next door, just to hear the mother, a young woman, calling her son Ossa. And I want to see the boy too; he's terribly manly and reminds me somehow of you. If I have a boy, I'll definitely call him Oskar and start using Ossa as his nickname. I've talked about it to Ervin too; he doesn't have anything against it, because he doesn't know that your name is Oskar too and I could call you Ossa, even now. Were you called that when you were little? Ossa, Ossa, Ossa! It sounds like music, it sounds like divine music. Do you still want to hear that music from my lips? When I am no longer around, you can know that I died with that music on my lips.

"The young lady next door, the same one who calls her little boy Ossa, has said to me several times that I'm looking terribly ill. It won't end well like this, she tells me. She says my workload is too heavy, I should look after myself, my husband should keep an eye on me, to see that I don't do too much. When she talks like that she always calls me a young madam who shouldn't live like other people, like farm people, used to everything at ground level. Have some mercy on yourself and your child, young madam, Ossa's mother says to me, and sometimes she has tears in her eyes – why? I haven't asked her. It's good for me to be soothed with words, because she can't do anything else, and perhaps I go so many times to that farmhouse to hear Ossa's mother's soothing words.

"Everything turned out differently to what anyone could expect or assume. Here I am now. In everyone's faces I read my own death, even grandfather's face, whom they brought here at my request, and I will certainly die, because I want to die. My child is already dead. She was a daughter and I couldn't ever have called her Ossa if we had both lived. That is good, it's best that way, because I feel I loved the name I hoped to give her more I loved than her. It's also good that there is something in the world that brings oblivion; it's just a shame that oblivion also expunges love, which is so miraculously beautiful, such a terribly beautiful thing, as you yourself once said, when I still didn't know what a dreadful thing love is – that it should never vanish.

"But perhaps even death doesn't bring oblivion? No, no, that cannot be! God cannot have brought people into this world with allowing them a death that leads to oblivion! God could not have given people love without adding the means to obliterate crimes of mercy from their memories! And my last wish, my last anguished cry on this earth to Him is that He forgives me my crime, for which I cannot forgive myself. By keeping my pledge I lost my happiness in life, our dream of life, and now what was killed is dragging me with it, as if the dead were ruling over the living.

"Yet I'm not complaining, I have no grievance. I only feel sorry for you. My pain for your sake is so terrible that I rejoice in death. I don't have the courage to ask your forgiveness for my crime; it's much easier for me to die. But if you had to forgive me after all, then I know that we were two foolish children, who took account of a thousand things, in the past, present or even the future, but not of our own love. But when I am no longer here, don't think of anything else but our love; it will comfort you. Love me a little longer as you loved me when I was alive. It is so easy to die beloved. Not to regret, not to mourn, only to love!

"A couple of those objects that I had in that worn suitcase, which you also carried that evening and which I didn't let out of my hands later, will accompany me; all the others I have destroyed. Thus I leave together with my shame and love. Love me because of my great shame, which I am taking with me.

"My last wish is that my death notice be put in an Estonian newspaper. That is for you. If you read that announcement – it is complete, so you won't mistake my name, you will recognise me – and if you are still interested enough in my fate to go to my grandfather's place within three days – he's expecting you – then you will receive this letter from him. He promised that, and I believe he will keep his promise as well, just as I once kept the pledge I gave him. But if you don't go to grandfather within three days, he will burn this letter without reading it himself or letting anyone else read it. Thus no one apart from grandfather and us two knows of this letter, not even Ervin, and only I know its contents, and you may know it too if you appear within three days.

"I have said everything I have to say. Now I feel pure and blessed, at least before you. I only ask, love me a little longer, a little while longer! If I don't come to your mind at any other time, perhaps I will when you happen to pass along the Avenue of Lies, where you once clutched my legs and where I committed my crime. Think of me for just a moment with love. Think because, although I killed our life's dream, I wanted so much to be like an open book to you, and if I couldn't be that in my mortal body, then I am that now with a living soul. Take it and love it, as long as you live. I will never cease loving you. Erika"